Hay...
don...
than...
She...
she...

much prettier than me. You're the one giving her the nervous breakdown now."

Her lips began to tremble. "You're killing her," she said, and started to cry. Then she began to rock in her chair, hugging herself again. "It's cold here, isn't it? Why? I'm tired. Why? You look very good. Why?"

"Stop it," I said. "You're just trying to avoid answering me."

She stopped rocking, but she sat there, her arms locked around herself, and stared at me.

"I came to talk to you sensibly, Haylee. I almost died. I did everything I could to survive, but it was horrible, nights without sleep, chained, my very breathing controlled. You knew it would be horrible. You knew him, and you left me there."

What surprised me about the way she was staring at me was that she didn't even blink. It was as if I were looking at a picture of her face.

"Do you hear me?"

She didn't move; she didn't stop staring.

"Haylee," I said sharply. "Cut it out. You know I can tell when you're pretending. Stop it!"

There was no reaction.

"Stop!" I screamed, and slapped the top of the table so hard that I hurt my palm.

Still, she didn't move, didn't even wince.

V.C. Andrews® Books

V.C. ANDREWS®

Shattered
MEMORIES

POCKET BOOKS

New York   London   Toronto   Sydney   New Delhi

Pocket Books
An Imprint of Simon & Schuster, Inc.
1230 Avenue of the Americas
New York, NY 10020

Following the death of Virginia Andrews, the Andrews family worked with a carefully selected writer to organize and complete Virginia Andrews's stories and to create additional novels, of which this is one, inspired by her storytelling genius.

This book is a work of fiction. Any references to historical events, real people, or real places are used fictitiously. Other names, characters, places, and events are products of the author's imagination, and any resemblance to actual events or places or persons, living or dead, is entirely coincidental.

First Pocket Books paperback edition November 2017

V.C. ANDREWS® and VIRGINIA ANDREWS® are registered trademarks of Vanda Productions, LLC

POCKET and colophon are registered trademarks of Simon & Schuster, Inc.

For information about special discounts for bulk purchases, please contact Simon & Schuster Special Sales at 1-866-506-1949 or business@simonandschuster.com.

Manufactured in the United States of America

10 9 8 7 6 5 4 3 2 1

ISBN 978-1-4767-9238-5
ISBN 978-1-4767-9247-7 (ebook)

Shattered
MEMORIES

Prologue

I was dozing when my therapist, Dr. Sacks, entered my hospital room. I didn't know how long she was standing there, but the moment I realized she was there, I sat up. She smiled and sat at the foot of my bed.

A dark-brown-haired woman in her mid-forties, with hazel eyes that held you firmly in her gaze, Dr. Sacks had an overpowering intensity. During our sessions, it wasn't easy to avoid an unpleasant memory she wanted me to confront. Despite her diminutive size, standing just more than five feet tall, I saw that she had a very strong presence wherever she was or whomever she spoke with. Other doctors and nurses moved quickly to satisfy her demands.

"You're going home tomorrow," she said, in the tone of a fait accompli.

After all I had been through trapped in Anthony Cabot's basement, chained and starved at times, my self-respect all but crushed, crying until there were no more tears, pleading and praying until I was struck dumb and resigned to die, anyone would think her words would make me happier than I had ever been.

But the thought of going home had become almost as terrifying as Anthony Cabot's basement. I had never lived a day in my house without my sister, Haylee, who right now was incarcerated in an institution for the criminally ill because of what she had done to me and our family. She had enabled Anthony Cabot to abduct me, and she had kept silent about it while my parents and the police frantically searched for me. My mother had suffered a nervous breakdown. She and my father had divorced before all this had occurred. If anyone should feel like Humpty Dumpty, it was I. I had no reason to believe that even a skilled therapist like Dr. Sacks could put me back together.

"What about my mother?" I asked.

"It will be a while more for her," Dr. Sacks said. "Your father has moved back to be with you until your mother is well enough to return. I've spoken to her therapist, Dr. Jaffe. He doesn't think it will be much longer, but she will need home care for a while."

"Maybe I do, too."

"No. You'll be fine," Dr. Sacks said, with that now familiar firm assurance. "Your father will help. However, I think it would be better if we kept you from attending school for the time being. In fact, I've been discussing the idea of your transferring to another school, perhaps a private one, sufficiently far away to enable you to get a new start.

"But before any decisions are made," she quickly followed, "I think it would be best for you first to reacclimatize yourself to your home, get stronger, regain the weight you lost, and try to regain something of a normal life."

"A normal life?" I smirked at how ridiculous that description sounded to me now.

"You'll recuperate, Kaylee. You're young and you're strong. Not many could have survived what you have endured. You're very bright and resourceful."

"Am I? How did I misread my sister? How did I fall into the trap she set?"

"You trusted and you loved. In the end, you've given her more reason to be envious," Dr. Sacks said. She stood. "The truth is, you won't have time to pity yourself, Kaylee. When your mother comes home, you'll have a lot to do. I find that's the best medicine for anyone who's suffered: to care for someone suffering more.

"I'll see you weekly until the new school year starts, and then we'll figure out what you need in terms of therapy sessions. I've said it many times, Kaylee. If you constantly think of yourself as a victim, you'll be a victim. You're a survivor now. You're not a victim anymore."

"Okay," I said, my voice sounding small, like the voice of a child. Despite what she said and how she said it, hope, like a newborn canary, still struggled to sing.

"Your father will be here soon. I'm taking you completely off the medication." She stared at me a moment. "I'll be here for you, Kaylee." She squeezed my hand gently and left.

I lay back on the pillow. Vivid memories of the terror I had endured still came up like some sour food. Dr. Sacks once told me I was suffering from post-traumatic stress disorder, not unlike the psychological illness some soldiers suffered after being in horrible battles. Just like them, I experienced flashbacks, nightmares, and severe anxiety. She had just said she was taking me off the antianxiety medication, and while I knew I should be happy about that, surely she saw how frightening it sounded to me. I felt like someone who was learning how to ride a bike. Someone else was holding the bike as I mastered balancing and pedaling, and then suddenly, he or she let go, and I was on my own, sailing along but terrified of crashing.

In our therapy sessions, Dr. Sacks had worked on my finding ways to avoid thinking about the horrible experience and fearing their recurrence. At one point, she even had me visit the basement in the hospital with her to face down my fear of dark, closed-in places.

"Most people suffer some claustrophobia, Kaylee," she said, "but yours has been heightened. You've got to defeat it every chance you get."

I had so much more to overcome than anyone else my age. I longed for normal fears and anxieties, like taking an important test, being accepted by friends, meeting a boy you liked and hoped liked you, choosing the right things to wear, styling your hair so it flattered you, and dealing with the rules your parents laid out for your social life. Would that ever be all I faced?

About an hour later, my father appeared. I had been so centered on my recovery and therapy, I really hadn't considered how all of this had affected him, but when I looked at him now with clearer eyes, I saw the fatigue in his face and hated how it was aging him. I hoped he would enjoy a recovery, too.

"So, good news," he said. "Dr. Sacks believes you're ready. Tell me what clothes to bring back for you."

How easy it would be for any other girl my age to rattle off a specific blouse, a pair of jeans, a favorite light jacket, shoes and socks, I thought, but the request seemed enormous to me. Our mother had been a major decider of the simplest decisions in Haylee's and my life. Her neurosis, as Dr. Sacks described it, to keep us similar in every way had a major influence on how we perceived ourselves. I couldn't simply tell him, "Anything. It doesn't matter." It would always matter, because I would always wonder what Mother would want me to wear, want us to wear.

For a few panicky moments, I couldn't recall my wardrobe and where things were. He saw the fear in my face. How was I going to adjust to what Dr. Sacks called a "normal life" if I couldn't even deal with such an ordinary request? What made her think I was ready?

"I could pick things out for you," my father said quickly, seeing my hesitation. "I warn you, however, that your mother never thought I had any sense of fashion. Whenever I dressed myself, she would pounce like a drill instructor in a marine training camp and send me back to the closet. Remember?" he asked, smiling.

"Yes. Just choose any pair of jeans. I have some white blouses in the closet, and you'll find a light pink sweater on the shelf. There should be a blue denim jacket beside it." I almost couldn't say the words, but I did so quickly. "You'll find my bras and panties in the dresser drawers with my socks. Just any pair of running shoes."

"Got it," he said. "They're doing your paperwork, so I'll be back in an hour or so."

One of the nurses stepped in to take my vitals. She told my father she would help me take a shower and get ready to leave. I still didn't have enough hair to brush. One of Anthony Cabot's punishments was to cut it down to my scalp. After the nurse left, my father sat on the bed and took my left hand in his.

"We're going to be all right, Kaylee. Both of us will help each other through all this. I promise."

He leaned in to kiss me, and instinctively, I cringed and turned my head. He kissed me on my temple.

He didn't have to tell me. I thought it myself instantly.

The longer I suffer, the longer I fear, the more I will hate my sister.

Mother, of course, would say, "The longer you will hate yourself."

1

It had taken me almost two months after my rescue and recuperation to build up the courage to visit Haylee in the juvenile detention center where she was undergoing psychiatric evaluation and counseling, the result of an agreement between the district attorney and the defense attorney my father had to hire for her. With Mother also still in a mental hospital at the time, my father, despite how disappointed he was in Haylee, was the only one who really could be involved in her present and future. Our grandparents and my father's brothers and their families were too far away to be of real assistance and still in quite a state of shock over what had happened to me and what Haylee had done.

My father was overwhelmed himself by all that had occurred and had decided to take a leave of absence from his work for a few weeks after I was released from intensive psychiatric care following my rescue. He wanted to spend more time with me. Dr. Sacks had explained to him as well as to me that I had constantly to learn how to live with the memories of my horrible entrapment. He wanted to be there to help. Even though he needed the quiet time to handle all the legal and family issues, I knew he had put aside his professional life mostly to be there for me. In his mind, one of his daughters was probably lost forever. There was still a chance to save the other.

My father had lived with Haylee alone, too, while I was still trapped in Anthony Cabot's basement apartment, because Mother was in a mental hospital. No one at the time, including him, knew what Haylee had done. My father admitted that the police detectives had some suspicions concerning Haylee, but he wouldn't let them pursue her because he couldn't imagine her doing what she had done. A central part of her plan was never to reveal to Anthony Cabot that she had a twin sister, so he was convinced that I was Haylee when I met him at that clandestine rendezvous my sister had arranged.

Returning home felt so strange. Everything reminded me of Haylee and Mother, and it was weird at first not seeing either of them or hearing their voices and footsteps. Everything familiar had a different look to it. During those early hours at home, I anticipated Haylee popping out of a room or rushing up the stairs to tell me something "we must never tell anyone else or hope to die!"

The silence was loud and in some ways was the most difficult thing to contend with, especially those first few nights, when I had to have my bedroom lights on and the door open. I don't think my father slept very much, either. He was probably lying there in his bed, poised to jump up and rush to my side because a nightmare had exploded behind my closed eyelids.

Gradually, things improved, but almost as soon as my father brought me home, he and I immediately began to talk about my attending a private prep school, just as Dr. Sacks had intimated. From the things my father said, I realized he had obviously done a good deal of research on them.

"I agree with Dr. Sacks. I think you need a fresh start," he said. "Make new friends. I found what I think is one of the best schools for you, Littlefield. It's about sixty miles northeast of here. It has a great academic reputation. I took a ride to see it. It's on a beautiful campus just outside the city of Carbondale, and what I like the most is that the class sizes are pretty small. You'll get a lot of personal attention."

"Personal attention? More counseling?" I grimaced. "All my teachers will know and be expected to handle me in a special way?"

"No, no, of course not. Nothing concerning what has happened will be anyone's business," he quickly said. "We'll tell no one anything, not even the administration. You'll be just like any other student transferring in from a public school or a different private school."

"What if someone looks me up on the Internet? There were newspaper stories."

"Why would anyone do that, Kaylee? Look," he added, leaning forward, "you have to let it go, too. I know it's very difficult to do that, but if you don't, then, as Dr. Sacks says, you'll always be a victim. Right?"

"Right."

I wasn't going to disagree about the school. I was still quite fragile, and talk about making so dramatic a new move frightened me. However, Dr. Sacks and I had spent a great deal of our time together talking about how I thought I was going to feel when and if I returned to my present school and my friends began asking me questions, hoping to get me to give them the disgusting details. I knew what concerned her as well as me. How could I not think everyone would look at me and think of me as a victim forever? Most would assume I had been raped repeatedly during my abduction. They would see my denial as some sort of mental defense, smile, nod, and tell me how happy they were that it hadn't happened, but surely they would whisper about it when I wasn't around. Their suspicions would haunt me. Their eyes would study my face, my hands, my arms, any part of me that was exposed, looking for scars.

Actually, that sort of thing began as soon as people heard I had come home. Friends began to call, each one eager to be the first who had heard something, but I refused to speak to anyone. I knew what really lay beneath something as innocuous as "How are you now?" or "Thank God you were rescued." They would all hope to trigger a flood of information from me, information they would take and spread like birdseed at the front door of every other classmate.

My silence was unambiguous. I wouldn't tell anyone anything, no matter who it was. Some tried a few times and finally gave up. Soon no one called. I wouldn't accept any visitors, either, nor did I go anywhere on my own. My father was aware of how troubled I was about having to face down those inquisitive eyes. He tried to fill my time by taking me to restaurants out of our area and shopping in Philadelphia. At times, I thought he was in almost as deep a depression as Mother, who remained in the hospital. His emotions were inside a ping-pong ball bouncing from rage at Haylee and, of course, my abductor to sympathy for me, even sympathy for himself, and sometimes careening to compassionately consider Mother's condition, although I always had the sense that he countered her accusations against him by placing all the blame on her.

For weeks after I came home, he and I tried to make sense of it all. We talked for hours sometimes after dinner, and when I was finally able to describe in detail some of the terrible things I had endured, his face would redden and his lips would drip his rage at Haylee. I didn't want to upset my father, but Dr. Sacks had urged me to do this, to confront the demons. "The more you do, the faster you will defeat them," she said. Nevertheless, I knew it gave my father nightmares, as it still did to me.

Ironically, however, the more he voiced his anger at Haylee, the sorrier I felt for her, which also made me sorrier for myself. I guess I couldn't help it. It was instinctive. We had lived this long protecting and sympathizing with each other. How could I stop doing it now, no matter what the circumstances? Mother was never angry at one of us without being angry at the other. That was still true.

Haylee wasn't in a terrifying basement of terror like I had been, but just like me, she had a seemingly impossible challenge to overcome. How could she ever return to this world, her friends, and our school? The story was out; she was quite the villain, and I was quite the victim. Neither of us could face familiar faces. The irony was that we were still looking at the world in a similar way, and it was still looking at us the way it had. We were never able to throw off the oddity of being so similar in appearance. People called us the "Mirror Sisters," no matter what we did, apparently.

Would my visiting her now change any of it? Even when my father's anger simmered down to a low boil, he didn't push for me to visit Haylee and certainly never even suggested that I find a way to forgive her. In fact, he said, "If you never wanted to see or talk to her again, I'd understand. Who wouldn't?"

However, even though time has a way of frustrating vengeance, I'd be a liar if I said I didn't want to see her where she was suffering for what she had done and enjoy her pain. During the early days after my rescue, when I was in the hospital, I found relief in raging about Haylee. Dr. Sacks thought that was healthy. "Get it out. It's like steam. You need the release," she said. But even before that week ended, I was tempering the things I was saying about my sister, and if I did say something nasty, I always added, "But I bet she's sorry now."

I guess I was hoping that she was. Was I being stupid? I always looked quickly at Dr. Sacks to see if she would tell me any reason I should think Haylee was feeling sorry, but she either had no knowledge of Haylee's situation or didn't think it was wise to say. Whenever I asked my father about her, he would only say, "She's being processed through the system." That made it sound as if she were some sort of product being manufactured. She was placed on the assembly line of rehabilitation. What about me? Could I ever really be rehabilitated? Haylee could finally realize her guilt and feel remorse, maybe, but how would I really recover? The nightmares might hibernate, but they'd be back. I could go to another school, but could I make new friends? Would I ever trust anyone again? Friendships needed trust. Love especially needed it.

As my rage subsided, though, my curiosity about Haylee increased. Just what sort of state of mind was she in now? Did she really regret anything? And if she did, did she regret it only because she had been caught? What had been her real intentions for me? Did she want me gone forever, or in the back of her mind had she been planning to rescue me herself and become a hero instead of a villain? How much was she really hurting now?

Once, after I had come home from the hospital and after my father had visited Haylee for some legal reason, I asked him, "Did she ask about me?"

"I wouldn't let her," he said.

"What's that mean?"

"I made it clear to her from the start that I wouldn't believe she was asking sincerely about your condition, and I didn't volunteer any information. She's never going to work me again. I can assure you of that. Fool me once, shame on you; fool me twice, shame on me."

His eyes were steely cold.

I understood what he was saying, of course, but I also believed he had been away from us too long after the divorce to tell whether either of us was speaking sincerely. Haylee had burned him badly with her shrewd performance after Anthony Cabot had abducted me. My father described how she cried and went to my room to embrace my pillow and sob for hours. She broke everyone's heart by playing the piano while her face was streaked with tears, moaning that she could still hear me playing on mine and that it tore her heart. We had two pianos, and she and I would do duets. One of us never played without the other. Of course, she knew that. My father described how she had milked our friends of their sympathy and had taken advantage of everyone she could, getting classmates to do her homework for her and having them bring her gifts whenever they did visit. She was the "suffering princess," while I was practically being waterboarded by a psychopath.

My father listed the details like a prosecutor before a jury, a jury of one, me. If I mentioned something that reminded him of one of her conniving achievements, he went on and on from that example to another and then another.

"She had me up nights crying for her," he moaned, now feeling sorry for himself, too. "I couldn't work; I couldn't think. I did all sorts of things to get her not to worry about you and bought her all sorts of things, jewelry, dresses. I was even setting her up with her own car!"

He was still smarting from all that. He never stopped talking about it. It took little to set him off like a firecracker.

I knew that he was thinking she had made a terrible fool of him in the community. His reputation and self-respect were seriously damaged. He had to face the police, his friends, and his fellow employees and somehow explain how his own daughter had pulled the wool over his eyes. The memory of every call he had made demanding more action and more attention after I had been abducted stung him now. He had the answer to the mystery living in the same house with him all the time and didn't know it. If Haylee hadn't gone too far with her wild behavior, he might never have gone to her computer and discovered what she had done. I was sure that realization also gave him additional nightmares.

He insisted on keeping the door to her room shut now. He suggested that he might sell the second piano. He considered giving away all our duplicated toys from the past—iPads, cell phones, even her jewelry and especially anything new he had gotten for her. Of course, Mother would never give away anything, even after all this. Everything, no matter how small, carried an important memory for her.

"You would sell the piano?" I asked him when he rattled off his list.

"Why would we still need two? I can't imagine hearing another duet," he said. "I can't even imagine her back in this house! I want to get all her things out of here and nail the door to her room shut."

"Daddy, stop!" I cried. "You're worrying me!"

He calmed. I really was concerned. He might give himself a heart attack, and then what would happen to me? I couldn't imagine living with my grandparents or my uncles and aunts. I couldn't imagine them wanting me. I was damaged goods.

Of course, I understood his personal rage and why he blamed himself as well. On more than one occasion, he told me that a parent should know his own child well enough to realize when she is lying to him. I didn't come right out and say it, but I didn't think he should feel stupid for missing any clues. I just didn't know how to say it without making it look like Haylee had some special talent or gift, making it look like I still admired her for something.

But the truth was that even if he hadn't been away from us as long as he was, he wouldn't have been able to tell whether Haylee was lying. Haylee and I were truly closer to each other than any two sisters could be. Mother had brought us up thinking and behaving as if we were halves of one person.

If I was fooled, why should he be surprised that he was?

Maybe Haylee did have a special talent for lying, although *talent* seems like the wrong word. That should be reserved for good things, but some people were gifted when it came to deception. They were born politicians, diplomats, and poker faces. Haylee was especially good at lying and looking innocent. Sometimes when we were very little, she was able to get me out of trouble when I accidentally had done something wrong or had forgotten something Mother wanted neither of us ever to forget.

I had listened to Haylee twist the truth often. She did it so well that I almost believed her myself sometimes. Perhaps I was just as guilty of encouraging her because I appreciated the results she was able to achieve. I did admire her for how easily she could get people to believe what she wanted or question any criticism made of us, especially when we were permitted to attend public school at grade three after being homeschooled so long. She was always able to distort things to make us look better to the other students and our teachers.

Few would challenge her, and I did feel sorry for those who had. Woe be unto the person who triggered Haylee's ire, I'd think, by the time we were in junior high. She would find ways to get that person in trouble either with our teachers or with other students. I'd seen her do it successfully many times. Her picture was right beside the word *manipulator* in the dictionary.

But when I analyzed it all, I realized it was really my love for her more than her skill in deception that blinded me to what she had been planning for me with Anthony Cabot, the man who had abducted me. She wouldn't have been able to hook onto my concern for her and cleverly manipulate me to put myself in danger if I didn't love her as much as I did. It wasn't that I trusted her so much as that I was worried about her. Foolish me, I wanted to protect her. It was my chance to do something for her. I wanted so much to do it, when all along she had set the trap well.

Anthony Cabot was convinced that I was the one who had tempted him on that computer and promised him we'd have a life together. Many times in his basement apartment, my dungeon, he threw that back at me to justify what he was doing to me. I quickly realized that Haylee had told him that *her* name was Kaylee. When I tried to explain, he didn't even believe I had an identical twin sister, especially one that clever. How she must have laughed at my attempts to keep her safe—me, Kaylee Blossom Fitzgerald, trying to shelter her from trouble, pain, and even death itself, when all the while it was going to be my own life that was placed in danger.

Was she still laughing? Had she finally realized what a terrible thing she had done? How was she explaining it, justifying it, in her therapy sessions? What clever twist of the truth had she tried this time? Could she even manipulate psychiatrists? How evil was my sister after all? I couldn't stop wondering.

"I think I'm ready to see and speak to her, Daddy," I finally concluded one day.

Mother was making progress. Dr. Jaffe, her therapist, was talking about her being released soon, but with home care for a while, of course. As soon as she'd come home, I imagined her asking me about Haylee. She would be troubled that I knew nothing more about Haylee than what others had told her. How could I not be interested in my sister's fate, no matter what? How could I not find ways to know more? I was sure that to Mother it was still like my being interested in myself.

The truth was that I was interested, very interested, but not for the reasons Mother would hope. At night, before I went to sleep, I would lie awake and think about Haylee. *She's thinking about me, too, right now*, I told myself. I wanted so to believe it. I could almost hear her and see her lying there in her bed in whatever Spartan room she was in, a room perhaps with bars on the windows. In my mind, she had no television or anything to provide

her with her own music. She certainly had no telephone, and she wasn't much of a reader. Haylee
hated loneliness. She was terrified of the pantry
when Mother locked us in it as punishment when
we were little girls, far more terrified than I ever
was. Now she surely had a lot of time on her hands
to think. She had to be wondering about me and
how much I might hate her. She had to.

Did these thoughts haunt her as much as I
hoped they did? Did she ever ask her therapist to
contact me for her? Did she dream of speaking to
me on the phone? Did she stare out a front window
and imagine me coming to see her?

I tossed and turned in my sleep, thinking about
it. I was bouncing from anger to simple curiosity to
sympathy. Which would win out? I wondered.

It was time to stop wondering.

"You're really ready for this?" my father asked.

"I think so, yes."

"I haven't been there much, but during the
times I have been there, I haven't seen any significant remorse in her," he warned. "Maybe it's too
soon."

"You haven't been to see her for a while, Daddy,
and when you do go, you admittedly spend as little
time with her as you can."

"I don't need to go regularly or spend time with
her. I keep informed about her," he said, but not
convincingly.

"Do you? Frequently? Tell me honestly, when did you speak with her doctors last?"

"That's not the point," he said, a little annoyed. Like me, he was conflicted about Haylee and didn't want any reminders of his difficulties in coming to terms with that. "I don't want her to hurt you in any way anymore," he said. His lips still whitened a bit from his inner rage whenever he referred to her. "She's not going to hurt anyone in this family ever again."

"She won't," I said, with as much self-confidence as I could muster.

Was I at least a little frightened? Of course, but I couldn't let fear stop me. If I could overcome Anthony Cabot so often in that basement apartment that was a torture chamber, I could visit my twin sister and dare look her in her eyes, our eyes. I wanted her to see that I had not only survived but grown stronger. I might even thank her for it. She'd hate that, of course. It amused me to think of some ways to get back at her, to give her some pain. No question, there was some Haylee in me, too. The question was, was there any Kaylee in her, at least enough to feel regretful and help me quiet my own inner rage?

"Okay, if that's what you want," my father said, with obvious reluctance. "As you know, she's been undergoing psychotherapy, not unlike what you had but obviously for different reasons and under different circumstances."

"Will she eventually go to a real jail?"

"I don't expect so," he said. "She has no previous record of anything illegal. There's no proof she was working with this horrid man, conspiring directly with him. The police are convinced that she simply placed you in his path, in the danger, not that it makes much difference to me."

Or to me, I thought but didn't say.

"You know I had to hire an attorney to represent her. The most they were going after her for was obstruction of justice, preventing the police from finding you. Why she did it is, of course, why she's in counseling."

"Yes," I said. He wasn't telling me anything I didn't already know, but now I was even more determined. Despite what my father had said, I couldn't help but wonder how successful Haylee's counseling had been. How could any therapist even begin to unravel that knotted rope of emotions inside her? How deep had her anger and hate toward us all been? How could she possibly recover?

"I'd like to go to see her, Daddy," I said, now more insistent.

He nodded. He could see that it was time to put his rage in a closet and find a way to go forward. "I'll make arrangements for us."

"I want to see and speak to her without you being there in the room with us, Daddy."

He looked at me sharply, his eyes filling with concern. "Without me? Is that wise?"

"She's still my sister," I said. "I'm not afraid of her."

"Yeah, well, I am," he said, and then almost laughed. He shook his head. "She's a piece of work. Your mother's work," he added.

I didn't respond. Haylee and I were both pieces of our mother's work. He should see that. Maybe I was more interested in Haylee now because I was afraid not of her but of myself. I had to get over that fear to complete my own recovery. Despite my resistance to it and Haylee's resistance, too, Mother had us convinced we were too alike ever to be comfortable being different.

Would she prove to be right? Was I becoming more and more like Haylee, especially hard and vengeful, one of the side effects of my incarceration and my battle to survive? Her bedroom might be empty and her voice and footsteps gone from the house, but she could never be completely gone, not as long as I was here. I felt like I was absorbing her lingering spirit, keeping it part of me.

Two days went by without my father mentioning anything about a visit. Even though I wasn't ready to return to any school, much less mine, I occupied myself by reading my textbooks and following the recommended literature list. I made our dinners, baked cookies and a cake, and looked after the house.

I even washed windows. No matter what I did, time seemed to trickle like drops of honey or molasses.

I couldn't get interested in television shows, especially soap operas. There were too many memories of Haylee, Mother, and me watching them together.

Every time I walked past Haylee's room, even with the door shut, I'd stop and listen, recalling the sound of her voice when she was talking on her phone. Sometimes she would pause and call to me. "I know you're there, Kaylee," she would say when I was standing just outside. She'd laugh. "My sister is eavesdropping. She's looking for pointers on how to talk to you boys," she'd tell the boy she was toying with on the phone, and then laugh at something he might have said.

I'd hurry away, trying to deny to myself that she was right.

Finally, on the third day, when my father returned home from work, he announced that Haylee's doctor had approved the idea of my visiting.

"As your parent and guardian, I gave Dr. Sacks permission to send Haylee's doctor your psychological therapy report," he told me. "Dr. Alexander, Haylee's psychiatrist, asked to see it first before deciding whether to allow the visit right now. She received it yesterday."

"Why did she want my report? Why did she want to know about me?"

"She likes to know the minefield she's crossing," he said, half kidding. "Anyway, she's approved the visit, so I'll take you there this Saturday."

Now that I was going to do it, I grew very nervous and questioned whether I really should see her. I certainly didn't want to forgive her, at least not this soon and not without seeing her show some shame and regret.

My father sensed my hesitation. "You don't have to do this. No one, least of all me, would expect you to care one iota about her ever again. I mean it."

"We can't hate each other, Daddy. It's just not possible," I said.

Did I believe it myself, even though I sounded so sincere?

He didn't look disappointed. It was, after all, difficult, if not impossible, for a parent to hate his own child, even a child who had done so much damage to all of us.

After a moment, he smiled. "I wonder if she'll ever say the same thing about you."

I couldn't help but wonder myself. There was only one way to find out.

And like most things you're not sure of and fear, you half wonder if you're better off not knowing after all.

2

It was a beautiful September day, too beautiful to spend in the confines of a mental institution, especially one housing people who had committed evil and illegal acts, although I was surprised at how perfectly the grounds were kept. Men were mowing the grass and trimming hedges as if it were some wealthy person's estate. There were flower beds with a mixture of red, white, and pink evenly spaced along the front and pretty maple and oak trees with redwood benches beneath some of them. From the road, no one could recognize what this place was. Even the sign announcing it as we drove up the long approach to the stark L-shaped, three-story white stucco building was written in small letters, more like a whisper voiced by someone embarrassed or ashamed.

The windows on the second and third floors were smaller than those on the first. I imagined one of them to be Haylee's room, but there were no bars. In fact, other than the guard at the entrance, there was nothing dramatic to indicate that the people inside were kept there against their will. No walls or high fences surrounded the property and certainly no barbed wire.

I was still thinking prison. My father hadn't told me much about the place. He didn't like talking about his visits here, and I had stopped asking, but a part of me was hoping at least to see it as austere, cold, and ugly. I wanted Haylee to be unhappy from the day she had been brought here. I wanted her to immediately see something that would tell her she was a person not welcome in society and that there would be no rewards for what she had done. This was supposed to be where people were sent when they were wrong, whether they could help it or not.

I was disappointed when we drove up, imagining the first day Haylee was brought here. She hadn't cringed at the sight of it; that was for sure. Knowing her so well, I thought she had probably smiled, laughing inside at how successful she had been in convincing a judge she wasn't really responsible for what she had done.

Off to the right, I saw a tall man in a light blue short-sleeved shirt and dark slacks talking to a teenage boy dressed in a black T-shirt with some rock-band insignia in bright green letters around a stark-white skull. He wore jeans and a pair of white running shoes. The man had his right hand on the boy's shoulder and looked like a coach talking to a member of his team. The boy was nodding his head and listening. He was obviously not an employee.

This answered one of my first questions. The inmates or patients—I wasn't sure what to call them—weren't wearing uniforms. It was another disappointment. I knew how much Haylee would have hated that, and I'd been looking forward to seeing her in something drab, something that clearly identified her as a prisoner and not a visitor, and something especially unfeminine.

At least, there was a guard in a dark blue uniform with a large silver badge at the booth you had to pass in order to enter the parking lot. He looked up from a magazine he was reading and waited for my father to lower his car window and hand him his driver's license. The guard nodded like he recognized him. Nevertheless, he copied my father's information on a clipboard and handed the license back to him. Then he nodded at me. My father had told me to make sure I brought my driver's license, too. I dug it out of my purse quickly and handed it to my father, who handed it to the guard. The man looked at my picture and at me, pausing a moment like someone suspicious, and then wrote the information on the clipboard.

How much did he really know about us? I wondered. Had he ever seen Haylee? Did he think my father had somehow gotten permission to take Haylee out for a while and was now returning her? Perhaps he didn't know or see any of the inmates or patients here. If he was able to see Haylee, I was sure he'd be amazed at how alike we looked, just as most strangers were when they first confronted the two of us, and maybe he'd wonder why one of us had ended up here.

My father gave me my license and drove into the parking lot. I could sense from how tight his jaw was and the stiff way he held himself that he hated being here, detested it, in fact. He had his shoulders hoisted like someone anticipating a blow. After he shut off the engine, he sat for a moment, his teeth clenched, and I was thinking he might be changing his mind.

"Okay, here's how this is going to work," he began, sitting there and looking forward as if he were reciting. "There is a lobby much like a hospital lobby. We're going to sign you in there, too, and then we'll wait for Haylee's doctor, Dr. Laura Alexander, to come for you. She will take you to her office and talk to you for a while. She's going to want to feel comfortable about your visit with Haylee. I'm not sure if she'll let me go with you to her office."

"She's going to want to feel comfortable about

my visit? Why does she have to feel comfortable about it?"

"Maybe *comfortable* is the wrong word. I mean she has to be sure she's doing the right thing in allowing the visit. She knows what Haylee has done to you. Ordinarily, people who have been victimized by the people in there, injured in some way or another, don't visit them, even when they are members of the same family. Dr. Alexander doesn't want anything unpleasant to happen here that might disturb Haylee."

"What? Disturb Haylee? She's worrying about disturbing Haylee?"

"You'll have to understand that her first concern is for Haylee and not you, Kaylee. You're not her patient; Haylee is. From what I've gathered from talking to her about this, I think she's agreed to your visit because she wants some confirmation that Haylee is truthfully regretful or moving clearly in that direction."

I smiled. "Haylee could convince anyone of anything if she thought it would help her or make her feel better about something."

"Dr. Alexander is an experienced psychiatrist, Kaylee. She's been practicing for more than fifteen years."

"Haylee's been practicing for nearly seventeen," I said.

"If you think she can successfully lie right to

your face and anyone else's, why do you want to see her?" he snapped back at me.

"It'll be different now," I told him confidently. "I have better lenses on my eyes. And I know her better than any doctor ever could."

He thought a moment and then nodded. "I bet you do; lenses better than mine, for sure. Okay. Let's go," he said, and opened his door.

I followed him to the front entrance. He hesitated just a little before he opened it. I was sure he was still struggling with the fear that he was doing me more harm than good by permitting me to see Haylee. But it was foolish to think, even to hope, that she and I would never see each other again. Better that this happened sooner rather than later, I thought, and I believed he reluctantly thought so, too.

Inside, there was another uniformed guard waiting near a metal detector. It buzzed when my father passed through, and the guard moved a wand over him and inspected his keys and his money clip. Nothing buzzed on me. He nodded for us to continue entering.

My father was right. It was like a typical hospital lobby, with a shiny light brown tile floor, some rust-colored leather or imitation leather settees, and a few chairs and side tables with magazine racks on both sides. There was even a table with a coffee machine and cups. The one thing that struck me as different were the walls—bare, no paintings, nothing. Straight ahead of us was a glass enclosure with a window that was slid open. Another man in a blue uniform similar to those of the other guards was behind the desk. On his right was a woman in the same uniform working on a computer. They both looked at us curiously. I had the feeling they didn't get many visitors who were otherwise not professionally involved with the patients.

"I'm Mason Fitzgerald," my father said immediately. "And this is my daughter, Kaylee. Dr. Alexander is waiting to see us."

The uniformed receptionist looked at some papers on his desk and then nodded at the clipboard on the counter in front of us. We had to sign in again, and again we were asked for our licenses. The guard copied down the numbers. I couldn't miss seeing the video camera on us. If anything finally convinced me that I was in a secured institution, it was all this care and observation and double-checking of those who visited.

"I'll let Dr. Alexander know you're here," he said, handing us visitor passes and nodding toward the settees.

My father indicated that I should stick on the pass just above my right breast. It was plain white, with the date and time and the prominent word *VISITOR*, with a tracking bar and some numbers.

We sat, neither of us saying anything. I was

impressed with the stillness. I had all sorts of frightening images in mind, most from movies that took
place in such places. I imagined mentally disturbed
inmates screaming, guards yelling, and some eleva-
tor music playing. The quiet was more disturbing,
however. I felt myself fidgeting, shifting in my seat,
and twirling some strands of the wig I wore over
my too-short hair. It was something Haylee often
did as well when she was nervous, fingering her
hair. It was practically the only way I could tell that
she ever *was* nervous.

My eyes wandered toward the magazines. I
was going to reach for one but stopped. I thought
I'd feel like I was waiting to see the dentist, and I
wouldn't comprehend anything I read anyway. I
forced myself to sit still and stare ahead. The guard
at the metal detector watched us for a few moments
and then walked over to the window and began
talking to the seated guard. Haylee was behind
those walls somewhere. I could feel my heartbeat
quickening from the moment we had entered, and
it had yet to settle down.

"Dr. Alexander will be out soon," my father
said, sensing my discomfort. "She strikes me as a
very efficient person who hates to waste her time or
anyone else's."

I nodded, but now that I was here and what I
was about to do was imminent, a part of me wanted
to get up and run out. How had we come to this,

my mother's precious, perfect twins? How do you know someone almost as well as you've known yourself all your life and suddenly realize she's betrayed you so dramatically that any love or affection you cherished between you was popped and gone as quickly as a soap bubble?

Of course, there were many things Haylee had done to me in the past that were irritating, if not outright painful, such as trying to steal a boyfriend or driving away my friends because she was jealous of my friendship with them or knew they didn't like her. Even though we were taught to share and be fair with each other all our lives, I would have to admit she forced me to do the things she wanted far more than she did anything I wanted. Maybe it was my fault for being so forgiving. Maybe I should have listened more closely to the adage "If you give them an inch, they'll take a mile."

Haylee would be the first to say that if someone was fooled by someone else, it was her own fault. She loved that "buyer beware" idea and often excused students who hurt other students. "It's her fault for being too trusting," she would tell me, speaking of the victim. "I don't feel sorry for her."

Why didn't I listen to the subtle warnings she was giving me about herself and me?

Shouldn't I have seen it coming? We breathed the same air, ate the same food, and heard the same things almost every day of our lives. People were amazed at how we moved together, pausing and turning simultaneously. Only conjoined twins were more *simpatico*. Yet I hadn't detected the biggest deception of all. Despite the fact that I hated agreeing with her about anything, especially now, I had to admit that I was more angry at myself for being stupid than I was angry at her.

Dr. Alexander stepped into the lobby. I heard the clicking of her heels on the tile floors just before she appeared. She was wearing an ankle-length light green skirt and matching blouse. In her high heels, she looked more than six feet tall. I wasn't surprised that my father hadn't mentioned she was African American. Neither of my parents ever showed any prejudice. My father had some very clever and accomplished African American men in his company and one of them, Al Daniels, used to play tennis at our home.

Dr. Alexander's striking ebony eyes immediately fixed on me as she approached. I felt like a target in someone's gun sights. She walked with a runway model's poise. My first thought now was how Mother would definitely compliment her on her posture and say, "There, that's how I want you to walk."

The doctor's demeanor reflected the self-confidence and efficiency my father claimed she had. His reminder that Haylee, not I, was her patient resonated. I felt immediately that she wasn't at all interested in making me feel comfortable or welcome. She didn't exhibit any sensitivity to how this visit was difficult for me. Instead, her eyes were full of stern, suspicious questions. We stood, and she offered me her hand. She barely glanced at my father. Only now, when I was confronting her, did it strike me that of course she'd have to be on guard against me wanting to do Haylee harm. She was visually frisking me for signs of anger and vengeance.

"I'm Dr. Alexander," she said. She looked at my father but held my hand. "I have seen other monozygotic twins, but I must say, these two girls are remarkable." She let go of my hand. "Kaylee, I'm happy to meet you."

There wasn't much feeling behind that. It was more like scientific curiosity. Her voice was a little deeper than I'd expected and even, I thought, had a slightly foreign accent, perhaps Caribbean.

"Thank you," I said, sounding just as mechanical.

"We'll go to my office for a chat first. Mr. Fitzgerald," she added, nodding and giving him permission to come along.

I hesitated. "My sister knows I'm coming?"

"She knows," Dr. Alexander replied, then led us through the lobby and to a long hallway. "My office is right down here on the right."

I remained a step or two behind them. When

she turned to speak to me, there was no polite smile on her face, and those eyes didn't warm. Whether it was her intention or not, she was very intimidating. If I had come here to do my sister any real harm, meeting Dr. Alexander would have given me second thoughts, if it didn't send me into a quick retreat immediately.

The first thing I thought of when we entered her office was that this probably was where Haylee came for her sessions. There were two pictures on the walls, one a seascape and the other a view of a lavender field with mountains on the horizon. They were both prints, pretty but not in any way extraordinary. Her desk was a light wood, like some school desk, with not much on it besides a long notepad, a closed laptop, and a receptacle for paper clips and pens. I saw no pictures of family anywhere. I didn't even see the usual plaques doctors and dentists keep on their walls to reveal their degrees and schools. There was no sense of her. Actually, it appeared to be an office anyone could share. Maybe it was.

The window behind the desk faced the rear of the building, where there was nothing more than grass, some rolling hills, and patches of woods. There was very little activity to distract a patient in counseling. To the right of the desk and angled to face it was a soft black-cushioned settee, and to the left of the desk were shelves with binders organized by date. On one of the shelves was a small clock in a wooden cabinet that looked like a cheap souvenir clock bought at some store for tourists in Switzerland.

Haylee would feel uncomfortable here, I thought, because I did, and not simply because it was a psychiatrist's office. It was too austere. She'd hate the view and hate that there was so little to distract her. Maybe she'd look down and count floor tiles. I remembered how she could frustrate our school guidance counselor, Ms. Lothrop, with her clear disinterest, interrupting her constantly with questions about her family pictures and her plaques.

Dr. Alexander sat behind her desk and nodded at the settee. "Please," she said.

My father waited for me to sit and then sat himself.

"What do you hope to accomplish with this visit today?" Dr. Alexander asked me immediately. It sounded more like a demand, almost an accusation. Someone cruder would have asked, "Why did you come here? What do you want? Why can't you leave her alone and let her get well? Why the hell are you interfering?" She leaned forward in anticipation of my reply.

"I'm not going to start yelling at her or anything," I said.

She stared, obviously waiting for another, fuller

answer. I glanced at my father. He looked just as interested in my response as Dr. Alexander might be.

"Nothing my sister has done to me was as bad as this, of course," I began, "but I always felt, hoped, that she was sorry for what she did. I don't think she hates me, and I don't want to hate her for the rest of my life, either. I thought we still might share that idea."

I didn't see a smile on her face as much as I saw a glint of approval in her eyes, even a little appreciation. She resembled how one of my teachers would look if I had grasped a particularly difficult problem or concept well, something he or she had taken great pains to explain. She gave my father a slight nod, confirming, I imagined, that what he had told her about me was correct.

"Very well. I'm going to take you to a sort of interview room. It's just a room with a metal table and two chairs," she said. "You can be alone with your sister, but I will be watching and listening to the two of you. Only me," she added, raising her eyebrows, I thought, for my father's benefit as much as mine.

"Through one of those one-way mirror windows?"

"Yes," she said, finally giving me a real smile. "I'm sure you appreciate why."

"Do you consider my sister dangerous?"

Her smile flew off her face like a frightened

bird leaping off a branch. "I don't answer questions about your sister asked by anyone but official personnel," she said. "But if I considered her dangerous, I certainly wouldn't allow the visit."

"Has my sister been in that room before?" I asked, ignoring her indignation.

"Why?"

"Because she'd realize what the mirror really was. She might not be honest. She would know she had an audience. My sister always likes an audience. More than I do," I quickly added before she could ask.

All my life, whenever anything was said about one of us, whoever heard it always asked if either Haylee or I felt the same way, happy or unhappy about it. We knew Mother wanted us to say yes, but she wasn't with me now, and even if she were, I wouldn't say yes. I didn't think I ever would again, even if it was true.

Dr. Alexander thought a moment and sat back like she was reconsidering the wisdom of my seeing Haylee. "What are your feelings right now?" she asked. "Now that you're here and about to do this."

Since I had brought up Haylee's dishonesty, I wondered just how honest *I* should be. At the moment, this felt like another security scan. If I didn't answer correctly, I'd be turned around and marched right out and off the grounds.

"A mixture of fear, anger, and curiosity," I replied. "I'm nervous about seeing her. Maybe once I do, I'll just turn around and walk out. Maybe I'll start crying. I don't know. That's why I came, to see what my reaction to her would be and her reaction to me. Someday we have to meet, and I thought, why not now? Enough time has passed for me. I hope it has for her as well."

Does she stare at Haylee like this after she answers one of her questions? I wondered. I didn't look away or down.

Because of the long pause, I thought that just as I expected, she was going to tell us she had changed her mind, but instead, she rose.

"You are free to remain here, Mr. Fitzgerald," she told my father. "The session your daughters will have together will be for fifteen minutes."

"Thank you," my father said. He nodded to me, and I stood. Then he reached for my hand. It was just a gentle squeeze, a little assurance that he was right here for me.

"This way," Dr. Alexander said, and she opened her office door.

We walked down the hallway. It was still much quieter than I had expected. It was a long, immaculate hallway with coffee-white tiled floors similar to the ones in her office and gray walls that resembled steel. I could see windowless double doors at the far end and thought we'd be passing through them, but she suddenly paused at a door on our right. She turned to me, and although she didn't smile, she spoke in a softer tone.

"I want you to know that I do feel sorry about what happened to you, Kaylee. However, I have learned a great deal about your family and what you both have endured, so I feel sorry for your sister, too. You understand?"

"Yes," I said. I didn't want to share any sympathy with Haylee, but I did understand.

"She's not here yet. I will have her brought. Don't expect to see a monster," she added. "She's just as frightened about this visit as you are."

I couldn't imagine it, but I kept myself from smirking with skepticism. *Remain as impassive as you can*, I told myself. *You're being scrutinized almost as much as your sister.*

"Okay," Dr. Alexander said when I didn't say anything, and she opened the door.

The room was as simple as she had described, with its metal table and chairs. However, the chairs had black cushions. There was nothing on the table. The floor was covered with the same large tiles that were in the hallway and her office. There was recessed lighting from above and a telephone on the wall that I imagined was for emergencies. I went to the chair on the other side of the table and sat. The one-way mirror window was to my left. I glanced at it and saw myself sitting there.

This morning when I woke up and got dressed, I had taken a long time to choose what to wear and how to do my makeup. Recently, my father had taken me shopping, and I had bought a new dress, which I was wearing today. When I was looking at the new fashions for the season, I couldn't help but think the way Haylee would. She was always pushing me to get something sexier. Since Mother wouldn't buy either of us anything the other didn't like or want, even when we were teenagers, I usually agreed with Haylee's choices. Otherwise, she'd be so unhappy and I would feel so terrible that neither of us could be satisfied with what was purchased for us. It was better to go along with Haylee's selections.

When I had taken this dress off the rack, my father was standing behind me. He stepped forward as I held it up, and he shook his head.

"What?"

"There's not much to it," he said, and I laughed. Those words would have clinched the choice for Haylee.

He felt the material and shrugged. "I could fold it up and put it in a business envelope."

"I'll try it on," I told him, and went into the dressing room.

The dress was a kaleidoscope print, in poly-blend stretch knit with a cap-sleeved bodice. It had a deep V neckline. Thanks to Haylee, I had just the right bra for it. The multicolor print was in shades of pink, teal, blue, and yellow. It fit me like a second skin. The banded waist topped a bodycon skirt that I thought was flattering, if not revealing, the way it traced every muscle in my hips and buttocks. The hem of the skirt was a good six inches above my knees. It was truly a Haylee dress.

When I stepped out of the dressing room, my father's eyes flew wide open. He shook his head, a slight but fearful smile on his face. "I'm sure you need some sort of license to wear that," he said.

I turned to see myself from every angle as I considered myself in the mirror. I surely felt like Haylee would feel, I thought. The dress was exciting on me, and I was happy I had gained back all the weight I had lost in Anthony Cabot's dungeon basement apartment. There was no question; the dress possessed me. I could hear Haylee beside me whispering, *Say you want this. Say it because I want it.*

"I like it, Daddy."

"Whatever," he said. "What do I know about clothes for teenage girls today?"

Afterward, he bought me a pair of black suede platform heels to go with it. I knew just the earrings and bracelet I'd wear with it, too.

When I looked at the dress this morning, I envisioned Haylee seeing me in it. The very sight of me looking so healthy and sexy would be a vengeful blow to her ego. She was probably expecting to see a meek, terribly wounded person who could be nothing but ultra-conservative with her fashions now. Sexually abused girls would be terrified of lustful looks. But I wasn't, and that would surely drive home how bad a situation she was in because of her own actions.

I couldn't imagine they would let Haylee have makeup, so I put mine on a little heavier than usual. My hair had grown about two inches since my rescue, which was not enough, of course. My father had bought me three wigs by now, all in my natural hair color but in three different styles and cuts. The one I chose today was the shortest. I wondered if Haylee would realize it was a wig, and if she did, would she dare ask why I was wearing one? I'd tell her, I vowed. I'd tell her every detail about that.

"You're wearing that to the institution?" my father had asked when I descended the stairway in the morning.

"I'm not going to look like a victim, Daddy," I said. I saw the glint in his eyes. He knew what I was up to, and at that moment, he was happy about my choice and my reason for it.

But it was a moment he would regret later.

Maybe we all would.

3

I was holding my breath when the door began to open. I was anticipating that all-too-familiar smirk on her face the moment she saw me. Of course, I wanted to see her beaten down, defeated, even something that was so unfamiliar to her that she had trouble wearing it: a look of apology and regret. Instead, she was none of that. She was expressionless, almost indifferent, but I think what shocked me most was her hair.

It was as short as the hair on the wig I was wearing, practically the exact same length. Even though it was impossible, of course, I even wondered if Mother had called to tell her to have her hair cut. I still had the childhood fantasy that she could envision us both whenever she wanted to and wanted to be sure we were alike.

Haylee was dressed in a plain white short-sleeved blouse and a pair of dark blue jeans, with no socks and a pair of black slip-on sneakers. As I expected, she wore no makeup, not even lipstick. She was thinner than I had anticipated, and despite how long I had been in Anthony Cabot's basement, in the hospital, and inside my house, she was paler than I was.

She hesitated and stared at me. The attendant who had brought her remained outside but closed the door, so we were now alone in the room, except, of course, for Dr. Alexander behind the mirror. Haylee glanced around and then looked at me without an iota of surprise, like I had been visiting her daily.

"Did you just get that dress?" she asked, as casually as she would if nothing at all had happened and we were still at home.

"Recently, yes."

"Did Daddy buy two?"

"Hardly," I said. "Why would he?"

She nodded, not even a small wrinkle at the corner of her lips. But I didn't think she looked angry or even disappointed.

"When did you cut your hair?" I asked, not hiding my suspicions.

"Yesterday," she said. At first, I thought she wasn't going to sit. She gazed at herself in the mirror and brushed back what hair she had. "Does it look terrible? I only spent ten minutes on it."

"You mean you literally cut it yourself?"

She spun around. "Attempted to. Someone else finished. They get hairstylists in training here to work on the poor jerks like me." She started to circle the table. "Stand up. I want to see the dress."

I did.

"Daddy bought you that without me whining for it or telling you to demand it?"

"I'm wearing it, aren't I?"

"You don't look bad at all," she said, still trying to sound indifferent, but I thought I also heard disappointment. "Overall, you look very good. A little overly made up, maybe, but nice hairstyle. You would pass our famous Haylee inspection."

"I did look bad," I said. "Very bad. I'm wearing a wig. My hair was butchered—but not by a stylist in training."

She shrugged and flopped into the chair across from me. "Whatever. It looks very nice, natural."

"Whatever? It took me weeks to gain some of the weight I lost. There were times he starved me and times I couldn't eat."

She shrugged again. "I wouldn't have noticed any weight loss if you hadn't told me. I lost some weight, too."

Her indifference triggered frustration inside me, frustration that felt like a hand tightening into a fist. "You lost some weight?" I said. "How unfortunate. Do you remember how long I was locked away?"

"Time is the stream I go fishing in," she replied, following with a trickle of a laugh.

"What?"

"That essay on Thoreau we had to write—you had to write, I should say. I was so bored. I hated writing essays."

"Essays? That's what you're thinking about now?"

"I can't believe Daddy bought you that dress. I guess you're his favorite now."

"Can you blame him?"

She looked around and then directly at the mirror, but obviously not trying to see through it.

"I just woke up one morning and thought I should cut it," she said, patting her hair again. "I was beginning to look too drab." She turned back and stared at me a moment before she smiled. "You were always his favorite anyway, Kaylee. You didn't know it, but I did. You were everyone's favorite, even Mother's. I learned that pretty quickly when you were gone."

"Is that why you did it?"

"That's the million-dollar question, isn't it? Why did I do it?"

"I don't have a million dollars, but I'd like to know."

"Why? Would it change anything?"

"I don't know. How can I know the answer without knowing why?"

"Oh, you're so . . . logical," she said, and then,

taking me by complete surprise, she burst out laughing. But it wasn't simply laughing; it was a strange combination of laughing and crying, and it was loud, too, very loud, insanely loud.

I didn't think she was going to stop. Tears were streaking down her cheeks. She gasped and laughed, looked up and then at me, and laughed again.

"You're . . . so . . . logical. You always were. You're so . . . Kaylee Blossom Fitzgerald," she said. She stopped smiling. "Why? Why? Why? Why?"

She started to chant. "Look at you, look at you. You look good. You lied. You pretended to be abducted. Where were you? Logical Kaylee? Where were you? Watching us all the time and laughing?"

"Stop it," I said. "You know very well where I was and why."

"Yes, why? Why? Why?" She sat there smiling.

"Aren't you even a little sorry?" I asked.

"Sorry? Everyone feels sorrier for you, don't they? You don't need me, too. You have everyone's full attention now, don't you? Thank you. I'd like to hear a thank you."

"Thank you? Don't you have any idea what happened to me? You think I went on a picnic?"

"What happened to you, yes. Everyone wants to know what happened to you, right? Yes? Questions. We get questions, only you get the most. I get only Why? Why? Why? I hear it even in my sleep."

"So what's the answer?"

"There's no answer. Don't you understand? There's no answer. There's never been an answer." She hugged herself and looked up at the ceiling.

"You haven't asked about Mother," I said.

She continued to stare at the ceiling for another moment and then lowered her head and leaned toward me. "Mother is in here," she whispered. "I don't have to ask about her. Mother is with me. I've got Mother now. You know why? Why? Why? Because she wants to know why, too."

She laughed.

"Mother wants to know more than anyone else, so she's here," she said, and pressed her right hand over her heart. "She's right here, and she won't leave until she gets the answer. Anyway, you can't have her back. You can't have her without me. It's not logical, Logical Kaylee."

"Mother's not here," I said. "I know exactly where she is. I've visited her. She's not well. She's suffered a lot, Haylee. I feel sorrier for her than I do for myself, and you should, too."

She stared at me hard, her eyelids narrowing. "She's here," she said. "Here." She pressed her hand even harder against her heart.

"No, she's in a hospital. Stop pretending you don't know what I mean. She had a nervous break-down, Haylee. You knew that. You knew why Daddy had to come back home to live with you."

She shook her head.

"Did you hear what I said? You've got to stop lying, Haylee, to everyone and to yourself. You're hurting only yourself now. Why did you do this to me? What did I do to you that you should have wanted to hurt me so much?"

She smiled, but there was no warmth in it. "You don't look like me anymore, Kaylee. You're prettier than I am now, but Mother can't stand that, I'm sure." She leaned forward to whisper. "Did you forget how she wants us to be? You're killing her by being so much prettier than me. You're the one giving her the nervous breakdown now."

Her lips began to tremble. "You're killing her," she said, and started to cry. Then she began to rock in her chair, hugging herself again. "It's cold here, isn't it? Why? I'm tired. Why? You look very good. Why?"

"Stop it," I said. "You're just trying to avoid answering me."

She stopped rocking, but she sat there, her arms locked around herself, and stared at me.

"I came to talk to you sensibly, Haylee. I almost died. I did everything I could to survive, but it was horrible, nights without sleep, chained, my very breathing controlled. You knew it would be horrible. You knew him, and you left me there."

What surprised me about the way she was staring at me was that she didn't even blink. It was as if I were looking at a picture of her face.

"Do you hear me?"

She didn't move; she didn't stop staring.

"Haylee," I said sharply. "Cut it out. You know I can tell when you're pretending. Stop it!"

There was no reaction.

"Stop!" I screamed, and slapped the top of the table so hard that I hurt my palm.

Still, she didn't move, didn't even wince.

I looked at the mirror, and a few moments later, the door opened, and Dr. Alexander came in with two male attendants. She looked at me first.

"Please return to my office," she said.

"What?" I looked at Haylee. She still hadn't moved, nor had anything changed on her face. "Stop it, Haylee," I said. "You have to talk to me."

"Please," Dr. Alexander said, but sharply. "Return to my office."

I rose slowly. Haylee's eyes didn't follow me. She sat there looking forward, as if I were still in front of her. I started out, looking back at her. Dr. Alexander put her hand on Haylee's shoulder, but she didn't turn. I hesitated in the doorway, and then Dr. Alexander looked at me.

"Return to my office," she commanded. "Now!"

I hurried out and down the hallway, almost as terrified as I had been in Anthony Cabot's basement. My heart was racing, and I was gasping for breath.

"Something happened," I told my father as soon as I entered the office and he looked up. I was crying now, too.

"What?" He leaped to his feet. "What's wrong? What happened? What did she do to you?"

"We started talking, and then she stopped and just stared at me. She didn't even blink. It was horrible. She froze. It was a nightmare," I said, and continued to cry.

He quickly embraced me. "I knew this was a mistake. I knew it," he said, holding me against him.

"I couldn't tell whether she was acting or not, Daddy. I couldn't tell. She was so weird. She said so many crazy things. She told me Mother was here, with her."

He led me to the settee. "All right. Take it easy. I'll see what I can find out," he said. "Just stay right there. I'll get you a glass of water, too."

I covered my face with my palms and sat there. A few minutes went by before he returned with a glass of water for me.

"Did you see Dr. Alexander?" I asked, and drank.

"No. An attendant told me to wait here," he said. "He got me your water."

He sat beside me and held my hand. I could see the anger boiling in his face, but I didn't know what to say to calm him. I was still too stunned. Almost ten full minutes went by before Dr. Alexander came to her office. My father continued to mumble under his breath, blaming himself. We both turned to the doctor when she entered.

"What happened?" my father demanded, even before she closed the door.

She didn't speak. She went behind her desk as if she wanted to keep it between us like a barrier and sat.

"I want to know exactly what's going on now," my father insisted.

"Please," she said, nodding at the settee.

He and I sat.

"Well?" he asked.

"Your daughter has been suffering periodic catatonia," she began.

I stopped my sniffling but held on to my father's hand.

"Catatonia?" my father asked.

"It's generally described as an abnormality of movement and behavior arising from a disturbed mental state."

"What mental state?"

"In her case, I'm pretty positive it's schizophrenia, Mr. Fitzgerald. I think she's been suffering with it for some time. Some time before she was brought here," she added.

My father sat back, his anger checked, but he was far from satisfied. "I didn't see any of this catatonia when I visited the last time," he said.

"It was coming on. You weren't here frequently enough to notice the developing symptoms." It didn't sound like a criticism but more like a simple fact. "Catatonia can take different forms. In Haylee's case, it takes the form of rigidity. If it took the other form, catatonic excitement or excessive movement, she'd be taking violent action against herself. We should be grateful for little things," she added, which I guessed was her attempt to lighten the mood.

My father didn't look like he appreciated it. "So exactly what just happened with Kaylee?" he asked.

"Disappointingly, the confrontation was too much for Haylee. She went into a catatonic stupor. She was, and still is at this moment, mute and rigid."

"How long will she be like this?" he asked.

"It's hard to say. It could last a while, even though a prolonged period would be painful. If it goes on too long this time, I'll put her on some medication that will help, but the principal cause of it is what we'll be spending most of our time on now."

"You said schizophrenia?"

"There are complicated things happening to her right now, Mr. Fitzgerald. One of them is, naturally, her paranoia. She believes everyone, even people who don't know her, knows what she has done and is out to harm her in some way. I was hoping that confronting Kaylee might ease that symptom."

"Maybe it did," my father said hopefully. He looked more like a parent concerned about his child now.

"I don't think so, Mr. Fitzgerald. What I saw was a reinforcement of her deeply seated sibling rivalry. She was hoping to be stronger, prettier perhaps, considering what Kaylee has experienced, but instead, Haylee suffered some deeper disappointment. She was not prettier."

"But she cut her own hair," I said. "She didn't want to be pretty."

"Contradictions. Yes. She was punishing herself, but I think when she entered the room, she was anticipating you would still look worse. As I said . . . in her eyes, you were the one who had suffered."

My father's eyes narrowed for a moment. He glanced at me and then back at Dr. Alexander. "She doesn't feel any guilt, then. Is that what you're saying? We shouldn't have come after all," he said. "There was nothing good that could come of it."

"Maybe not. I was, as I said, hoping for some retreat in these symptoms, especially the paranoia."

She turned to me.

"You and your sister have had such an unusual relationship. It was and remains perhaps only you who can get to her. She wants that, but she resents

it, too. Complicated," she said again. It was beginning to annoy me. It seemed like an easy way out,
an explanation for everything.

"What will happen to her now?" I asked.

"More intense therapy." She leaned forward.
"Did you know how your sister would react to
your looking so pretty, Kaylee? You do know each
other so well, better than most sisters know each
other, right? Is that why you wore that obviously
sexy dress and made up your face before you came?
You wanted some sort of revenge?"

"Stop that!" my father snapped instantly, and he
stood. "I won't permit an iota of guilt to be placed
at this girl's feet after what her sister did to her. You
read her psychiatrist's report."

"Did you really come here to see whether you
and your sister could stop hating each other, Kaylee?" she pursued, ignoring my father.

"Yes," I said. "I did. I'm sorry if everything's
become . . . more complicated now."

My father reached for my hand so that I would
stand, too. "That's enough," he said. "I'll be in
touch. Perhaps through my attorney."

He almost physically turned me toward the
door.

"It's important that you and I talk again, Kaylee," Dr. Alexander called to me, totally ignoring
my father. "When you're ready."

"Go," my father ordered, opening the door.

I didn't look back. He closed the door behind us.

"Psychiatry is a form of voodoo," he muttered as we walked back to the lobby.

He was walking so quickly now that we almost didn't stop for the guard at the front entrance. Apparently, he had to take back our visitor passes and check to be sure an inmate wasn't being smuggled out. He wanted to see my license again and look at me, but I could have told him that it wouldn't do him much good.

We were identical in too many ways.

I had the odd feeling that in a sense, I was being left back there and Haylee was the one walking out with my father.

Neither of us spoke until we were off the grounds and well on our way home.

"Under no circumstances do I want you returning here to see that woman," he said. "These people can screw with your mind so much they can turn you into mental cripples. They're always looking for ways to excuse the guilty, especially here. They should call the place Palace Equivocation or Palace Excuse Abuse," he said. He was so angry that he was talking through clenched teeth.

"And did you hear the way she gave me that little dig about not visiting enough?" he added, turning to me. "Like I don't have enough on my hands visiting your mother and having consultations with her doctor and making sure you're going to be all right while trying to hold on to my business. Who put Haylee in that place? Certainly not me. She put herself there with her deceitful, evil actions."

He went into his silent thoughts a while and then seemed to calm. After taking a few deep breaths, he turned to me. "I'm sorry. I should be worrying about how you are, not how she is."

"I don't know. Maybe I shouldn't have gone to see her. Maybe you were right. Maybe it was too soon."

"Sure, I was right. I don't care what Dr. Alexander says. And I told you I wasn't going to let her hurt you anymore. I'm sorry. You just put it out of your mind for now. We'll concentrate on what's best for you and not spend any more time worrying about her."

"I'm all right, Daddy."

"Sure. You're strong. You're the strong one after all." He took another deep breath. "I have to see your mother's doctor tomorrow. We might be bringing her home."

"Really?" This was a surprise. He hadn't hinted at it. Maybe he was waiting to see the results of this visit first.

"We'll see. I want you to think about that prep school now, Kaylee. I want you out of this whole thing as soon as possible. Okay?"

"Okay, Daddy," I said.

He shook his head and then smiled. "What say

you and I have some of that Thai food you love tonight? We'll go to that place in Philly, okay?"

"Okay."

He sat back. "You'll be fine," he said, nodding.
"You'll be just fine, Kaylee. Once you start somewhere new, you'll do just fine."

Would I? I wondered. Maybe.

But was Dr. Alexander right to ask if I had
really gone there to see if Haylee and I would stop
hating each other? Did she allow me to come so she
could observe me almost as much as Haylee? Was
she smarter than my father thought?

I couldn't say I was unhappy that he didn't want
me to return to see her.

The truth was, I was afraid to see her anymore.

I was even afraid to look at myself in a mirror
right now.

If I did, I was sure I wouldn't see any regrets
or any sadness about Haylee going into catatonic
states. I felt good about it, actually. I felt as good as
Haylee would surely feel if the roles were reversed,
as Mother once proposed.

Thai food sounded very good. In fact, my new
future sounded very good.

For the first time, I thought I might be able to
have a future without thinking about Haylee every
day.

I might not think of her at all once I was gone.

I remembered years ago one of Mother's friends

saying we were so like conjoined twins that it would take an operation to separate us.

Maybe that just happened, I thought . . . I hoped. A mental operation, but one just as effective.

It was something I felt my father obviously wanted for me, too. When we got home, he did some work, and I went to my room to rest and change into something I thought was more appropriate to wear to dinner with him. I wasn't sure I would ever wear the sexy dress again. It would bring back the memory of what I had just experienced or, perhaps more accurately, what I had just done.

I chose a simple black dress and wore only lipstick. I saw that he was pleased. It was as if I had put away my anger, locked it in some drawer to forget it. On our way to Philly, he began to talk about some of his business ventures. It was almost like old times before he had divorced Mother, back when we were something of a happy little family.

He was behaving as if he had gotten a weight off his back, too. I hadn't seen him so up since I had returned from the hospital.

Once we were in the restaurant and had ordered our food, my father sat back, looking thoughtful again. I thought perhaps he had received darker news about Mother than he had anticipated and she wasn't coming home after all, but as it turned out, he had other things on his mind.

"The thing about unexpected events that can impact your life is just that, they're unexpected," he began. I imagined he was going to start talking again about how what Haylee had done had taken him by such surprise, but he surprised me by smiling. "Sometimes those can be good things."

The waiter brought his drink and my Arnold Palmer. I was happy that I wasn't on any medications anymore, but it wasn't so I could sneak some of my father's alcohol to drink like Haylee and I occasionally used to do. He sipped his drink and leaned forward, as if we had to be sure no one could overhear our conversation. What great secret was he about to tell me?

"I've met someone new," he said. "I've held back telling you until I was more confident in your recuperation."

"Someone new?"

"Actually, she's been working for us in accounting. We hit it off immediately. Her name is Dana Cartwell. She's not a divorcée," he quickly added, as if he thought I believed that was the only sort of woman he could date. "She was engaged once but, as she says, woke up before it was too late. She has a great sense of humor. I think you're going to like her."

"If you do, I'm sure I will, Daddy," I said.

He smiled, took another sip of his drink, and sat back.

I imagined he was holding his breath the whole time. It struck me how much of an emotional minefield we were all living in now. I was sure he was afraid I would think he was deserting me just when I needed him the most. How could he spend his emotions on anyone new, especially at this critical time? Most children of divorced couples resented it when one or both of their parents started new relationships. After all, how much love was there to go around? This was especially true for me under these terrible circumstances.

However, deep in my heart, I knew things couldn't last the way they were. Mother was going to come home; he would leave to live in his own apartment again. He would be more active in his work, and as soon as the prep school was all set up for me, I would leave as well. At this moment, of course, I didn't know what condition Mother would be in and how she could get along with everyone out of the house.

"Nothing will change between us," he promised. "I'll pay so much attention to you that you'll have me reported for stalking."

I laughed. It suddenly occurred to me that I really hadn't done much laughing lately. I also wished now that I had something stronger than an Arnold Palmer to drink and might ask to sneak a little of his vodka and tonic.

"Does Dana know all about us?"

I realized that knowing all about us took in quite a lot. How could anyone digest it and still want to be with him?

"Pretty much," he said. "You can't work for our company and not know the horror we've endured. She wasn't nosy or anything like that. I just felt comfortable talking to her about it. That's how you know you're with someone special, when you don't feel you have to disguise things or tell half-truths."

Our food began arriving.

"And all that didn't scare her away?"

"Not yet," he said. There was a lot more he had to tell her, obviously. "She's a pretty centered woman—and pretty, too, on the inside as well as the outside."

I forced a smile.

How do you tell your father that you're happy he's found someone to love other than your mother? No matter how open-minded and mature you think you are, it's still a strange feeling when you do congratulate him. You can't help thinking you're betraying your mother, and you hate the idea of another female taking your father's attention and devotion from you, but if you love him, you also can't help but be happy he's found some happiness, too.

"I look forward to meeting her, Daddy," I said.

"And she feels the same about meeting you. You'll like her, I'm sure. So let's eat," he said, and began dishing out the food we had ordered.

A couple of hours later, we were on our way home, both of us quiet now, settling into our own thoughts.

Later, in my room, I couldn't help it.

I sat in front of my mirror and tried to be catatonic. I was close to what I saw Haylee do but not perfectly the same.

It was real, I thought. She wasn't putting on any act.

She was locking herself up in herself.

And in a way, she was finally escaping.

But to what?

4

My father left the day my mother was sent home, and almost immediately, there were shadows within shadows in our house. Lights were often not turned on or were kept dim for most of the day. Mother felt safer and happier in the darkness. She wrapped it around herself the way someone would snuggle in a warm blanket on cold evenings, and she was not eager to have her curtains drawn open in the morning. She knew she would be shocked by the reality that came pouring in on the back of the sunlight, a reality she'd rather not face: none of it was simply a bad dream.

When Haylee and I were little and still shared a room and a bed, Mother was always up ahead of us and eager to sing us the "Good Morning Song," telling us how nice it was to have us there with her each day. Many times she said she wished she could freeze time so we would never grow older and nothing would ever change. She would kiss us each twice and stroke our hair twice before dressing us in the duplicate outfits she had chosen for us the night before. Afterward, when we were standing for her inspection so she could make sure that everything about us was the same, she would clap her hands and say, "You are like the sunshine warming my heart."

We were often compared to the sunshine in one way or another. Our faces lit up her day. One look at us wiped away the dark clouds that came from whatever worry or problem she had at the time. Like a planet, she was held in orbit around us. Neither Haylee nor I could deny that the exaggerated and happy way she described us made us feel extra special, even though the odds of having twins were far greater than for any other type of multiple births and the odds of having identical twins were about the same for every couple wherever they lived in the world. Because the reason one fertilized egg, or zygote, would split into two was still a mystery, Mother believed it was something spiritual and extraordinary.

Perhaps Haylee soaked up all the praise more, and more deeply, than I did, but because of the way Mother displayed us in public and talked about us, we believed that anyone looking at us would surely think, *There go two diamond-studded little girls, dazzling whomever they meet.*

Now, however, the early sunlight didn't tiptoe softly into our house and gently wake the sleeping walls the way Mother surely remembered. Like a clumsy bull in a shop of fragile antiques, it pushed its way through the rooms and hallways, up the stairway, and to our bedrooms, smashing aside the contents of any obscure, dark corner in which Mother might hover to find relief from her haunting dreams.

For hours after the sun went down, she would avoid turning on the lights or asking Irene Granford—her forty-two-year-old live-in nurse and caretaker, someone her therapist, Dr. Jaffe, believed she still needed, at least for the immediate future— or me, when I was home, to turn them on. A mere table lamp had become a powerful spotlight forcing her to face blinding reality. It made it more difficult for her to escape behind the fortress of her memories, where she could see and hear Haylee and me the way she wanted, even now, as two identical and perfect little girls, with dark brown hair so light and fluffy that it seemed woven from clouds, two identical and perfect little girls with our mother's amber eyes, who loved each other as much as they could love themselves, two identical and perfect little girls who had the same thoughts, had the same tastes and feelings, and dreamed the same dreams.

Whenever Mother did sit in a well-lit room, she spent most of her time thumbing slowly through albums filled with pictures of us from birth up to the year before my abduction. There were also many videos of us that my father had taken before our parents divorced. In every picture and in every video, we wore the exact same clothes and had our hair trimmed and brushed in the same style, not a strand on either of us longer than on the other. When I stood in the background and watched Mother looking at those pictures or saw her watching the videos with her face frozen in that nostalgic and sad expression, I felt as though Haylee and I were long dead and gone. In her mind, we might very well be, at least the two daughters she had once cherished. The girls who existed now were practically strangers, invaders trespassing in the bodies of her precious, perfect children.

I could see it in the way she looked at me whenever I came into a room. Gone was that deep familiarity and love, that obsessive attachment to every movement in my face and body, to every word I said, and to every breath I took. It always had been the same whenever she had turned or looked up to see Haylee enter. Now, after all that had happened, there was coolness, indifference, her kisses sitting on plastic lips, her touch almost always accidental.

In the past, whenever she would see one of us without the other, the first thing she would ask

was "Where is your sister?" Regardless of the time
of day or the circumstance, whenever one of us
appeared without the other, her eyes would flame
with fear. We could never claim that we didn't
know. She had us believing we'd feel each other's
heartbeats in another room, even outside the house.
It was as if she had a premonition from the day we
were born, a vision of us separated, one of us lost
forever. And of course, there was that deep-seated
belief that one of us couldn't exist without the
other. That idea was embedded in her so firmly that
accepting any alternative was not only impossible
but, to her, practically murder.

During the days that followed her return, I
could easily read the desperate thoughts in her
eyes. This current situation we were all swimming
in frantically couldn't last; it was only a temporary
hiccup. All that had happened would be wiped
away, vacuumed into the bag of things forgotten
forever and ever. How she could look at me and
have any thought similar to that was incredible, but
this was the hope that sustained her. It was now the
only dream she had left, in a house where dreams
had once swum as gracefully as so many goldfish
in a bowl.

Mother's mental breakdown had begun when
I first disappeared. After my rescue and before
she returned home from the hospital, Dr. Jaffe,
her psychiatrist, had assured my father and me

that she finally had come to accept all that had happened and fully understood what Haylee had done to cause my abduction. She realized and acknowledged that Haylee had been lying and had been deceitful, from that first night in front of the movie theater from which I had disappeared through every minute, every hour, every day, and every week that had followed. Now she knew that lies, not dreams, had been swimming around her, and she had nearly drowned in them. Every ugly fact she faced was another jellyfish sting. I had no doubt that when she first heard them, she winced with real pain.

Although acknowledging the whole truth helped lift her out of the dark pool of mental illness that had made it impossible for her to have any sort of sensible daily life at the time, it did not return her to the person she had been. There were too many scars, too many deeply felt wounds in her heart. Reluctantly, she had swallowed the ugly facts like bitter medicine or sour milk. In one sense, she had recuperated. She no longer denied what Haylee had done, but the side effects left her crippled in so many other ways. For the time being, we were alike in that sense.

Sometimes when I saw her step out of the shadows now, she looked like she had absorbed them. Her eyes were gloomy, her eyelids half-open. She seemed to drift, to slide along the walls, seeking the darkest places, periodically glancing back to be sure the light or the sunshine wasn't following her and, along with it, the ugly truth: one of her precious daughters had nearly destroyed the other. Frantically, her gaze darted around the room she was about to enter. She looked like a frightened mouse quickly seeking a safe haven, a place to hide, a place that would serve as a sanctuary. But how did you flee from reality forever?

When Mother wasn't reminiscing through photographs or videos, she would spend hours at a time simply sitting and staring out a window, turning her extended fingers clockwise and counterclockwise, as if she were winding an old watch, perhaps hoping she could turn back time and would see us both returning from school. She slept a great deal, and when she was up and was somewhat energetic, she would talk about us constantly, eager to describe what we had been to her—but not how we now were. Usually, I slipped away.

Irene was her audience most of the time. For a woman nearly six feet tall, with manly shoulders and large hands, with long, thin fingers that reminded me of spider legs, Irene was surprisingly gentle, even graceful. Her patience and compassion were something to behold. I thought it was more than simply her good training. She sincerely liked Mother and appreciated the pain she had suffered and continued to endure. Early on, I suspected there was something dark in Irene's own past that enabled her to empathize, but she didn't like to talk about herself. "Let's concentrate on your mother," she would say, if our conversation drifted too far into her past. *Everyone has secrets*, I thought.

In any case, she was better at sympathizing than I was, because despite the truth she had accepted, Mother still searched for ways to excuse Haylee for what she had done to me—and to her. The blame was as easy to spread as warm butter. To her, my father was obviously the one who bore the most guilt. After all, he had chosen to desert us, to divorce her. How could she have been expected to carry the burden of bringing up two young girls with such extraordinary needs on her own? No wonder something unfortunate had happened.

Unfortunate? I would think. *That sounds too much like something accidental. There was nothing accidental about this.*

Nevertheless, this sort of logic of blaming my father settled in her mind and comforted her, even though she knew that from day one of our lives, she had instructed him about how he should behave toward us, and she had presented herself as an expert on girls who shared the design of every cell in their bodies. So the truth was that he couldn't contradict her; sometimes he couldn't even ask questions. Whether she wanted to face it or not, she was, in fact, bringing us up on her own and always had been. It was a major part of what eventually drove my father out of the house and into his new life.

And then there was the blame that stained me. Somehow, in Mother's mind, I had failed my sister by not directly addressing her growing jealousies. Mother had repeatedly told me that I should have revealed what Haylee had been doing on the Internet with the man who had abducted me. Keeping it a secret from Mother was to her as good as causing what had happened. There was, after all, such a thing as a conspiracy of silence.

Didn't I understand? Haylee had needed our help. Because of my silence, the sickness of sibling rivalry was permitted to grow and get stronger. Identical twins were far more susceptible to it than ordinary siblings. It was the bogeyman Mother had feared the most. He was always there in the shadows, waiting for his opportunity to pounce on us, and by not seeking Mother's help early, I had helped give him that opportunity. To Mother's way of thinking, Haylee was just as much a victim as I was. Mother once said, "She really didn't want to do that to you. She couldn't help herself. Just like you wouldn't have been able to help yourself if the roles were reversed."

But the roles weren't reversed and never could be! I wanted to shout back at her. *I would never put my sister into a spider's web.*

However, Irene, my father, and Dr. Jaffe advised

me never to argue with Mother and warned me especially against giving her any nitty-gritty details of my abduction. She was still too fragile. One more nightmare would crack her like a fresh egg.

Yet I always wondered how she was able to cope with my having to have therapy, too. Why didn't she want to know why I needed it so long after I had been rescued and still needed it from time to time? Why didn't she ask more questions about my abduction? How could she not worry about how it had all changed me, damaged me? She never even asked me if I had been raped. Shouldn't that have been her first concern? She didn't ask about my hair, why I was nearly bald, or why I was so thin. When I think back about it all, I can't recall a moment when she had shed a tear over what had happened to me. Where was the mother I needed when I needed a mother the most? When was it her turn to be sympathetic? Wasn't that a big part of who she was supposed to be?

And when my father had decided, along with my therapist, that my attending a private prep school rather than returning to my high school for the new school year was a good idea, why didn't she question the reason? After all, I was being sent away. I'd be out of the house again. Why didn't she wonder why I was so eager to do it? Why didn't she fight for me to stay with her?

In my heart, I concluded that she understood

but simply would rather avoid facing up to it. That much self-denial she couldn't keep hidden. Otherwise, she would only end up back in the hospital, not that she was making much of an attempt to return to the world.

She didn't want friends to visit or call. She had no interest in going anywhere, doing any shopping, having her hair and nails done, or taking me to do any of those things. She didn't even appreciate her own mother, my grandmother Clara Beth, making the trip from Arizona to Pennsylvania to see her. She frustrated Nana by refusing to talk about anything but the needlework she was doing or a chicken recipe she had discovered. She behaved as if nothing terrible had happened to this family, and whenever she made a reference to me, she cloaked it in words and images that made it sound like she was referring to Haylee as well. Clara Beth finally threw her hands up in frustration and fled from our house as if she were breaking free of any guilt herself. She didn't even say good-bye to me.

I supposed, in some ways, I couldn't blame her. In a real way, our house was on fire. Despite Mother having been released from continuous psychiatric care, she was as good as in a hospital in our own home, which was another reason I was happy to go off to a private prep school and avoid every opportunity but Christmas and spring break to go home.

I would much rather have spent my holidays with my father, but by now, he had found someone new to love again and was trying to make a new life. In a real sense, he was fleeing from the past as much as I was. I couldn't blame him for it. How else could he go on? How else could I?

Once, before all this had happened, when I criticized Haylee for being so selfish, she smiled at me the way an adult might smile at a child for being so innocent.

"Sometimes," she said, "you have to be selfish in order to survive, Kaylee. You'll figure that out on your own, I'm sure." Her voice dripped with condescension.

I didn't believe her at the time, probably because I didn't want to believe her.

But she was right. She was right about many things.

And when I permitted myself to think about my captivity and the brutality inflicted on me in that basement apartment, I realized I had survived because of what I had learned from my twin sister, the sister who had maneuvered to put me there and whom I couldn't imagine ever forgiving, even after I had seen her in her dreadful catatonic state.

But I knew in my heart that eventually, somehow, that was precisely what I had to do to help her survive, and what I had to do to help myself survive—forgive.

Mother knew nothing about my visiting Haylee and what had happened. My father had told Mother's therapist, who had advised us to keep it from her. Her doctor said that the news could send her reeling backward and return her to the psychiatric ward. Keeping it from her was no problem. I had no trouble not talking about my visit. I wanted to forget it for as long as I could. It was another reason I was willing to leave and try to start anew.

Several weeks after Mother had been brought home, my father was there to help me bring down my luggage. It was the start of a new semester at Littlefield. Mother knew I was leaving and was in the living room with Irene. All the arrangements had been made. The pamphlets about Littlefield had been received, and I had deliberately left them on the coffee table in the living room for days after they had arrived. I could see, however, that no one had picked them up, not even Irene. This morning, Mother didn't—as I had expected, actually hoped— offer her opinion on what I should pack for my stay at Littlefield.

"Does she fully understand what's happening, Daddy?" I asked, pausing at the foot of the stairway and nodding toward the living room.

"Oh, she understands. I went over it with her in great detail last week and again yesterday. You probably forgot how your mother could pout sometimes. There were days when she wouldn't say a word to me, answer a question, anything, until I said I was sorry for whatever innocent thing I had done or uttered."

I nodded. Of course, I remembered days like that. None of us could stand the silent treatment. Haylee was probably the least concerned of the three of us about upsetting Mother, but she was bothered by silence and hated it. When she wasn't with me or Mother, she was constantly wearing earphones or on the telephone. I had no doubt she would have had more trouble than I had surviving in Anthony Cabot's basement apartment with no one but a cat to talk to most of the time.

I walked to the living room and stood in the doorway. Mother and Irene stopped talking and turned to look at me. Mother was in a housecoat and her pink and green slippers. She had yet to get to the stage where she would dress nicely, with concern about her hair and makeup, even if she wasn't leaving the house. The one exception was the half dozen or so dinners we'd had with my father since her return. Never once during any of those dinners did Haylee's name come up. Periodically, Mother would gaze at the chair Haylee would have occupied, but then she would look away quickly or down.

There were long moments of silence at these dinners, followed by my father talking about the house or his work. Irene showed interest and asked questions, but whenever my father mentioned the prep school looming on the horizon for me, Mother stared blankly at him and just ate. My father and I exchanged looks, but neither of us forced her to comment. It was like tiptoeing over thin ice. Neither of us wanted to be blamed for causing her to have a relapse.

"I'm going now, Mother," I said now. "To my new school," I added with emphasis. I was really leaving. There was no point in pretending otherwise.

Normally, whenever Haylee and I left for somewhere, even just to go to school in the morning, we always kissed Mother good-bye, me kissing her on her right cheek and Haylee kissing her on her left. Since she had returned from the hospital, whenever I kissed her, she always brought her hand to the other cheek to confirm that Haylee hadn't kissed her, and then she would grimace. It was disturbing, giving me the feeling that my kiss was insufficient or that it stung. It was eerie for me, because I imagined Haylee there, giving me her confident smile to say, *See! Mother likes my kiss better.*

However, my father told me that before Mother had gone to therapy, when I had been abducted, she would act as if I had kissed her, too, that I was there. Now that he thought about it more, he said it really bothered Haylee, who would go into a pout.

"I should have realized something from that,"

he said. "I should have realized what she had done. There are none so blind as those who refuse to see."

I never dreamed that something as simple as a kiss good-bye would become such a deeply traumatic thing, but it was. When we were younger, Haylee was especially embarrassed about Mother's special kisses and her demands that we kiss her so much, even in front of our classmates. Haylee complained to my father, but he told us that kisses were important to Mother because she had so few when she was a little girl. Neither her mother nor her father was a very affectionate person.

"People who have suffered great thirsts of any kind are more obsessive about satisfying themselves when they finally can," he said. "That can often be overwhelming. Try to be understanding."

I thought that made sense, but Haylee grimaced and continued to complain whenever Mother wasn't around. "Why do we have to suffer for what our grandparents did to her? That's unfair!"

Now, as I stood in the doorway, holding my luggage, I knew Irene was waiting, along with me, for my mother to say something, to wish me luck, a good trip, anything. She simply stared at me blankly, the way she had at dinner when the private school was mentioned. Finally, Irene said, "Have a nice trip. We'll be anxious to hear how the school is and how you are doing."

Mother looked at her, not simply surprised

but a little annoyed that she had put words in her mouth by including her.

She pulled herself back on the sofa and, sitting stiffly, added, "I'll be here. I'm not going anywhere."

I could practically hear her thinking, *I'm waiting for your sister to come home.*

I was afraid to approach her and kiss her. Her face would feel like cold marble.

"'Bye," I said, and hurried to the front door, where my father was waiting. He saw the disappointed look on my face. I told him what Mother had said. "I'm surprised they let her come home," I added, not hiding my anger.

"Oh, there's a difference between being mentally disturbed and behaving like a spoiled child because you're not getting things your own way or, more important, deciding them. She'll get over it," he said confidently.

He loaded my suitcases into the car's trunk, and we got in.

"Kaylee, I know I sound like a car stuck in low gear or something, but try to put all this behind you for a while so you can give yourself a chance for a fresh start. It's going to be great. You'll see," he said, reaching over to squeeze my hand gently.

Before we turned out of the driveway, I looked back and saw Mother standing at the living-room window, looking out at us. I felt more of a sting than an ache in my heart. She looked forlorn, abandoned, and much smaller to me than she ever was. It wasn't all that long ago when she had both Haylee and me in her life, in our home. Now, I thought, with my father gone, of course, she would have no one but her caretaker, Irene. She hadn't reconnected with any of her girlfriends. The echoes and the memories hanging in every corner like woven spiderwebs might easily drive her back to the hospital.

I knew that it was selfish of me to desert her, but there was no way I could return to my school or any school near us. Our story was too infamous here. I was afraid even to go to the local supermarket, maybe especially the local supermarket, or any place where people who knew one another gathered. They would see me and begin their chatter. *There she is. She doesn't look normal. How could she be?*

If I stayed, I wouldn't leave the house very much. I'd become as much of a prisoner as Haylee was, and how would that do Mother any good?

"This is like going to college," my father said, now eager to fill every moment of silence. "You're on your own more, and you meet new people. It's exciting. Don't you think so?"

"I guess," I said.

"Oh, it will be. Makes me wish I was eighteen again."

"You wouldn't be going somewhere specifically

to get away from people who knew you," I said bitterly.

"You gotta stop thinking of it like that, Kaylee. Look at the positive side. The school will have better teachers. It's more beautiful. You'll make lots of new discoveries along with new friends. And when it does come time for you to go to college, it won't be as traumatic as it is for most high school kids. You'll grow up faster."

"Is that good? I think I've had to grow up too fast as it is."

He looked at me.

"You know what I mean?"

I felt guilty now about how I was treating him. He was right, and he was only trying to help me. I had to pull myself up and out of this pool of depression and self-pity.

"You never have to mention what happened to you," he said. "You don't have to react to any nasty questions. You'll see. You'll feel differently when you get there."

"I know. I hope," I added. "I'm sorry, Daddy. And I do feel sorry for Mother, too. I realize she is struggling for a way to forget and start anew, just like I am."

"Yeah. Well, I promise I'll look in on her regularly," he said. "It might even get to where she thinks we never divorced," he added, reaching for some humor.

I did smile. I sat back. "Tell me about your first day at college, Daddy," I said. "You never told us much about that."

He had, but I wanted to hear him talk. I didn't want to think about what was happening and what I was doing, and I didn't want him to feel any more uncomfortable than he was. Once he began, he was on a roll. As he spoke, memories returned. I could recall exactly where I was, or I should say where Haylee and I were, when he told us things. Sometimes it was at dinner; sometimes it was when we took long car trips. Mother was laughing then at his stories, too.

Despite their arguments concerning how Mother was raising us growing in intensity almost weekly, neither Haylee nor I had believed that divorce was an option. My father seemed endlessly patient and tolerant. However, as the disputes about us—really about her and the things she was doing with us and to us—continued, he eventually reached his limit and was tired of backing down. I saw that he wasn't just walking away anymore. He'd linger and argue longer, the reasonableness in his voice darkening into anger until that anger became a different kind of retreat. Mother never gave in, not even for something as small as letting us wear different-colored hair ribbons. My father began to avoid us, all of us. He was coming home later and later, taking more business trips, and eventually even missing our birthdays. Mother didn't seem to care until it was too late, and then she worked to turn us against him, putting all the blame on him.

I've got to stop thinking about all that now, I told myself.

When we drew closer to Littlefield, my father told me that there were about a dozen other girls enrolling today, too.

"I'll hang around until you're settled in. There's a meeting with the principal, Mrs. Mitchell, right after we get your things into your dorm room. She's very nice but also very firm." He leaned toward me to whisper. "I overheard two of the teachers talking about her. They call her Mrs. Thatcher."

"Thatcher?"

"The Iron Lady, British prime minister."

"Oh."

He laughed. I wanted to hear more, of course. He hadn't told me all that much about Littlefield, other than that it was a senior high school, with students in grades nine through twelve, and that the population was about three hundred.

"The dorms are quite nice, but you have to share a room with one other girl," he finally revealed. It brought a new fear to my doorstep.

"Who? What other girl?"

"We don't know yet," he said. "I saw a typical room. There's plenty of space for two." He smiled. "It's twice as large as the dorm room I had when

I went to college, and we had to share with two others. Plenty of closet space," he continued, "and two desks, although your dorm has a study lab and a recreational area. There are no televisions in the dorm rooms, but you can play music, and you have your computer. A new computer," he added. "It's a surprise I have in the trunk. A great new laptop. There's Wi-Fi at the dorm, of course, so we can email and Skype and stuff."

For a moment, I considered asking him to turn around and go back. I'd rather return to home-schooling, something Mother had made us do until we were eight and ready for the third grade. My father saw the reservations and fear in my face. Although he was involved with computer software, and both Haylee and I were quite educated when it came to computer use, neither of us had mentioned the word *computer* since I had been rescued. It was through a computer that Haylee had designed my abduction, and it was fortunately because of a computer that my father had made the discoveries leading to my rescue. I hadn't even turned mine on since I had been rescued and brought home. I had nightmares that if I did, Anthony Cabot would im-mediately appear on the screen.

But more important, I had never slept in a room with any other girl without Haylee sleeping over, too. Mother never permitted either of us to sleep at some friend's house without the other. Consequently, neither of us did. I had never shared a bathroom or sat beside another girl and fixed my hair in her bedroom, any of the things other girls in our class had done, if Haylee wasn't right there as well. I wasn't simply too shy to share a room now. There was a bigger reason, a bigger fear.

Girls who had such an intimate relationship couldn't be as secretive about their lives as I wanted to be. I had envisioned myself comfortably alone at this new school, taking my time to make friends and taking baby steps toward any social life. I dreaded the first question my new roommate was sure to ask: "Do you have any brothers or sisters?" My father had assured me that my horrible recent past would remain unknown at Littlefield. This was the main reason I was attending a school sufficiently far away from our community. How would I do that if I had a roommate?

"I don't care about the space or a computer, Daddy. I don't know if I can live that closely with another girl yet. Can't you get me a room by myself?"

"Now, stay calm, Kaylee. They don't have single rooms. They want their students to develop a social life as well as an academic life. It's part of what Littlefield sees as its educational goals, its philosophy. I've had a nice discussion with your therapist, of course, and she agrees that it's time you had new relationships. There's a great danger that you will retreat so deeply into yourself that you'll never be able to do these things again. She believes you're ready for it. I believe you are, too. You're a very strong person. Look what you've survived. This will be a piece of cake," he said, smiling. "You'll figure out how to handle touchy subjects."

I couldn't help it; I was trembling.

"I don't know," I said, near tears.

"Look," he said, "if you have a big problem with it, we'll think of something else, but give it a chance, okay? Please, Kaylee."

"Okay," I said. I was sure he and my therapist were right. I had to find the strength to do this. "I'll try."

"Thatta girl," he said.

We drove on until he slowed, made a turn, and nodded at the campus ahead of us on the right. A sign in what looked like brass read, *Littlefield*. Under it was a quote: *I am still learning. —Michelangelo.*

Nothing was truer for me, too. The difference was, I had more than simply knowledge to learn. I had to learn how to be a different person.

5

My father hadn't exaggerated about the beauty of the campus. The pictures on the brochure also did not do it justice. It was close to two hundred acres. There were two main academic buildings side by side, Matthews Hall and Asper Hall, each named for the philanthropist who had paid for the buildings. Asper, the building on the left as we drove up the driveway, had been constructed nearly twenty-five years before Matthews, which was built to accommodate a growing population. My father explained that Matthews contained an updated library with computers and more than forty-five thousand books.

There was a separate gymnasium building, Holmes Gymnasium, built shortly after the first classroom building was constructed. The school had tennis courts, a baseball field, and a running track. Everything appeared to have someone's name attached.

"Successful early graduates and their families contributed to the campus," my father said when I mentioned that. "This started as an all-girls school," he said. "That's why the girls' dormitories, two buildings on our left, were across campus from the two buildings that housed the boys."

I was in the Eleanor Cook dormitory, the one farther on the left.

There were parking lots in front of all the dormitories and parking areas in front of the gymnasium and both academic buildings, but it was the grounds that were most impressive, with their fieldstone walking paths; maple, hickory, and oak trees; trimmed hedges, fountains with statues of birds, one circular fountain with a giant peacock; and redwood benches and flower beds evenly spaced. I saw that the area had extensive lighting, with lampposts and fixtures on the outsides of all the buildings.

"It's hard to believe this is just a high school. There's a lot of money in here, isn't there?"

"A lot," my father said, smiling.

"How expensive is the tuition?"

"Worth every penny," he said, without telling me.

We turned toward the Eleanor Cook dorm. I saw two other cars with their trunks open and parents helping the girls move their things into the dorm. We pulled alongside one. A tall, slim girl, easily five-foot-eleven, with long arms and a small, almost flat bosom, stood a little to the right, watching her father pull her suitcases from the Lincoln Town Car trunk. She was wearing an ankle-length black skirt and a gray long-sleeved blouse. The man was tall, too, with a similar shade of dark brown hair, and he wore a gray pin-striped suit and a black tie. He put a smaller bag beside the two suitcases, but the girl made no effort to pick it up. I saw him raise his arms, and she moved forward reluctantly to take it and press it against herself, as if she would never let it go.

Her father closed the trunk and picked up both suitcases. I wondered where her mother was. But that signaled that others would wonder where mine was. My father popped our trunk.

"Your new home sweet home," he said, smiling and holding his arms out toward Eleanor Cook Hall.

I got out slowly and watched the tall girl walk behind her father, her head down, her steps slow and small, almost like a geisha. My father began to take out my suitcases. I picked up my smaller bags and waited, looking out at the campus.

There was a warm breeze gently swaying some of the tree limbs. If I were a little girl, unafraid of her imagination, I could easily believe all of them were waving to me, greeting me. The grounds were so beautiful and calming, with the fountains and flowers, that it was difficult not to feel welcome, optimistic.

Maybe I really could start a new life here, I thought. My father was right. It would feel good to be on my own and not have all the heavy emotional turmoil to wade through every day. It could drown someone, especially someone like me. I was lucky to escape.

"Ready?" my father asked.

I nodded, and we started for the front entrance. Just inside were two girls, both with light brown hair, the taller one wearing thick-lensed glasses, her hair short and curly, dressed in a dark blue jumpsuit with a keyhole neckline. The other was cuter, with bright green eyes and diminutive facial features. She wore a white polka-dot flared skirt and a black short-sleeved top. She stepped forward first. Her right cheek had a dimple that flashed on and off when she smiled.

"Welcome to Eleanor Cook," she said. "I'm Marcy Ross, and this is Terri Stone. We're sort of a welcoming committee."

"We *are* the welcoming committee," Terri said. "Marcy will escort you to your room, and I'll show you the facilities."

"Facilities," Marcy mocked. "Toilets and stuff. You're Kaylee Fitzgerald," she said, as if she was assigning me my name.

I looked at my father, who was smiling widely.

"And I'm her father, Mason Fitzgerald."

"Welcome to you, too, Mr. Fitzgerald," Terri Stone said, again sounding more official.

"C'mon," Marcy said, before I could say anything. She hooked my right arm and started marching me ahead, through the small lobby and down the hallway on our left. "I was going nuts waiting for you. Mrs. Rosewell assigned me to you. Terri is assigned to everyone. She's the official facilities guide," she added, her face beaming.

"Who's Mrs. Rosewell?"

"Our house mother. Platypus," she added, leaning in to whisper. "Only don't call her that to her face or say it closely enough for her to hear."

"Platypus?"

"She's nice, but she's built like one and has a way of pressing her lips out like a duck's bill. She waddles when she walks, too."

"Where is she?"

"She's with two other newlyweds," Marcy said.

"What?"

"That's an in joke. We call new students newlyweds. You have to take so many oaths, follow rules that make it seem like you're marrying the school. Don't worry about it. Maybe we don't break the rules, but we bend them."

She stopped and turned me sharply to go down a short corridor on our left.

"I'm here, too, right across the hall with Facilities," she said, pausing at an open door.

My father and Terri Stone caught up to us. Another girl came to the door. She was a buxom redhead about my height, wearing a Littlefield basketball team T-shirt and a pair of jeans, so I assumed she was not a newlywed and had probably been assigned to bring my roommate here. Her light complexion was peppered with freckles over the crests of her cheeks. She widened her eyes at Marcy and nodded to her right. We couldn't see around the doorframe yet, but it was obvious someone was already in my room.

"Hi," she said, offering her right hand. "I'm Toby Dickens, dorm president."

"Kaylee Fitzgerald," I said.

"She's in here?" she asked Marcy.

"Good guess."

"Good luck," Toby muttered, and stepped past us.

When I looked back through the doorway, I saw the man who had carried in the tall dark-haired girl's luggage standing there looking out at us. Marcy smiled at him and led me into the room. The man was studying me too hard, I thought. He looked like a research scientist peering through a microscope. What was he checking for, a sign of measles?

I couldn't help being paranoid, of course. Maybe he knew who I was, knew everything, and wasn't happy to have his daughter share a dorm room with me.

"You're on the right side," Marcy told me, nodding at the single bed with a gray blanket and a large white pillow. The bed looked like it had been made by a drill sergeant—tight, perfect. I saw the desk at the foot of the bed. To the immediate right of the door was a closet about a quarter of the size of mine at home, but Haylee's and my rooms and closets were way bigger than the rooms and closets our classmates had. Mother had insisted on that.

Something had kept me from turning to my left too soon. It wasn't that I realized my roommate was the girl I had seen in the parking lot, a girl who struck me as strange to start with. I was still trying to get used to the idea that I would share my intimate places with someone new.

She didn't smile or offer to introduce herself. Looking at her more closely now, I didn't think she was unattractive, but I did think she was almost sickly thin. She had her lips folded inward, her gray-black eyes wide like someone very frightened. Her dark brown hair fell straight to the base of her neck. It looked dull, lifeless. Her shoulder bones were prominently outlined beneath her thin blouse.

Marcy was the first to blow up the pregnant silence with a big "This is your roommate, Kaylee Fitzgerald."

"Say hello, Claudia," her father ordered.

"Hello," she said, and immediately raised her eyes toward the ceiling.

My father was right behind me, still holding my suitcases in his hand, but he dropped them both quickly and offered his hand to Claudia's father.

"Mason Fitzgerald," he said.

"Bob Lukas."

Again, there was an uncomfortable silence.

"Facilities," Marcy sang, and Terri stepped forward.

"Before you two unpack and get settled, I'll show you our bathrooms, showers, study, and recreational area, and the extra storage room, should you need it. Mr. Fitzgerald, Mr. Lukas, Mrs. Rosewell is waiting in the recreational room with some coffee and cakes. Marcy will take you to her."

"Daddies, this way, please," Marcy said.

My father looked at me. I gave him a quick nod.

"So where are you from?" he asked Mr. Lukas as they followed Marcy out.

I looked at Claudia. She didn't smile as much as she relaxed her face. She folded her arms, lowered her head, and followed me as I followed Terri out. Terri obviously had a memorized tour, describing how to use the bathrooms and showers, with that added "Always be considerate" tag to everything she said. We followed in single file, because Claudia seemed to want it that way. I had yet to say another word to her. We met two other girls in the bathrooms and then were shown the extra storage space before being brought to the study hall, which was furnished with half a dozen desks, one large one with eight chairs, and two brown leather settees. The floors were a dark wood, and there were four windows with views of the grounds.

A doorway led us into the recreational area, now populated with half a dozen parents besides Claudia's and mine. Terri brought us quickly to Mrs. Rosewell.

I immediately understood why Marcy had referred to her as a platypus. She had a narrow face but with protruding lips that looked like some plastic surgeon had tried to drown them in Botox. She was short, maybe only five foot one, with wide hips and a heavy bosom. Her grayish-brown hair was too short for her face, barely reaching her earlobes, but she had a very warm smile, motherly, and hazel eyes that should have helped any nervous newlywed to relax a little. She hugged us like a grandmother, her large breasts forcing both of us to stand straighter. Claudia looked terrified at being so warmly embraced and kept her arms stiff, her fingers extended.

"Now, girls, we'll have our little chat about the house rules after you're settled in and after you and your parents visit with Mrs. Mitchell," she explained. "If you like, have some cake and milk. We don't encourage our girls to ingest caffeine and urge them to avoid soda. Too much sugar," she told the parents standing nearby. I saw my father smiling at me, holding back a laugh. That, more than anything, helped me unwind a bit more.

"You want some cake or a cookie?" I asked Claudia.

"No," she said, grimacing. "She just said soda has too much sugar. Why do they have cake and cookies?"

"She didn't say no sugar," I said, shrugged, and walked over to the refreshment table, where I met two other new girls, Jessie Paul and Estelle Marcus, who were rooming together. I looked back at Claudia. She was standing alone, just a few feet behind her father, my father, and two other men with their wives.

I guess I shouldn't worry about my roommate asking too many questions, I told myself. She looked more terrified of meeting other girls than I did. In fact, seeing and meeting her practically convinced me completely that I was back to being as normal as I ever was.

"Your father hanging around to take you to dinner?" I heard Marcy ask, and turned to see her right behind me.

"No. He hasn't said so, I mean. I don't think so."

She laughed. "Don't make it a world crisis. You want help unpacking? I'm not especially good at it, but I am nosy."

"What?"

"C'mon. You don't have to hang out here. You have a half hour or so before you meet Mrs. Thatcher and get your panties inspected," she said, seizing my hand.

I started to resist and then gave up and followed her out, looking back at my father, who saw me and winked. Claudia was still standing like someone who belonged with Haylee.

Maybe I attract them, I thought, and surprised myself by laughing.

"What's so funny?" Marcy asked as we continued down the hallway.

"I don't think I could explain it easily."

"Good. I hate long stories. But," she said, pausing and looking back, "I think you might have your hands full. You might have Dracula's daughter for a roommate."

"Her I could handle," I said.

Marcy's face brightened even more. "I'm going to like you," she said. "And you're going to like me."

She said it with such confidence that I couldn't help but laugh.

Maybe it was possible, I thought. Maybe I could escape the past, just as my father hoped I would.

6

Marcy went at my luggage like a starving resistance fighter behind enemy lines who had just had an airdrop of needed supplies. She moaned and groaned about not being my size every time she took out something and held it up to see how it might look on her. It reminded me of how Haylee would put on something Mother had bought us both and tell me why it looked better on her than it did on me, even though we had identical bodies and there was nothing different about our dresses, blouses, or skirts. According to Haylee, the color would do more for her complexion, her eyes, and her hair because hers was subtly different. If Mother had heard her say it, she would have punished her severely, which would mean I would suffer, too. The logic was that if there was the seed of something wrong in one of us, it would be in the other. Punishment wasn't just retribution to Mother; it was preventive, protective.

While we were unpacking, Claudia entered, practically tiptoeing to her side of our room. I realized quickly that she had a way of moving about surreptitiously, making hardly a sound, and keeping her eyes from meeting anyone else's. She wasn't simply shy; she wanted to be unnoticed, to completely disappear, which was not something easy to do in this place, I thought.

There was a window across from each bed, and each of us had a bedside light, a side table, and a small pink area rug beside the bed. The flooring was similar to the wood floors in the study hall. There were dark brown paneled walls and, to the right of the door, a bulletin board on which we could tack any reminders or schedules. Already pinned to it were the dormitory rules in big black letters.

"Need any help?" Marcy asked Claudia, peering around her at her suitcase.

"No," she said quickly. "Thank you," she added after a long moment, like someone who had just remembered she should say that.

"So where you from?" Marcy asked her.

"Allentown."

"First time in a private school?"

She looked like she wasn't going to answer as

she took out clothes and began to hang up blouses and skirts.

Marcy shrugged, and we continued with mine.

"No, it's my third," Claudia finally said. It was as if sounds entered her ears and then took their time reaching her brain.

"Third? Did you say third?" Marcy asked.

"In three years," Claudia added. Then she smiled, but it wasn't so much a smile as a smirk that said, *So shut up about it.*

"Say," Marcy said, turning to me as well. "Now that I think of it, how come your mothers didn't come along to see you guys enrolled and moved into the dorm?"

"My mother's recuperating from a long illness," I said.

Claudia thought a moment, obviously deciding whether to answer Marcy.

"My mother's home with my younger sister, Jillian. She's six now. Our little princess," she added. "Jillian didn't want to take the ride, and when she whines, it's like a thousand church bells ringing. I usually put my hands over my ears, but my mother says I should stop doing that because I might give Jillian a complex. So my mother stayed home with her to keep the peace. That's the slogan that hangs above our heads in my house: 'Keep the Peace.'"

Neither Marcy nor I spoke. Marcy turned to me and widened her eyes. We finished getting my things into the drawers built into the closet. We could hear Terri marching up and down the hallway and calling for all newlyweds to join their parents in the lobby to go to Mrs. Mitchell's orientation meeting. She paused in our doorway.

"Watch out for Marcy," she said, staring at her like a schoolteacher reprimanding a first-grader. "She tends to borrow everything she can and then conveniently forgets to return it. That's why she helps newlyweds unpack."

"It's not doing me any good," Marcy whined. "Nothing Kaylee has fits."

"You can borrow anything I have," Claudia said. "And forget to return it."

Marcy and I looked at each other and then started to laugh.

But Claudia didn't. She looked like she meant it. We all started out.

"Her bark is worse than her bite," Marcy called after us as Claudia and I joined our fathers, who were standing together in the lobby.

"How's it going?" my father asked, looking at both of us for an answer.

"Good," I said. Claudia didn't respond, and her father didn't wait to see if she would.

As we walked across campus to Matthews Hall, where the administrative offices were, our fathers remained ahead of us, talking. I imagined they had a lot to share, both apparently having daughters who needed some special tender loving care. My father, of course, would mention nothing about Haylee or what I had survived. I wondered what reason for my being here he did tell Claudia's father. He would probably give him the reason most were here. Their parents had little faith in public schools and could afford to send their kids to one of these places, so why not try it?

I glanced at Claudia, who walked with her arms folded tightly across her chest, her head high and her neck stiff. Three private schools, I thought. She'd been through these orientations twice. No wonder she looked only vaguely interested.

"So why have you gone to so many private schools?" I asked her.

She shrugged. "My father says it's like trying on shoes. Even though a pair might be your size, they might still squeeze here and there or simply be wrong for your feet." After a moment, she added, "However, if Littlefield doesn't work for me, they'll ship me to a nunnery."

"Seriously?"

"Who knows?" she said. "My mother thinks I'm an unhealthy influence on my little sister. If she could, she'd keep Jillian in a plastic bubble or keep me in the attic."

"Oh. I'm sorry."

"I've stopped feeling sorry for myself," she replied. When she spoke, she quickly glanced at me and then shifted her eyes to look down before she finished a sentence.

Everyone had family problems, I thought. Some were only skin deep and could be shrugged off, but some were so deep that they'd affect who you were forever. Here I was arriving with so much emotional baggage that I thought there was little chance I would succeed at anything, especially making new friends, and the first person I had to get along with seemed to be a walking tragedy.

Since I had arrived, I hadn't thought much about Haylee, and, more important, I wasn't thinking about how she would react to things. I had begun to feel optimistic. Now I couldn't help wondering what Claudia would think if she knew my story. Would she avoid complaining about her own life? She did have that "top this" attitude, as if she were the poster child for parental neglect, and as funny as it might sound, I was betting she didn't want anyone else to draw more pity than she could. Maybe she didn't feel sorry for herself any longer, but she sure seemed eager to get others to feel sorry for her, whereas I wanted to avoid it like the plague.

"Do you have any brothers or sisters?" Claudia asked, as if she could hear me thinking. It was like a bell I was waiting to hear ring. Marcy had yet to ask, but I knew she would as soon as she could.

"No," I said. It wasn't an instantaneous decision

for me to deny Haylee's existence. I had been thinking about the question constantly during the ride
to Littlefield and concluded that for now, being an
only child was the best answer. Besides, right now,
as far as my father was concerned, and apparently
even Mother, I was the same as an only child.

"You're lucky," she said. "Is your mother seriously ill?"

"She'll be all right," I replied, rather than making up something. There was obviously no way to
tell the truth.

We walked silently for a while. I saw that my
father was having a good conversation with Claudia's father.

"What's your father do?" I asked her.

"He's a private business manager."

"My father runs a very successful software company," I said, then decided not to sound too perfect.
Misery, after all, loves company. "My parents are
divorced."

"Are they?" She paused and looked thoughtful.
"I wish mine were."

"What? Why?"

"Children of divorced parents get more attention, because each parent wants to show the other
that their child or children love them more. My
mother had been trying to get pregnant again for
years, so when my sister, Jilly, came, they treated
her like she was a gift from the angels. I became the

back-burner child. Everything I wanted was put on
the back burner until Jilly's needs and desires were
met. My mother hates when I call her Jilly instead
of Jillian. That's why I do it."

She walked faster.

"I'm sorry," I said, catching up, "but being the
child of divorced parents is not better than being a
child in a happy family, believe me."

"I wouldn't know," she said. "I haven't had
either type." She sounded like someone who had
been deprived of food.

Our fathers waited for us to catch up when
we reached the entrance to Matthews Hall. They
were of one serious face full of worry. Suddenly,
the beautiful sunny day looked overcast to me, and
there weren't more than a few puffy, cotton-candy
clouds moving lazily across the sky. Depression
was insidious, crawling over the grounds toward
me, smiling and reminding me that I was always
only a short memory away from its firm, tight grip.
My father started to reach for my hand, but he
stopped when he glanced at Claudia's father, who
was already turning to enter. Maybe he thought I
didn't want to seem like a little girl next to my new
roommate, when in truth, that was really what I
felt like.

A lean woman in a gray skirt suit and high-
necked blouse was there to greet us. She wore her
dull gray hair severely drawn back and pinned with

a black hair clip. She easily looked like she was in her sixties, but I bet myself she was probably no more than forty, someone who thought the older she looked, the more respect she'd command. Later I would learn that she was Mrs. Mitchell's personal assistant, Pamela Cross. Marcy would tell me, "She's the cross Mrs. Mitchell bears."

"Right this way, please," she firmly directed us and the others entering the hall. She held her arm out as though she were preventing us from going anywhere else in the building. We entered a conference room on the right. Inside, a female student in a midlength black skirt and a frilly white blouse handed out pamphlets to both parents and students. She barely smiled and wore a tag that read, "Student Government President, Kim Bailey." Some of the information on the pamphlet was also in the brochures my father had brought for Mother to see, but there were two pages of rules that applied to both classroom behavior and dormitory behavior. The list for the latter looked longer than what was pinned on our room's bulletin board. Everyone stopped talking in anticipation. Some looked like they were even holding their breath. I imagined a drumroll.

Everyone turned when Mrs. Mitchell entered. She was about five foot nine and quite pretty, with small facial features and dazzlingly bright blue eyes. She had her light brown hair styled in a classic bob. Her smile was warm and friendly, and I couldn't imagine why my father had heard and why Marcy and the others thought of her as an Iron Lady, a Mrs. Thatcher. Her makeup was subdued but tasteful, complementing her natural beauty. She wore a dark green skirt suit in the same style as the one Pamela Cross wore, with a white blouse and a string of small pearls matching her pearl earrings.

"Welcome, everyone," Mrs. Mitchell said, stepping behind the podium. She held out her arms. "Welcome to Littlefield. I'm so glad we have been able to provide you with a beautiful fall day for your first impression of our campus. We're very proud of it. It's truly our home away from home, something I have high hopes your children will come to believe as well."

Her voice was crisp; her words, although spoken sharply, made her sound refined and proper, and they seemed genuine.

"Please, take seats if you haven't. I promise I won't keep you long. I know how eager your children are to become part of Littlefield."

Her posture firmed, and the warm smile evaporated. The dazzle in her eyes quickly changed to a steely, sharp, and intense focus on us all.

"What I want to do is assure you that you have placed your child in a responsible, efficient school where every child is treated like an individual. Everyone reaches his or her goals in a different way, but we'll provide the foundation for your child to exhibit his or her predilections freely and success-fully. To our way of thinking, there is no such thing as a normal child or an average child. Perhaps it's been well hidden until now, but we'll know and nourish what makes your child special.

"To do all this, we ask a few things of everyone. We are not here to reform anyone," she continued. Now I could hear the firmness in her voice, but it wasn't simply gritty and unwavering. There was a clear suggestion of intolerance. "Littlefield is not a solution for children who have been in constant trouble in their public schools. We have little time for disciplinary problems. And we know you parents aren't spending all this money to have your child waste time or effort or be responsible for wasting someone else's. That is a belief set in concrete here.

"The pamphlet you've been given has the latest update to our rules. We are aware of the growing problems educators and parents are having out there," she said, nodding at the window as if those problems and troubles were peering in at us. "I can guarantee you that you left them behind you when you passed through our gates. We believe we have a contract with you and your children. We'll provide the best education possible, and in return, we ask your child to provide the best behavior possible, characterized by cooperation, obedience, and respect for others as well as him- or herself."

She smiled, but her smile was ice-cold now, more like a mask.

"No DSD," she said. "Drinking, smoking, drugs. A single violation of that rule is a breach of our contract. Children, your parents signed a document that establishes they will lose all the money they've invested in Littlefield. There are no exceptions, no special circumstances. Violators who plead will plead to deaf ears.

"Read the rules, obey the rules, and enjoy your school life and education," she said. "Parents, you all have my direct phone line should you need anything. We have our own medical facilities. Mrs. Cohen, our school nurse, comes to us from service in the U.S. Army."

Mrs. Cohen stepped forward. She was in a nurse's uniform and looked to be in her late thirties, even though there were strands of gray in her dark brown hair.

Mrs. Mitchell continued. "You will soon meet our guidance counselor, Mr. Hedrick. We are proud of all our staff. Every teacher at Littlefield has a master's degree.

"For now, let's get everyone settled in comfortably. Tomorrow, after all, is a school day."

It was so quiet when she paused that I could hear heavy breathing behind me. Mrs. Mitchell nodded and started out. Someone's mother stopped her to ask a question, but the rest of us began to leave. My father was at my side, Claudia and her father ahead of us, looking like they were fleeing a fire.

"I set up an account for you," my father said as we walked. "The business department handles it. You can withdraw cash when you need it for things."

"Thank you, Daddy."

"So what do you think?" he asked. I knew he was eager to hear me say encouraging things.

"So far, so good. My roommate is a bit much, but I'm sure it'll be fine."

He nodded. "You might end up doing some psychotherapy yourself. Her father told me a little about her. This is her third private school in three years."

"She told us."

"She's also a bit of an anorexic," my father said.

"Maybe more than a bit. So she's in therapy, too, huh?"

"Be careful you don't start trading stories," he joked, but my slipping and saying something I didn't want anyone here to know was something I feared. He saw the fear in my face. "Look, Kaylee, when it comes to your roommate, just be a listener. Maybe that's all she really needs."

I stopped walking abruptly.

"What?"

"Did you tell Claudia's father about Haylee?"

"Not a word. He didn't ask about any other children."

"Good. I don't care to mention her, either, and I won't. I'm an only child now."

"Very wise," he said. "You're a lot stronger than you think, Kaylee. I'm sure you'll be a great help to some of the other girls besides your roommate."

I looked down and shook my head. "How did this happen? In hours, it all turned around so that I'm the normal one here."

"You always were," he said, and hugged me. "You were always the normal one, Kaylee."

He kissed me, and we walked back to Eleanor Cook Hall holding hands as if we never walked together without doing so. We paused at the parking lot.

"So I guess I'll just take off," he said. "Girls don't want fathers hanging around. I feel confident you're in a good place with good people, and I'll impress that fact on your mother."

"Okay, Daddy." My voice sounded so young, so helpless. I hated it.

"Hey, hey, you're going to be fine, honey, fine."

I nodded.

"I'll call you, or you call me whenever you feel like it, no matter what time of day or night," he said. "I'll stop by to see your mother as soon as I get back and give her a report. She'll come around. You'll see." He hugged and kissed me again.

I stood there and watched him go to his car, get in, back up, and start out. He paused and opened his window.

"You're never alone, Kaylee, never," he said, and then he drove off. I stood there until he was gone.

Finally, out of his sight, I started to cry.

Then I saw Claudia with her father at his car. He was lecturing her forcefully about something, perhaps telling her this was her last chance. The whole time, she had her head down. When he stopped, she kept her head down. He gave her a quick, mechanical hug during which she remained stiff, her arms extended downward, her hands like claws, and then he got into his car and drove off without waving to her or anything.

She turned and saw me. She looked surprised to see me waiting for her when she stepped forward.

"How does it compare?" I asked her.

"What?"

"Littlefield, our orientation with the principal, any of it, to your other private schools."

She shrugged. "I don't think I ever noticed," she said, and walked faster, like someone who didn't care to walk together.

I kept up with her, and we entered the dorm. Mrs. Rosewell was waiting for us.

"Right this way, girls," she said, and led us to her office. She had a small desk, but she had us sit on the settee and then pulled a chair up to face us.

"I want you both to feel comfortable here at Cook Hall, but I want you to treat the building with respect and at least as well as you would treat your own home. It is, after all, your home away from home," she added, smiling.

She reached over to her desk and picked up copies of the rules that were posted on our bulletin board.

"Let us begin to read them together," she said, handing us each a copy. She read the rules as I imagined Moses read the Ten Commandments to his people. She emphasized no alcohol, drugs, or cigarettes dramatically but seemed self-conscious when she read the rule forbidding any boys in our rooms.

"Okay," she said. "We've done what we're supposed to. I have no doubt you two will be ideal residents. If either of you has any problems, no matter what, you should know my door is always open. I wish you both luck." She stood.

We thanked her and went to our room. The moment we arrived, Marcy popped out of hers and threw herself onto my bed.

"First impressions of Mrs. Thatcher," she declared, and pointed to me.

"That's loading the question," I replied. "If you call her that, you'll influence our opinions."

"What?" She widened her smile. "Are you going to be a lawyer?"

"Maybe," I said. "I'm right, right, Claudia?" I asked as she continued to organize her things.

She paused and looked at us. "Sorry," she said. "I wasn't listening."

"Not listening?" Marcy sat up. "There's not a lot of conversation going on in here, so you have to pay attention. We might say very important things."

Claudia simply stared at her. Her dark eyes weren't registering anger. In fact, they were almost void of any emotion and more like glass marbles.

"Whatever," Marcy said. She looked at me. "So what about you? Do you have any brothers or sisters, spoiled or otherwise?"

"No."

"Neither?"

"It's not unusual," I said, smiling to keep her from having any suspicions.

"I'll say. I'm a child of divorced parents."

"You, too?" I said. "Divorced?"

"You mean yours are?"

"I'm afraid so."

"Wow. We're almost the majority here at Cook Hall. There are eight others. My parents divorced when I was only five. I grew up thinking that marriages were supposed to last only five or six years and people traded in wives and husbands like they do cars. I thought there could be too much mileage on a marriage, too."

I looked at Claudia, who suddenly seemed very interested in what we were saying.

"No wonder you're so happy," she told Marcy. "Your divorced parents probably spoil you."

"Probably," Marcy sang. "*Viva la Divorce!*" she cried, and even Claudia had to smile. Finally.

I finished my unpacking and glanced at the pamphlet.

"The cafeteria is in Asper Hall?"

"We call it Regurgitation Central," Marcy joked.

"Do we have to wear anything special to dinner?"

She tapped the rules on our bulletin board. "No shorts, no bare midriffs, no bare feet, and this vague reference to no inappropriate blouses, shirts, or otherwise. Otherwise anything else. Terri Facilities and I will escort you two. You can get rid of us after today, if you like," Marcy added, more for Claudia's benefit than mine. She looked at me.

"Well, we certainly don't want to be a burden," I said, sounding as if I meant it. Almost as soon as the words left my lips, I thought I sounded more like Haylee, dripping with sarcasm. I quickly smiled.

"No worries. We're both trained professional busybodies," Marcy said.

"I think I'll take a shower and change," I said.

"Good idea. There are a few boys you'll want to impress," Marcy said, looking at both of us.

Claudia raised her eyebrows at being included.

"I mean, we're not really here just for an academic education, are we?" Marcy added. She did a little pirouette and headed out.

"I like her, don't you?" I asked Claudia.

"Sure," Claudia said dryly. "I like everybody."

She began to draw school supplies and her computer out of her bag and get her desk organized.

Later for that, I thought, and chose something to wear to dinner.

"Off to the shower," I said. Claudia glanced at me and then back at her computer.

"You need a password for the Wi-Fi," she said. "No one told it to us."

"I'm sure they will. See you soon," I said.

There was no one else in the showers when I entered. As the water cascaded over me, I imagined it was washing away all traces of my nightmare abduction. Perhaps my father's hopes for me could be realized. I could make new friends and create a world with only me in it, no Haylee to refer to, no Haylee to consider. There were only my feelings now, my dreams. The warm water felt wonderful. *This is a magic shower*, I thought. *It erases your past.*

When I returned to our room, Claudia was still in front of her computer. She had gotten the password and had put it on my desk for me. She looked like she was in a heavy instant-message exchange with someone. I didn't want to seem nosy, so I didn't look over her shoulder. Instead, I concentrated on what I would wear. There was a sense of freedom about it. I didn't have to consider what Mother would think or if Haylee liked my choice. Better yet, I didn't have to conform to what she wanted. I put on a turquoise blouse and a dark blue skirt.

"I *thought* you were wearing a wig!" Marcy exclaimed as I was brushing my short hair to give it some sense of style. There were obviously no locks on our doors. Right now, I looked like Joan of Arc or someone. There were women who had their hair cut as short as mine deliberately, of course, but I had always been so proud of mine, of ours.

"I'm sorry I got talked into that," I said. "My father felt sorry for me and bought me the wigs."

Claudia was now giving me her full attention. "My father forbids me to cut my hair," she said.

"What's he going to do if you do, disown you?" Marcy asked.

Claudia shrugged. "Too late for that. He did that years ago," she said.

Marcy widened her eyes and then laughed because she didn't know what to say. Neither did I. She turned to me.

"You have one of those faces that can't be damaged by a bad hairstyle," Marcy said. "I'll poke you in the ribs if one of the boys I'm after looks at you with too much interest."

"What?"

"Kidding," she sang, and smiled at Claudia. "You didn't change for dinner?"

"I had other things to do," Claudia said. "It's not the Ritz, is it?"

"The what? Oh." Marcy laughed. "No, it's definitely not the Ritz. It's not even McDonald's, but it's all we have," she said dramatically. "Cherish it, darling," she added. "Mrs. Rosewell calls everyone darling. Or dearie. I hate *dearie*, don't you?"

"Call me anything," I said, recalling one of my father's pet expressions. "Just don't call me late for dinner."

"That's good!" Marcy cried. "C'mon. Let's march in together like the Three Musketeers!"

"I'm really not hungry," Claudia said.

"Hey, wait until you see the food before you say that," Marcy replied, and shocked her by scooping her under one arm and then holding her other arm out for me.

It was going to be difficult to be depressed in Marcy's company, I thought, and for both Claudia and me, she was just what the doctor ordered.

The question was how long before she would flee our company.

7

An explosion of chatter and laughter confronted us when we entered the dining hall. Although the tables and chairs resembled any school cafeteria's furnishings, the walls had a rich-looking light brown paneling, and there was decorative framing around the large four-panel windows, most of which looked out on the manicured lawns and bushes. Hundreds of recessed light fixtures brightened the room, which had an immaculately polished dark brown tile floor. Off to the left were the familiar counters and metal shelf along which students moved their trays to choose their entrées and side dishes as well as drinks and desserts. Every table had a bouquet of flowers that looked real.

Although Marcy kidded us about the food, it looked quite a bit more elaborate than the usual public-school fare. Four women and a tall man who was obviously the head chef served the students. The kitchen was in full view and looked immaculate, with stainless-steel fixtures. Of course, it occurred to me that much of this was dressed up to appeal to the parents more than the students. The parents were paying the bills.

Obviously, most of the students in the dining hall knew one another, some for years, perhaps. As I had seen in the orientation meeting, there were only a little more than thirty new students. Most, like me and now Claudia, were still being escorted by girls who had been assigned to help them get oriented, but just like in my public school and probably every other school in the world, there were groups of students who clung to one another, cliques or what Haylee called "clacks." Marcy and Terri naturally steered us to theirs, a table with four other girls from Cook Hall and two boys, Haden Kimble and Luke Richards, both seniors. There was something about them that immediately told me they wouldn't be lusting after my or any other girl's bod. Right now, that gave me some relief.

What I really appreciated was that neither Claudia nor I was immediately bombarded with personal questions. In fact, it was as if we had always been students here. After Marcy introduced us, Haden and Luke continued their argument about face piercing as though we were simply a minor interruption. Someone else might have resented the lack of attention and interest, but both Claudia and I were grateful, for obviously different reasons.

"Teenagers are so damn predictable," Haden said. He wore a pair of thick black-framed glasses that settled comfortably halfway down the bridge of his thin nose. "A fad catches on, and most everyone who does it does it simply not to seem 'different.'" He made quotation marks in the air.

"Ditto," Luke said.

Estelle Marcus, the girl they were looking at when they spoke, had a silver dot in her left nostril. She hadn't had it when I had seen her earlier in the dorm hallway.

"It's not a fad for me," she shot back indignantly. "I wear it when I want to wear it and because I want to wear it. The emphasis," she added, imitating Haden's quotation marks in the air, "is on 'when I want.'"

"Don't you have to wear that all the time or the hole will close up?" I asked her. Mother wouldn't permit Haylee or me even to have pierced ears. There would be no deliberate changes in our bodies for fear that one would not be exactly like the other.

"I wear it enough to prevent that," Estelle snapped back. She took a second look at me to see if I was favoring the argument the boys were making.

"If she wore it to class, Mrs. Mitchell would have her expelled," Terri said. She almost added,

And rightly so. The words were spelled out in her disapproving look.

I thought that was that, but then Claudia suddenly blurted, "You wouldn't be at the last school I was at."

Everyone turned to her. She looked shocked at herself that she had spoken, as shocked as I was, especially because she sounded like she was in defense of piercing, but then she added, "However, they needed the money, so you could practically get away with murder there."

"What school was that?" Estelle quickly asked, sounding like she would transfer in the morning.

"Saddle Brook," Claudia said. "A girl was gang-raped the year I attended, but the school managed to keep it out of the newspapers."

No one spoke.

"She was my roommate," Claudia continued.

Marcy and I looked at each other, surprised at how talkative Claudia suddenly was, and how revealing.

"Really?" Luke asked. "How horrible for you, but, of course, more for her."

Everyone looked at Claudia as if she had just missed being gang-raped herself.

"She's in a nuthouse right now," Claudia said. "Catatonic."

"Catatonic?" I asked, too quickly perhaps. "I mean, I think I know what that is."

"It's like a coma with your eyes open," Claudia said. "Most of the girls there seemed catatonic to me," she added without the slightest hint of humor.

A heavy silence followed. In moments, Claudia had wiped away all smiles and excitement. The potential dangers and horrors of the world that hovered just outside the boundaries of our special, privileged, private world flashed behind everyone's eyes. The lesson was clear to me. If you brought sadness and horror in, you were as marked by it as Cain was marked with sin. It was a clear "blame the messenger" message. No one here, I vowed to myself, would learn what I had endured.

"Let's eat before I lose my appetite," Marcy suddenly declared, practically leaping to her feet.

Terri and I, with Claudia following slowly, rose and went to the food line. Marcy glanced back at Claudia and widened her eyes at me.

"I feel sorry for you if you get to tell each other bedtime stories when the lights are out," she whispered. "She's like a female Norman Bates from *Psycho*. You could ask Mrs. Rosewell to arrange a room change."

"I'll be fine."

"Just shout if it ever gets too much. I'll bring the depression extinguisher," she said, then moved quickly to deliberately bump against the boy ahead of us.

He turned with annoyance until he saw who it was and then smiled. "A bit clumsy?"

"Only around you," she told him. "You have that effect on *jeunes femmes*."

He widened his smile and looked at the three of us. "New victims?"

"Freshly served," she said, and introduced us to Rob Brian, a senior with curly dark brown hair and an impish smile. He seemed a perfect match for her. He introduced us to Ben Kaplan, a boy about Claudia's height with a similarly lean build, a face peppered with orange freckles, and short apricot-colored hair.

"Welcome, girls," Rob said. "Be skeptical of everything Marcy tells you about us."

"Kaylee doesn't need to be warned. She can handle herself. She was prom queen at her last school and is a brilliant student with a four-point-oh. I plan on stealing all her homework," she declared, "and raising my grade average enough to get my father to buy me a car."

I felt my face flush when the boys looked at me with even more interest.

"What about you, Claudia?" Ben asked. He looked like he would be a teenager until he was fifty.

"Claudia was arrested twice for speed dating," Marcy quipped. "Her bite is worse than her bark."

The boys laughed.

"Put me on your dance card," Ben told Claudia before they walked off. "I'm not afraid of being bitten."

I looked at her to see if she was offended, but she wore her usual indifference to everything she had seen or heard. I watched her select her food as if she were navigating through potential poison.

"Vegetarian?" I asked when I saw her avoid the chicken and beef dishes.

"Tonight," she said.

After we had gotten our food and gone back to our table, I attacked Marcy, but half-heartedly.

"How could you make up stories like that about me? I never said I was a prom queen, and I never told you about my grades. Did they believe you?"

"What did she do now?" Terri asked.

"She told those boys stories about us . . . exaggerations!"

"Marcy hasn't said a serious thing since I've known her," Estelle said.

"What difference does it make?" Marcy said, shrugging. "No one will check up on it. We can be whoever we like here." She turned sharply to Claudia. "You don't have to be yourself anymore. Forget all that about your old school. You can be reborn here. Pick out a new you. I have a catalogue in my room if you need choices. I try to be a different person every week."

I looked across the room at Rob and Ben. Everyone at their table was gazing at us as Rob spoke to them. Who knew what he was telling them now? Once you cast a lie into the sea of gossip, it was like trying to find a drop in the ocean, impossible to retrieve.

"She's not kidding," Terri said. "Wait until she starts with her fake English accent. She has a terrible crush on Mr. Edgewater, our lit teacher, and thinks if she speaks more like him, he'll ravish her."

"He will . . . someday."

"Dream, dream, dream," Estelle said.

"Why not dream? The truth is so boring," Marcy continued. "Right, Claudia?"

"We are what we pretend to be, so we must be careful about what we pretend to be," she replied dryly. She began to poke at her food as though she were looking for something disgusting, like a hair or a dead fly.

"Huh? What's that mean?"

"Kurt Vonnegut," Claudia said.

"He's an author, right?" Terri asked.

"Yes."

"I don't care what he is. I hate warnings," Marcy declared, souring her face. "They are such downers. There are too many 'bewares' in the world. We don't need to add any."

Claudia retreated after that and didn't utter another word.

"What did you think of Rob?" Marcy asked me, keeping her eyes, still full of reprimand, on Claudia, who had closed herself like a clam.

"Cute," I said. "Is he your boyfriend?"

"Not yet, but I'm going to sleep with him," she predicted without the slightest hesitation. "Not my first, but my first was a disaster, in ninth grade. How about you?"

Everyone, including Claudia, leaned toward me.

"Abstinence makes the heart grow fonder," I said.

Marcy tilted her head. "Isn't that supposed to be *absence* makes the heart grow fonder?"

"Oh, damn, I made a mistake all these years."

Everyone but Claudia laughed, and Marcy poked me with her shoulder.

"We're going to be great friends . . . or else . . ."

"Or else what?"

"Bored," she declared, and I laughed, too, probably the most free and honest laugh in a very long time. Claudia looked surprised, but in her look, I detected a desire to be part of whatever was forming between Marcy and me.

Something was, for sure. As our conversations continued, I did begin to feel more and more relaxed. Everyone who had advised me was so right. Attending a new school with people who didn't know me or my family was the prescription for a healthy, happier future for me.

As we put our trays and dishes on the shelves set out for them, I happened to glance toward the far right corner of the dining hall and saw a boy sitting alone at a table. I didn't want to stare at him, but it looked like he was staring at me. Of course, I realized he could be looking at someone near me. However, it struck me as odd that he was sitting completely alone and, instead of talking to anyone, had a textbook open. He wore his dark brown hair longer than most boys here, and he was dressed better, with what looked like a Robert Graham shirt and a pair of dark slacks rather than jeans. My father wore those shirts, so I knew about them and how expensive they were. I thought this boy was good-looking in a mature way. He had the air of someone quite self-confident.

I told myself I could be reading all this into just a glimpse and looked away quickly. But then I turned to Marcy and asked, "Who's that boy in the corner?"

"Corner?" She looked. "Oh," she said, dropping her voice. "That's Troy Matzner or, excuse me, Troy Alexander Matzner the Thirtieth or something."

"Why is he sitting alone?"

"There's no one here good enough to stand in his shadow. Even the teachers treat him special, like he's one of them and not us. There's a four-point-oh without pretending. Some people think he's gay, but I also heard a rumor that he's seeing an older woman."

"How much older?"

"Maybe in her thirties or something. I don't know anything for sure, but don't waste your time. He won't give you a minute, much less an hour, of his day."

"No worries. I have time to spare," I said.

She laughed and took my hand to pull me along. "C'mon. You don't have any homework yet. We can hang out in my room and tell each other secrets without either of us knowing what's true and what isn't."

I looked back at Claudia, walking behind us, her head down.

"I should get to know my roommate, don't you think?"

"The voice of darkness? Whatever," Marcy said. "I'll hang out with you guys and watch you open the coffin. Just kidding. She's a breath of stale air."

Just before we left Asper and headed for Cook, I looked back and saw Troy Matzner leaving the dining hall. I wasn't imagining it. He was looking in my direction. Despite all my fears and trepidations and especially Marcy's warnings, I couldn't help but be a little interested in him. Maybe it was more than a little.

I turned away quickly and continued walking.

The night air was chilly but sharply fresh. The moon wasn't visible, but the partly cloudy sky gave us glimpses of bright stars and familiar constellations. There was something liberating about being away from home and away from anyone who knew me. I felt invigorated, hopeful, and especially generous. I paused once to let Claudia catch up. She looked surprised at how I wasn't going to ignore her. She had fewer expectations for any sort of happiness than I had.

"Food wasn't really that bad, was it?" I asked her. I had watched her picking at her food. She ate little. "Maybe you should have tried the chicken. You'll probably be hungry later."

"No, I won't. Anyway, it wasn't worse than my mother's," she said. "Which isn't saying much."

"We're not supposed to keep any food in our rooms," Marcy said, "but I have some great energy bars if you do get hungry later," she told Claudia.

"Thanks," Claudia said, "but I don't think . . ."

"Oh, you'll get hungry later," Marcy insisted. "I'll give you one to hide under your pillow or in your pajamas."

I smiled at her. She was determined not to permit Claudia to cast a negative or depressing net over us. It amazed me. How did she become so optimistic and stay so happy with divorced parents and a broken home? Whether she was all pretend or not,

I thought, she was exactly what the doctor ordered, someone who could vacuum up any sad thoughts or at least sweep them under the rug.

"You guys know that we can leave the campus on weekends, go into town and to a restaurant, mall, or movie, right?" Marcy asked as we walked on.

"No," Claudia said, and shrugged as if to say *What difference does it make?*

"It's not exactly Fun City here on weekends, and you can get better things to eat, not to mention drink."

"No one said anything to me about that," Claudia claimed.

"It's on the contract your parents signed with the school. They had to agree that the school wasn't responsible for what you did off campus, but you have to obey the curfew. No later than midnight back in your bunk and no leaving the campus on school days except Fridays and holidays . . . or . . ." She traced a line over her neck. "Twelve is not hard and fast. The bed check is random, meaning if Mrs. Rosewell is still awake or not, and most of the time, she's drifted off. We also occupy her attention if we know someone is going to be late, so don't worry."

"How do we get to town?" I asked.

"There is a bus at the corner, but seniors have driving privileges. Most of the boys have their own cars. Rob does," she added, nudging me. She leaned in to whisper. "Double dates are possible. Interested?"

I didn't answer.

The concept of dating, starting a relationship, was truly at the tail end of my immediate concerns right now. Survival was number one. Survival meant somehow burying the immediate past so deeply that it wouldn't come up even in nightmares. Every time I saw a cat or heard a sound that resembled the rattling of a chain, I cringed. The sight of any man whose head and body from behind vaguely suggested Anthony Cabot, my abductor, still sent ice water flowing along my spine and seized my breath. My utmost fear was that someone, someone like Marcy or Terri, would notice my reactions and begin to ask questions.

I saw how everyone had responded to Claudia's reference to a girl at her last school being gang-raped. How would they react to having a girl who had been abducted and kept chained in a farmhouse basement, a girl whose hair had been chopped away and who was often naked and exposed? When and if that story spread, what boy would want to date me anyway, and what girl would want to become close friends with me? I would avoid all this as best I could.

However, soon the inevitable questions would come: *Why did your parents want you to attend Littlefield? Why did they want you out of the pub-*

lic school? If you're an only child, why would they want you out of the house so soon? The whys would come raining down around me and make my head spin, but my reaction had to be credible.

I had my stock answers prepared. *My classes weren't challenging enough. Even my teachers admitted it, citing their burden of having to teach so many of the basics that the other students never learned or mastered. They tried to give me individual attention, but the public-school class sizes were just too big. Cutbacks, you see.* Who wouldn't believe all that? Some or most of it was why they were sent here, too.

But a bigger question haunted me. I didn't think it would come up so quickly. That was naive on my part, I guess, a symptom of the overly protected life I had lived under Mother's rule. I knew that if our roles were reversed, Haylee would have landed a date by now or certainly wouldn't have shied away from any and every opportunity to date someone.

The question was, could I ever commit to or feel safe in any sort of relationship? I didn't have to have a daily psychological evaluation to know that my feelings and emotions were still quite fragile. Just the thought of someone touching me made me shiver. It disturbed me deeply to think I could be this withdrawn for the rest of my life as a result of what terrible things had been done to me. I could be emotionally handicapped, psychologically crippled forever. I certainly was feeling that way right now, and there was no one here I could go to for advice or help with these feelings. I'd have to go home and see my therapist, Dr. Sacks, whom I was scheduled to see again in six months.

"I think it would be best for me to get comfortable with my work and my teachers and my new dorm life first," I told Marcy.

"Dulllllllll," Marcy sang. "That's all easier than you think. Leave it to me. I'll fix you up with the right guy or guys. It will be easy, considering what you look like, and it will make things easier for me, too. Now, Claudia," she said, stepping closer and whispering, "that will be my biggest challenge."

"Then maybe you should begin with her," I suggested.

She stopped walking, but I continued moving forward. "What?" She hurried back to my side. "Find her a date? No way, José."

"She's my roommate. It would be terrible to leave her alone, especially on the first few weekends," I added.

Marcy's excitement dwindled quickly. I smiled to myself. Amazing how clever I could be when I was looking for ways to avoid a crisis, I thought.

Marcy looked back at Claudia and then shook her head. "And here I was thinking my social life was about to skyrocket," she moaned.

"Maybe it will," I said. "Think of how impressed everyone will be if you play Cupid successfully for her."

"Sounds too much like a homework assignment," she complained.

We walked on. When we got to the dorm, Marcy went quickly to her room and returned with some energy bars.

Claudia reluctantly accepted one. "I probably won't eat it," she said.

"If you change your mind, at least you'll have it," Marcy said.

Claudia put it in her night-table drawer. Almost immediately, Marcy began asking Claudia what she thought were key questions related to dating while I organized my desk. It took all my self-control to keep from laughing. But then I thought, *What if she's really good at this and finds Claudia a boyfriend?*

What excuse would I have then?

"So did you have any boyfriends at your two other private schools?" Marcy asked her.

"Not exactly," Claudia replied. "Not how you mean," she quickly added.

Marcy looked to me with an amused expression. She had planted herself on the floor between Claudia and me and sat in the lotus position.

"How do I mean?"

"Sex," Claudia said bluntly.

"You haven't had any sex?"

"No, not how you mean."

"What is this with what I mean? It's not rocket science. Are you a virgin? How close did you come to losing it? Was there a boy you liked enough to do it with? They are not multiple-choice questions."

"They are to me," Claudia said.

"Huh?" Marcy looked at me with frustration.

I looked away, secretly pleased at Marcy's frustration.

"If you could have the boy of your dreams, what would he be like?" she asked.

"I always felt hypothetical questions were a waste of time," Claudia replied. "Something like that should be spontaneous anyway. It's my big bang theory."

"What?" Marcy looked like she wasn't sure if she should laugh and turned to me for some hint.

I said nothing.

"Do you mean big bang like I think or hope?" she asked.

"I'm going to brush my teeth and wash up for bed," Claudia said instead of replying. She gathered her bag of toiletries and walked out.

"What language does she speak? Can you think of another reason to have a boyfriend? What did she mean by saying they are multiple-choice questions to her? And what is a big bang theory?" Marcy asked after Claudia was gone.

I shrugged. "I think I know what she means. Companionship could be one reason other than sex, I suppose."

"Companionship? With a boy?" Marcy grimaced as if the word left a bitter taste after it was pronounced. "That died for me once I had my first period. Unless he's gay, any boy has one thing on his mind, no matter how safe you might think he is. Which is fine by me," she added. "Don't tell me that when you look at a boy, especially a boy you just met, the vision of what it would be like to sleep with him doesn't come into it some way, sometime, even if it's a 'never happen' thought. It's still one of your thoughts, right? I mean, I'm not some nymphomaniac. I'm a well-adjusted, determined-to-be-sexually-active young woman. Okay, that's enough confession from me. She has my head spinning. Your turn."

"I suppose I think about it but not, as you make it sound, with every boy I meet. They have to be attractive and interesting enough for me to care."

"I'm not saying I'd do it with just any of them, but it helps to imagine what it would be like."

I looked away. All this sounded so immature to me now. Was it impossible for me to be a teenage girl again and have these kinds of discussions?

Marcy persisted. "All right. I'll start from scratch. How about you? Any special boy you left behind?"

"There was one once," I said. It seemed like decades ago. "My first real crush, I suppose. He moved away."

"Lost contact?"

"Yes, but he set the bar for me."

"Which means?"

"I tend to measure other boys against him, and so far, no one's come close."

She nodded, impressed.

I'm getting good at this, I thought, and again thought, *out of self-defense.*

Claudia returned, wearing her light pink robe and matching pajamas. "What time is lights-out?" she asked, putting away her clothes.

"Lights-out? This isn't exactly the army," Marcy said.

"Fine." Claudia scooped a sleep mask out of her smaller suitcase.

"We're trying to get to know each other," Marcy said.

"There's always tomorrow. I'm not leaving . . . for a while, anyway," Claudia said, and put her sleep mask on before crawling into bed and turning her back to us.

"You want to come to my room?" Marcy asked.

"I think I should go to bed, too," I said. "It's been a long day. I'll see you at breakfast, okay?"

Marcy was disappointed, but she stood up. "I hope you don't turn out to be a good influence on me or something," she said. "If you think of something shocking to tell me, don't be afraid to wake me up. 'Night, newlyweds," she chimed.

Claudia didn't respond.

I smiled. "Thanks. 'Night," I said.

She rolled her eyes and left. I changed into my pajamas and went to brush my teeth and wash up. When I returned, Claudia had turned onto her back and taken off her sleep mask.

"It's all right with me if you want to ask for a different roommate," she said.

"What for?" I asked.

She didn't answer.

"We haven't known each other long enough to dislike each other," I said.

She turned to me. "I have never had a boyfriend. I haven't gone to any parties or anything since I was in junior high school. I'm not gay, although I've been accused of being gay," she rattled off, like someone who had to get it said and over.

"I wouldn't frame it as an accusation if you were," I said. "And I haven't been Miss Popularity at my school, despite how Marcy thinks of me. She means no harm. Let's just get ourselves started and organized, Claudia. It seems like a good school. I hope we'll both be happy here."

She studied me a moment to see if I was just telling her what she would want to hear and then nodded. She apparently decided I was sincere. "Okay."

I got into bed, and after I put out the light, we were silent, but then she asked me what my class schedule was. We shared two classes.

"I'm better in math. If I wasn't, my father would be disappointed," she said.

"What about your mother?"

"She doesn't even ask about my grades anymore."

"I'm better in English and history, so maybe we can help each other."

"Maybe," she said cautiously.

"Good night," I said.

"'Night." She sounded so fragile.

Who was more broken? I wondered. Maybe it didn't matter. Maybe in some way, I was lucky to have pulled her as a roommate. I wasn't going to sleep worrying about myself for a change. And I would have less reason to think about Haylee.

That felt good. I never thought I would feel happy so quickly here. I was skeptical that I ever would, but I closed my eyes and considered that I might. I just might make something of a comeback after all.

That boy back at the dining hall came to mind again. Troy Matzner. I wondered why he kept to himself. Was it good to be curious or dangerous now? Why not start optimistically? I thought.

I might even fall in love with someone and come to the point where everything terrible that had happened to me would seem like it had happened to someone else.

Maybe I could pretend it had happened to Haylee.

After all, that was who Anthony Cabot thought he had kidnapped.

8

I liked my teachers at Littlefield. Although they dressed more formally than the teachers in my previous school, the men here wearing ties and jackets and the women wearing dresses with hems at least at midcalf, I felt a more relaxed atmosphere in their classrooms. There was definitely a different energy throughout the school. Everyone moved more slowly, and teachers especially spoke more softly.

In my public-school classes, imposing discipline always seemed to be the first order of business and a continual issue. Many of my teachers, male and female alike, often lost their tempers. They held themselves like people who anticipated unpleasantness, shoulders braced, eyes full of suspicion. Sometimes you felt you could cut the air because it was thick with tension. For some of my public-school teachers, there were classes that ruined their entire teaching day and students they'd like to put in front of a firing squad. However, if they let down their guard, those who were more interested in disrupting our classes pounced.

Cutups were sent to the dean. Students were frequently suspended. Smoking in the bathrooms was a constant problem, as was graffiti. We knew that teachers were often judged, especially the new ones, on how well they kept order in their classes and how often they had to give up and send someone to the dean. They were aware of it, too, and tolerated a great deal more than they should, which in the end hurt how well we learned. There were so many interruptions.

Here at Littlefield, the teachers had a great weapon: the cost. If you were misbehaving repeatedly or did something that required the dean to be involved, you risked all the money your parents paid to have you attend, and even for well-to-do people, that was a significant loss, not to mention the embarrassment.

I learned quickly that it was true: Mrs. Mitchell was the Iron Lady when it came to discipline. If someone was speaking too loudly in the halls or even jokingly punched or pushed another student and she witnessed it, she sent laser arrows from her eyes, and the student cutting up instantly turned into Little Lord Fauntleroy, the Harry Potter of his time, perfectly mannered, polite, and considerate. It was like slowing down when you saw a traffic cop with a radar gun ahead of you.

She didn't have a radar gun, but she had a way of looking so intently at us as she passed by or stood in an office doorway, watching us move from class to class, that most of us had to look away or down, soften our voices, or hold our breath. My fears were different, of course. I worried that she realized something more significant than what had brought the other students here had brought me to Littlefield, and I feared that one of these days, she would call me into her office to cross-examine me. I doubted I could lie to her.

Nevertheless, as the first week of school at Littlefield drew to an end, I did feel more self-confident. At breakfasts, lunches, and dinners with my classmates, I listened more than I spoke, but when I did speak, I talked about my school and social life before my abduction, answering the usual questions about friends and parties. Did we drink anything, take anything? How late could we stay out? Did I have parties at my house? How wild did our parties get?

I didn't want to appear too goody-goody, but I didn't want to make everything seem all right, either. I tried to sound just naive about it. Some were disappointed. They were like prisoners on an island who had hoped to hear raucous tales from the ones who had just arrived.

A number of times, I almost gave away that I was an identical twin, but I was able to rescue the references by assigning them to this mythical best friend. I made it seem like she and I were inseparable. I called her Audrina and fabricated her history, family, and personality, weaving in details from novels I had read.

Marcy asked the most questions about her, pressuring me for a detailed description, coming right out and asking if I thought she was prettier than I was. I simply put together some features from three or four girls and created an imaginary friend who was attractive by anyone's standards. Marcy pushed on, wanting to know how long we'd been friends. What did we have in common? Did we share clothes and things? Was she jealous of me, especially over a boy?

If anything, I thought Marcy was the jealous one, jealous of my admiration for this mythical best friend. I realized early on that despite her outgoing personality, Marcy had really never had a close friend. I sensed she was hoping I might be her first. I wasn't averse to it. For too long, Haylee had to be my best friend, and I had to be hers. The prospect of growing close to someone without Haylee looking over my shoulder and in some way interfering was exciting to me.

But Marcy's questions made me feel like I was writing a teenage soap opera, and finally, one day at lunch after she asked me whether I knew if Audrina was a virgin, I spun on her and said, "Please, no more questions about her, Marcy. I've left that world. This is my world now. I don't even email or Instagram anyone back home. To be honest, they were all mad at me for agreeing to attend a private school."

She both liked and didn't like my answer, but she stopped asking questions about the mythical Audrina. She did, however, want to know if any of the boys I liked or the ones who liked me felt I had become a snob or something when they learned I was going to leave and attend an expensive private school.

"That happened to me," she said quickly, to be sure I would answer.

"I wasn't really involved with any boy closely enough to care," I told her. That was the truth.

Of course, what she suggested had been of some concern when my father and Dr. Sacks proposed that I attend a private school. I did have friends whom I admittedly pushed away in the period immediately after my rescue. I regretted losing them and imagined that their way of writing me off forever now was to think of me just the way Marcy was claiming her friends thought of her. We thought we were too good for them. The difference,

I hoped, was that the ones who were sensitive and intelligent would realize how difficult it would have been for me simply to rejoin them.

Was it naive of me to expect that after a while, none of that would matter, that I would start a new life here and forget the horror I had endured? Can you really tuck away the painful memories in your life or bury them under new and better ones? How damaged was I? When, I wondered, would someone here look at me and realize it? I hadn't met that many of my classmates yet, but every time I got to speak to someone new, I held my breath, anticipating her or him to pause and ask, *What really made you want to come here? What happened to you, Kaylee Blossom Fitzgerald? Something did, so stop pretending otherwise.*

Claudia had yet to ask such a question, but sometimes I caught her looking at me with more curiosity, and I thought she was on the verge of doing so. Haylee used to tell anyone who criticized her for something she had done that, "It takes one to know one." There was some truth in that. Someone who was deeply emotionally wounded should recognize someone else who was, I thought, and that was why I feared Claudia would eventually get the truth from me.

Claudia tagged along reluctantly when we went to the dining hall, but I wouldn't let her drift into solitude, where she would surely only feel sorry for herself and thus make things gloomier for me. I always kept a place for her at our table in the dining hall and included her in any conversations. By driving her darkness back, I hoped I would be driving away my own.

I wasn't starting to like her so much as I was finding it easier to tolerate her, thanks a great deal to Marcy, who would swipe away Claudia's dour expression with a quip about Mrs. Rosewell or her own roommate, who she claimed was obsessive-compulsive, insisting that toothpaste tubes be squeezed from the bottom up.

"I do that, too," Claudia claimed, after which Marcy went into a dramatic faint, slapping her hand over her forehead, falling onto my bed, and claiming she was overwhelmed by efficient, organized people.

"You don't know what this means to confront another organized person. If this keeps up, I'll have to reform, get good grades, and behave myself. I'll choke on compliments!"

Claudia actually laughed. *She can be rescued*, I thought. I still wondered if I could, but she certainly did have good qualities. She wasn't one to raise her hand in class to answer questions, but when she was called on, she always had the answer the teacher was looking to get. As she had predicted, she started off well in math, getting a hundred on our first quiz and A-pluses on her homework. Thanks to her, I did just as well. She had no problem tutoring me and certainly showed more patience than I would have tutoring someone.

Maybe I'd learned more about psychology than I thought, but gradually, whenever Marcy wasn't hovering over us, I began to get more and more out of Claudia concerning her home life and her self-image. She was less reluctant to talk when I did what my therapists did and acted almost disinterested, clearing away any sense of pursuit or pressure. If she offered something, some detail, I made reference to someone I knew who had a similar experience, so I could say, "I know what you mean, Claudia." As a result of all this, she grew more comfortable with me, more comfortable, I thought, than she had been with any previous roommates.

Although I didn't think she would like it, I began to feel sorry for her. I had trouble believing and accepting the idea that a parent could dislike his or her own child, but the more she told me about her relationship with her parents, especially her mother, the more I accepted that it was possible and the sorrier I began to feel for her. My father was right. I was becoming a little more than an amateur therapist. You suffer a wound and watch how the doctor treats it, and nine times out of ten, when something similar happens to someone else, you can help.

I understood her bitterness when she told me how her mother, almost from the days of Claudia's infancy, never wanted to go shopping with her for clothes, shoes, or practically anything for her. She gave that assignment to their housekeeper and nanny, Beneatha Patterson, an African American woman, whom Claudia admitted she liked more than her own mother. Claudia never had the mother-daughter talks Haylee and I had with our mother, and she certainly spoke little with her about sex and relationships. I gathered that the icing on the cake for Claudia was when her mother decided she didn't need Beneatha to serve as nanny to her new daughter, Jillian. Now she would willingly and lovingly take on those motherly responsibilities.

I could easily understand why that was so painful for Claudia. After all, this was the exact opposite of how Mother had treated Haylee and me. There was never to be an iota of favoritism in our house, nothing to ever stimulate jealousy or sibling rivalry. Mother would practically lunge at my father to claw him if he complimented only Haylee or me for some reason, no matter how simple. Listening to Claudia describe her home life, I began to wonder if Mother was all that terrible after all. She had become something of an expert in parenting. She just went a little overboard. Well, maybe she went a lot overboard.

My father was the first to bail out, of course. The divorce still came as a shock to both Haylee and me when it happened, but Mother didn't seem as disturbed by it, as we had anticipated she would be. Now all of it, all the responsibility for us, had fallen squarely on him.

My father called me twice the first week. The first time was to be sure I was comfortable and happy. The second time was to talk about Haylee.

"I thought you should know what's happening, Kaylee. If you don't want to know, just tell me, but I wasn't going to shut you out of it all without your telling me to do so."

When I realized why he was calling, I left my room and went outside for privacy. When we were nearby, Mother used to warn her friends who were talking about other women that "little pitchers have big ears." People, especially girls in Cook Hall, snooped on one another.

Claudia, like everyone else at Littlefield right now, believed I was an only child. Probably, if I was going to trust anyone with the truth, Claudia would be the best one. The girls who spoke to her did so solely because she was part of Marcy's and my group from Cook Hall. She didn't actively pursue any friendships other than what she had with us. Except for Marcy, who did it because she thought it pleased me, no one asked her personal questions. I did tell myself that if I needed to confide in anyone here, Claudia would be the one, because whatever I told her would never find its way from her lips. It would almost be like talking to myself. Right now, I saw no urgent need to do it.

"What's happening with her, Daddy? I do want to know."

"Dr. Alexander called me yesterday. Haylee's catatonia was still severe, so they wanted to begin electric shock treatments."

"Electric shock?"

"Yes."

"Did they do it?"

"They did it just an hour ago, Kaylee."

Despite the cruel thing Haylee had done to me and all the deceit that followed, I couldn't erase the years we had spent together being more like conjoined twins than merely identical. For most of our lives, whenever one of us suffered pain or an illness, the other did, too, if not actually, then virtually. Of course, it was mostly psychological, but that didn't make it less painful for one of us than the other. Mother taught us early on that when one of us caught a cold, the other would for sure, and that always seemed to happen. She even began giving medicine to both of us, even if the other showed no symptoms yet. When we were little and one of us cut herself on something, Mother would cut the other in the same place—a finger, a hand, a leg, whatever. We were taught that each of us must always feel what the other felt. We must think of ourselves as halves of the same person.

There was some reality to it. Neither of us could be allergic to something without the other also being allergic. We suffered cavities in the same teeth, which absolutely shocked the dentist. If one of us developed a cough, Mother gave the other the same cough medicine, and soon after, we were both coughing. Maybe we began to cough out of sympathy or simply because we wanted to please Mother, but whatever the reason, we did it. It happened.

Standing there in the late-afternoon twilight, miles and miles from Haylee, practically in another world, I could still empathize with her. I even grimaced with pain as I did more than simply imagine the electricity passing through my brain; I felt it. My jaw stiffened. My whole body hardened with expectation. I felt myself tremble.

"Kaylee?" my father asked when I was silent for too long.

"What happened?" I asked after regaining my breath.

"It worked," he said. "She's much better."

"So you visited her?"

"Yes. I had to, both for her sake and your mother's."

"Yours, too, Daddy. She's still your daughter."

"Right. I saw her, but I didn't speak to her. Anyway, I wanted you to know so you wouldn't blame yourself for any of this. Don't tell me you didn't, Kaylee," he added quickly. "You wanted to punish her, get even somehow, and you believe you did."

"Yes," I confessed. We had discussed it, but now, with Haylee getting this painful treatment, I felt more guilt than pleasure. It was still true and maybe always would be. Everything I did to her, I did to myself, and vice versa, whether she wanted to admit it or not.

"Anyway, it's over," my father said. "Her therapy has begun again. Dr. Alexander and I decided I would visit her next week. I'll call you after I do."

"Okay."

"You can't let this interfere with your good progress, Kaylee. You're going to have a better life now, and that's that," he said firmly. "What's happening to Haylee she brought on herself."

"All right, Daddy."

"Are you making new friends?"

"Yes, and I like my teachers and the classes."

"Good. Your mother finally asked me about you."

"Did she? I did call to speak with her, but Mrs. Granford said she was sleeping, and she never called me back."

"Yes, well, I told her about Haylee, and I think it's all finally sinking in. In fact, she seems a lot better, too. Mrs. Granford said she is doing a lot more for herself. Maybe she'll call you soon. Things could get back to being . . . normal, whatever that means for your mother."

"Oh, I want that to happen, Daddy."

"It will, I'm sure. You enjoy yourself, understand? Dana and I are talking about driving over one weekend to take you to lunch, okay?"

"Yes, I'd like that."

"Okay, sweetheart. Have a good night."

"I will. Thank you, Daddy."

I stood there in the growing darkness for a while, thinking, remembering. You can be angry, you can hate, but you can't stop recalling better times. On nights like this, when Haylee and I were alone and Mother and my father were downstairs watching television or out to dinner during those happier years that my father vaguely referred to as "normal," the two of us would cuddle, either in her bed or mine, and talk about dreams and wishes. Back then, we wanted to please each other. Love wasn't only natural; it was the glue that held us together and made us special. We enjoyed being special then. We pranced about in our new shoes and dresses, knowing we were the center of attention, two sisters who mirrored each other so perfectly that we brought amazement to faces that hadn't been excited by much in their lives for years. Smiles and laughter rained down on us. We were Mother's perfect little girls. Surely only good things would come our way.

When we were little, we wanted so much to be older. Why was I thinking more often and more fondly now about my little-girl days, longing for them? In so many ways, I wished I was a little girl again. Other girls my age would surely think I was crazy, especially now, when you could do so much more on your own—drive, stay out later, and generally be responsible for yourself. Yes, I wanted to go back in time.

And yet, deep in my heart, I knew Haylee and I could never be those perfect twins again, certainly not the way Mother had envisioned us. Now it was difficult even to think of us as merely sisters.

"You didn't come out to smoke, did you?" I heard.

At first, I didn't see him standing there in the shadows, but he stepped out, and I recognized Troy Matzner. He was in a dark green pullover sweater and jeans tonight.

"What are you doing hovering in the shadows here?" I demanded. I felt spied upon.

"Not hovering in the shadows. I'm just taking a walk," he said, coming closer and into more of the light spilling from the building and the outside fixtures. "I wasn't hanging in the shadows listening to your conversation," he added without smiling. "If that's what you're afraid of."

"I'm not afraid of it."

"Old boyfriend left back home?" he asked, nodding at the smartphone in my hand.

"My father, if you must know."

He nodded and looked away, his arms folded. "You enjoying it here?" he asked, without turning back to me.

"So far," I said. "How long have you been here?"

"Three years."

I knew he was a senior. I didn't cross-examine the other girls to find out about him or ask Marcy anymore, but whenever anyone made a reference to him, my ears perked up . . . whether I wanted them to or not.

"So if you're not spying, what are you doing at Cook Hall?"

He turned back to me. "I'm getting some fresh air," he responded sharply. "Actually," he added, softening his tone, "I'm taking a much-needed break from my inane roommate."

"Inane?"

"I'd say he's about ten years behind on his emotional development. If I hear one more fart joke, I'll be on trial for murder," he said. I noticed that when he spoke firmly, he began looking at me but almost immediately looked to the side or down to finish.

Now that he was more in the light and closer to me than he had been, I could appreciate how handsome he was. His dark brown hair was layered softly with strands just over his forehead. It looked like it had been styled by someone who worked in

Hollywood, sculpted and trimmed and yet very natural-looking. When I had glimpses of him passing in the hallways, I thought his eyes were unique, but now that I could see them clearly and closely, that impression was verified. They were hazel with a slight tint of green, perhaps brought out more by the lighting. He had full, sensuous lips and prominent high cheekbones complementing his male-model perfect nose. His good looks and the way he held his firm shoulders back, the way he held his head and just slightly tucked in the right side of his mouth, did give him an aristocratic arrogance that I was confident turned off most of the boys here and intimidated most of the girls.

"I did hear that you've had a new roommate every year and one year had none for most of the time."

"Maybe I snore."

"Somehow I doubt that was it," I said.

He turned, and I thought he was just going to walk away, deciding he had given me enough of his royal time or something, but then he turned back.

"So were you complaining to your father? Is that why you came out to have the conversation? You were afraid someone might report you to the Iron Lady? She has her little informers, ass kissers, you know."

"No," I snapped back because of how condescending he sounded. "I'm not afraid of that. But now that you've brought it up, why do you continue attending school here if you're so unhappy?"

Instead of saying something nasty and walking away, he smiled. "Who says going somewhere else would make me happier? I just have one more year, half a year, actually. I'll grit my teeth and bear it."

We heard some girls laughing as they came up a sidewalk in our direction. I felt myself calm down.

"Do you take a walk every night?" I asked.

"Just about." He paused, like someone deciding if I was worth another few minutes. "So really, what's your impression of the place? You haven't been here a week, but it doesn't take long to decide."

"It's fine. I like my classes and teachers, and the place is beautiful. Maybe my bar for satisfaction is lower than yours," I added.

He didn't laugh, but he widened his smile and looked away. "Where are you from?" he asked, again not turning back.

"Ridgeway. And you?"

"Carbondale," he said, "but I consider myself an exchange student."

"What? How are you an exchange student if you're from Carbondale, Pennsylvania?"

"I speak another language," he said, turning back to me.

"What other language?"

"English," he said.

"Very funny."

"Is it?" There was that pause again. He looked like he was fighting with himself to continue talking to me, like he would just walk away. "What brought you here? Why didn't you begin your high school education here?" he asked, like a lawyer in a courtroom surprising a witness.

Of course, the question sounded alarm bells, but I also thought he wouldn't have asked it if he wasn't interested in me. Could flattery overpower caution?

"I had to finish my needlework project in arts and crafts before I could leave my previous school," I said.

He stared, first in disbelief, and then a real look of appreciation washed it away. "Do you always finish what you begin?"

"Of course, don't you?"

"Can't wait to see it, then," he said.

"I don't show it to just anybody. You have to earn the right."

"And just how do I go about doing that?"

"Figure it out," I said. "I'll give you the rest of the year. Got to get back to my homework and tease the Iron Lady's little spies. Enjoy the rest of your walk."

I didn't look back. Haylee used to be firm about that whenever we dated or flirted with a boy. "When you walk away, you don't look back. If you look back, you commit and give them an advantage. Never show how interested you are, Kaylee," she'd instructed.

I paused now, thinking about that, and then I shook my head and continued walking.

No matter what, as crazy as it seemed to me and probably would seem to anyone who knew about us, I was still relying on Haylee's advice.

9

What slows down time? What makes it pass faster? Certainly, the minutes felt like hours to me when I was locked in Anthony Cabot's basement. Even the days immediately following my release seemed to last more than twenty-four hours. There was so much recuperating to do, so much therapy to endure, and so much horror to hide, even from myself.

During the first few weeks at Littlefield, the days were long to me because I was under tension, despite how welcome I felt and how comfortable it was. On most of the early days, I became tired earlier than I expected and certainly earlier than Marcy wanted, but tension is subtly exhausting. She had boundless energy and an insatiable appetite for intimate conversations, which usually became more intimate the later it became in the evening. She was constantly fishing to learn about my experiences with boys. I knew when I was getting tired enough to slip and mention something that might lead to my real reason for being here.

"I hate going to sleep," she told me when I pleaded for a breather and time to prepare for bed this evening. "Either I lie there regretting things I didn't say or do, or I fill with fear that tomorrow won't be any more exciting than today."

"Why does every day have to be exciting? Try not to be so intense about it," I said. "Constant expectations diminish good results."

Her eyes widened. "Excuse me?" She looked at Claudia, who, despite how she would seem to be intent on reading or writing a paper when we talked, was really listening to every syllable we uttered.

Claudia didn't nod in agreement with me or say anything, but her face was full of reinforcement.

"All I'm saying is you've got to relax a little more, take your time, Marcy. Fools rush in where angels fear to tread." I smiled. I knew how old and wise beyond my years I was sounding. "We just read that in Alexander Pope's poem, remember?"

"Alexander Pope? That's what you're thinking about now?"

"What's the point of reading great things and great words if we don't learn from them?"

Marcy leaned back on her hands and looked up at the ceiling. "Oh, Lord," she said. "What have I done to make you bring back my grandmother?"

We both spun around when Claudia laughed. She finally laughed at something outrageous Marcy had said, and the first week or so not a day passed when she didn't.

"Sorry," she said, looking shocked at herself.

Neither of us spoke.

"When you mentioned your grandmother, I thought of my own," Claudia said. "She was a walking book of lessons concerning how I should live. Her claim to fame was having sex only to give birth to my mother and my uncle Matthew, who became a priest and moved to Canada before he was twenty-three. He joined the church to escape from her."

I glanced at Marcy. Neither of us wanted to interrupt her, especially Marcy. Sometimes Claudia was so quiet Marcy forgot she was in the room with us.

"She was always giving my mother advice about how to bring me up," Claudia continued. She had apparently loosened the knot that was choking her personal memories. "Her favorite expression was 'There will be time for that sort of thing later,' which was why I didn't go to parties when other girls my age were going to them or wear lipstick when they were wearing it. 'That sort of thing' took in everything that was any sort of fun. Sometimes I thought she was made of wood and I'd get splinters when she hugged me like a robot."

"And your grandfather put up with all that? I mean, didn't he want sex?" Marcy asked.

"My grandfather owned a car dealership, and although no one came right out and said it, he was in an affair with his bookkeeper at the company for years and years. When he died, the bookkeeper left to live with her sister in Cancún."

"Mexico?" I asked.

"Yes. She was Mexican and very pretty. I liked her a lot but could never admit it in front of my mother and father and especially not in front of my grandmother."

She paused and thought for a moment. "Funny," she said. "No one told me to be quiet about it, but even when I was only nine, I sensed I'd better be." She shrugged and returned to her reading.

Marcy looked at me and smiled. Then the smile flew off her face as her thoughts returned. "Never mind her grandmother. What makes you so wise?" she asked me. "Sometimes you act twice, even three times your age." She pointed her right forefinger at me. "I've been watching you. You've got secrets, Kaylee Blossom Fitzgerald."

I could feel my face flush. Claudia stopped reading again and looked up. Marcy was saying something that Claudia felt about me, too, I thought.

"Do you know when you're really naked?" I asked Marcy.

"I think I can figure it out without a mirror."

"Maybe not. You're really naked when you have no secrets."

She slapped her right palm against her forehead. "It's true!" she cried. "My grandmother has been resurrected. Okay. I'm exhausted. I might fall asleep without fantasizing about Rob Brian. Thanks to you." She stood and turned to Claudia. "If you find out any of those secrets that keep her from being naked, don't forget to share them. Good night, Grandma." She smiled and left us.

Claudia looked at the closed door. Despite the face she made and the way she seemed to be disinterested in anything Marcy and I did together or discussed, I realized she liked Marcy, too. Perhaps, just as I was on the days immediately following my rescue, she was locked away in herself, secretly hoping someone would find the key and let her out.

"I really had little to do with my grandparents," I said. "They lived too far away and visited too little, and we visited them too little, too."

"I wish I could say the same when it came to my maternal grandmother. My father's parents were okay, but they retired to Costa Rica, and my mother hates traveling."

"I want to do a lot of traveling," I said.

"Yes, so do I."

She glanced at her history text and quickly closed it. Then she sat there staring at me—or staring through me. Most people would have been put off by it, but I sensed she was struggling with the possibility of telling me something very serious, so I didn't want to interrupt the argument she was probably having with herself.

All the time we had been roommates and shared schoolwork, I avoided asking her any questions about her personal life. She dropped hints about herself here and there, but I deliberately avoided picking up on any and starting a more detailed conversation. Whenever you ask someone something most would consider personal, you inevitably begin to reveal personal things about yourself, and until now, I had been on constant vigil to make sure I didn't give even the slightest hints about what had happened to me, especially slipping and revealing that I had a twin sister. Despite all I had been through, including the therapy, it wasn't easy to be on constant guard, measuring every sentence, every word I uttered to anyone. All my life, even during my horrible incarceration in Anthony Cabot's basement, it was nearly impossible to think of myself and not think about Haylee simultaneously. The words *my sister Haylee* were practically engraved on my tongue.

I never doubted that was almost literally true. Even back when I was only eight and we were finally in a public school and not homeschooled, I mentioned her more than she mentioned me when I talked with other girls. Despite how alike Mother insisted we should be and were in her mind, in my mind, Haylee was stronger and especially wiser when it came to interacting with others our age. Common phrases for me were *My sister Haylee says* or *My sister Haylee thinks*. Whatever I was asked to do, my first thought was, *Would Haylee do it?* I'd even answer with *Haylee wouldn't do that.* Or *I'll see if Haylee wants to do it.*

Now, ironically, I believed I had to filter her out of my daily thinking in order for me to survive. Every morning when I woke up, I recited my mantra: *Don't mention or think of Haylee.* It was only natural for me to study the way others looked at me whenever I spoke, to see if they somehow had seen through me and sensed that I was keeping a very big secret from them. Never telling anyone that I had a twin sister, a perfect replica of myself, was certainly a very big secret.

Although Claudia was so introverted and shy, especially when it came to meeting new people and making friends, and although she was unsure of herself when it came to socializing, I couldn't help but suspect she was a great deal more perceptive than she made out to be or anyone thought she was. I often caught her looking at me intently at times and thinking deeply about something I had done or said. Perhaps there was something of herself that she recognized in me, or perhaps I wasn't as invulnerable when it came to protecting my secrets as I thought I was. Maybe there was something I did or was doing that stirred her suspicions. You can't live so intimately with someone without exposing something about yourself. The question was simply how perceptive was she?

Right now, I was expecting a question about myself, something she had sensed, but she surprised me.

"Despite what everyone thinks here, I'm not a virgin," she said. She didn't say it with any note of self-praise, nor did she say it like a confession to a priest. "Maybe I did it to get back at my grandmother or my mother. I can't think of any other reason."

"You didn't like the boy?"

"He was all right, I suppose, when it came to looks, but I didn't have that special affection for him I guess you should have. Everything I've read or heard told me it should be one of the most important events of your life, even for boys."

"You mean you weren't even that attracted to him? Didn't he arouse you first? I mean, didn't he . . ."

"Physically, yes. I don't know if I was that attractive to him. I think I was sort of an accomplishment. I certainly wasn't infatuated with him the way Marcy is with this Rob Brian. I didn't fantasize about him, exactly. I fantasized about the act."

"So for you it was more like experimenting?"

"No. I think it falls more properly into what school psychologists call 'acting out.' Anger and frustration brought me to it." She thought a moment. "Maybe it involved a little experimenting, too. After all, I had only what I read and saw in movies to go by. I wasn't exactly anyone's particular confidante in the schools I attended. And besides, that would be secondhand anyway. I'd say this comes under one of the things you have to do yourself."

"How long ago was this?"

"Last year. That's the real reason I'm here and not in the school I was in. The boy talked about it, and so did the girls when they found out. Somehow the story got to the dean, Mrs. Mintz, and she informed my mother that there were rumors she should check out. She had to be pretty explicit about the rumors, I'm sure. My mother is as good as any CIA interrogator."

"Really." I smiled. "No one would ever guess any of this."

I paused, thinking she was as good at hiding her secret as I was at hiding mine. We both had a need to keep a part of ourselves under lock and key. Serendipity had made us roommates.

"I was wondering why your father seemed so

intense when you first arrived. I don't think I saw him smile once."

"He was still quite angry. My grandmother had heart failure over the rumors."

"Seriously?"

"Well, she might have been having it anyway, but of course, my mother blames it on me."

"Did she die?"

"Not yet. She's in assisted living. I'm expressly forbidden to go see her, not that I was rushing out to do it."

There was a long moment of silence between us. It felt like a dark cavern into which all her words of confession had fallen. This was the moment when I knew that she, like anyone else, would now expect me to reveal my sexual experience, a sort of tit for tat. My most forward and adventurous was with my first real boyfriend, Matt Tesler. I was afraid of talking about my sexual relations with him. I was sure one thing would lead to another and I would eventually reveal how Haylee had fooled him into thinking she was me and then had sex with him the night we had a party and she and her boyfriend had gotten Matt high. Although that wasn't Haylee's intention, she had kept me a virgin.

I didn't ever want to think of how the sexual threats that occurred in Anthony Cabot's basement changed that. It was a nightmare, and nightmares are just bad dreams. I'd have to live with that theory or not live at all.

I wondered now if Claudia was looking for my approval or if she was trying to get me to respect her more and become a closer friend, probably the closest she'd ever had. I didn't want to sound superior and tell her it was okay with me. That would sound too condescending. I struggled to find a way to give her something intimate about myself. She trusted me with her big secret, and I had already admitted to Marcy and her that I did have secrets, too.

"I came close recently," I began. "I really liked this boy in my school, and I had him over one night when my mother was out on a date. We made out in my bedroom, actually got naked together."

"How did you stop from going all the way?"

"I didn't," I said. "I was going to do it, but he had taken something to get high earlier, and . . ."

"He passed out while he was having sex with you?"

"Yes," I said. "He was embarrassed and apologetic, but by then, it was too late. I had to get him out of the house before my mother came home so she wouldn't see how wasted he was. Then things just happened, and his family had to move away."

"So you never got another chance to be with him before he left?"

"No, but I won't deny that I was ready to do it then and if another chance had come up," I said.

Was she buying it all? It was partly true. Was she going to be upset now?

She surprised me by smiling. "Who'd ever think I was more experienced than you?" she said. She looked very pleased with herself. "However," she added, afraid I might be the one upset now, "I didn't have an orgasm. Can you really call it having sex if you don't have an orgasm?"

"I don't think I would," I said, happy with that definition. It helped me more than it could ever help her, but she had no idea why. "Why didn't you?"

"What do they call it? Premature ejaculation? I didn't have time. He was too quick. Of course, he never mentioned that when he bragged to other boys at school, and it got to the girls, too."

I smiled. "I bet he couldn't look you in the face afterward, not for too long, anyway."

"Oh, no, but none of the girls really cared to ask me about it. They were happier talking about me behind my back and would not have believed me no matter what I said."

"I hope your next experience is positive," I said. "It helps if you really like the guy."

"Really liking the guy was not that important to the girls I knew, so I didn't think about it. For some, even just liking him was okay. They acted like it's simply something else you do for fun. You think Marcy is like that?"

I smiled to myself. She was comfortable enough

with me to expect me to talk about Marcy behind her back.

"No," I said. "I think Marcy likes to talk, but I wouldn't buy into everything she says."

"That's what I thought."

"She's sweet, though, don't you think?"

She nodded.

I felt hypocritical saying it, but I thought I had to. "Thanks for trusting me with your experience, Claudia."

She nodded. I wasn't sure if she was disappointed or satisfied with what I had given her in return. "There is a boy who's been paying attention to me here," she added, almost like a bonus.

"Who?"

"Ben Kaplan."

"Oh, yes. He's very cute."

"He was the one who talked to me in the lunch line the first day. I guess I can thank Marcy for that. He's been talking to me between classes and walked me back to the dorm once."

"You sneak. I never even noticed you paying attention to him."

She smiled. "He noticed," she said, and then rose to go out and get ready for bed.

How surprised Marcy would be, I thought, if Claudia went on a date with Ben Kaplan and ended up double-dating with her and Rob Brian instead of me.

Later, instead of just turning off her light and turning on her side with her back to me to go to sleep as usual, Claudia first said, "Good night."

"Good night," I responded, and turned off my light. I didn't fall asleep for a while. I lay there instead and looked up at the ceiling. Dim light from the outside lamps still pierced our curtains and created what looked like a ganglion of twisted shadows on the walls. I could hear Mrs. Rosewell telling some of the girls they should be going to sleep as she patrolled the hallway. I heard the imitation quacks that followed her and smiled.

There was no question that I was happy to be here and avoid what would have been unmanageable challenges at my old school, challenges perhaps even more difficult because I was living with Mother. Most of the time when I was home, I would feel like I was walking on thin glass. Every time she looked at me, I knew in my heart she was looking for Haylee as well. Maybe the day would come when she would finally ask me questions about my abduction, but did I want that day to come? Did I want to relive it, even to win her full sympathy?

No, it was better to be here, where I could grow stronger and comfortable with myself. Talking to Claudia and listening to her intimate revelations renewed my hope. I could return to a full and normal life with relationships and maybe even enjoy the youth that was nearly stolen completely from me. Yes, I had to be careful. I had to continue to lie about my past and my family, but for now, at least, I was okay with it.

When something terrible happens, like what happened to me, you can't help but wonder who will be the stranger you eventually will confide in? Who will be able to win your trust? Can anyone ever? Would it be impossible to give that trust no matter what? *Keep up the baby steps*, I told myself. *Maybe it's slow going, but you're going in the right direction, hoping nothing will happen to send you reeling back.*

The following weekend, what I had humorously imagined happened.

Ben Kaplan asked Claudia out for pizza and a movie in town, and Rob asked Marcy. It was going to be a double date, because Rob and Ben were good friends. Claudia had told me first, but I hadn't mentioned it to Marcy. She looked stunned when she approached me in the hallway just before our last class on Friday.

"Claudia is going on a date," she said, pulling me aside. "With Rob's friend Ben. He wants us to double-date with them. What will I talk about?"

"She's really good at math."

"Very funny, Kaylee. This is my first big date with Rob. She could make it a disaster."

"No, she won't. Stop hyperventilating about it."

"Hyper what?"

"She'll be fine. Let Ben worry about her."

"I can still find you a date in time," she said. "Rob told me about four boys alone who'd like to ask you out. Why aren't you showing interest in anyone?"

"When someone is interesting, I'll be interested," I said, practically singing. "Let's go. I want to shower and change for dinner."

"Dinner here on a Friday night when you could go to town? Look, if you're gay, tell me, and I'll find you a girlfriend."

I simply smiled and started down the hallway.

She hurried to catch up. "Are you?"

"I'm not gay," I said. "I'm simply . . . very choosy. I don't want to make mistakes."

"So that's one of your secrets?"

"What?"

"Bad romances. How many?"

"Weren't you ever taught to put your disappointments in a bag of rocks and let them sink to the bottom of the sea?"

"Not that way, but yes, and you know who told me. Maybe you are the reincarnation of my grandmother," she said. "Oh, mercy. I hope Claudia doesn't wear one of her Amish dresses. I'll be such a contrast."

I laughed. "They're not Amish dresses. Maybe

we'll take her shopping on Saturday and find her something more appropriate for future dates."

"You mean something more twenty-first century?"

"Whatever."

As we started out, I saw Troy Matzner heading toward the boys' dorm. Marcy saw which way I was looking.

"Forget him," she said. "He's not worth wasting your eyesight on. He's never asked any girl out here, and I doubt he ever will. Or, more important, no girl would accept an invitation to go out with him."

"What does he do on weekends?"

"Dress up for his mirrors. I don't have the foggiest. I did hear that sometimes he goes home for the weekend. He's got that red Jaguar convertible all the boys swoon over."

"Really? I didn't notice it."

"You don't go over to the boys' dorm, or you would. Speaking of clothes, what will I wear? I want to be sexy but not obvious. And that's not something my grandmother told me. I just know it."

"I'll help you choose something."

"Thanks."

I glanced once more at Troy. He was walking with his head down. How, I wondered, could he be satisfied with his solitude? I was an expert with that challenge now. It wasn't something I thought I would ever choose for myself.

"Spending eyesight," Marcy warned.

I didn't argue. I hurried along and followed her to Cook Hall.

Claudia was very excited, and Marcy reluctantly talked up their double date. She came into our room to help Claudia choose something from her closet, swinging her eyes my way every time Claudia reached for something.

"You know what?" Marcy finally said. "Wear that dark blue skirt, even though it looks like my grandmother's, and maybe Kaylee will lend you that turquoise knit sweater. You can wear it over one of those granny blouses and with a pair of earrings and a necklace I'll lend you. You'll look great."

"Really?" Claudia looked at me. I was already taking out the sweater. Marcy knew my wardrobe better than I did by now. "Thank you," Claudia said.

Marcy raised her eyes toward the ceiling and then smiled.

Afterward, she got Claudia to come into her room to do her makeup and hair under her supervision. When Claudia stepped back into the room, I had to smile and clap.

"Who are you?" I asked.

Marcy stood behind her, looking very proud. "Imagine what I could do for you when you find someone interesting," she said.

I laughed and wished them both a good time.

After they left, I made my way over to Asper Hall to have some dinner. Later, I was planning on writing a long letter to my mother. Perhaps if I put my feelings into written words, they would have a good impact on her, I thought.

The cafeteria was about a third or so less populated. I saw the girls Marcy, Claudia, and I hung with already seated. Terri waved to me. I nodded and smiled, imagining their conversation was about Marcy's and Claudia's dates. That would lead to them talking about the boys they liked at the school and boyfriends they'd had in the past. Once again, I would feel their eyes on me, waiting for me to reveal more of myself.

Just as I stepped off the line with my tray, however, I heard someone say, "Thought you'd have a date by now."

It was Troy Matzner. I didn't see him behind me in the line and didn't anticipate seeing him. I thought he might have left for the weekend.

"More puzzling is why you don't," I replied, and he laughed.

"I'm what you call the more serious student," he said.

"Can't you have a serious date?"

He nodded, a glint of appreciation in his eyes. "I would if you would sacrifice dinner with the dissectors and join me at that table," he said, nodding at one in the far left corner.

He started for it. There was an invisible chain wrapped around my waist and anchored to the girls' table, but, more important, it was anchored to all my fears. Was I ready to get more involved with any boy? How could I do that and not eventually reveal my sister's and my horrid history? Right now, even when some boy accidentally grazed my arm in the hallways, I felt my insides cringe.

I took a deep breath. I could hear my father telling Haylee and me that if we fell off a bike, we had to get right back on, or the fear of it would sink so deeply into our hearts and souls we'd never ride again. Maybe riding a bike wasn't exactly the proper analogy to make, but it seemed to work.

I followed Troy, knowing that the moment I sat at his table, all the girls at ours would have the topic for the weekend, and it would get to Marcy with lightning speed. I watched him sit and neatly unfold his napkin to place on his lap, something I rarely saw any boy do, even here.

He looked up. "This open-faced turkey sandwich is surprisingly good, especially the gravy on the mashed potatoes." He looked at my Asian chicken salad. "That's all you're having?"

I sat across from him. "I like a light dinner sometimes," I said. "So why do you call them dissectors?"

"Aren't they? Don't they spend most of their time together tearing apart other girls?"

"Boys don't do that, sit and take apart other boys?"

"They usually do it with a single banderole."

"A what?"

"A diagonal cut across the chest or abdomen. It's a term from fencing. When I was in a junior prep school, we had fencing lessons instead of regular physical education. Sons of noblemen," he added.

"Your father is a nobleman?"

"My mother believes it and convinced him. So no one asked you out yet? Really?" He looked down and began to eat again, as if he had tossed the question into the air and didn't expect me to answer.

"Why is that so important to you?"

He shrugged. "It's a way of finding out what your defenses are," he said, as if no other purpose could even be suggested. "Fencing again."

"So, I repeat, why is that so important to you?"

He laughed and sat back. Then he looked up and nodded. "I'm always right with my first impressions of people I meet."

"You're always right? Doesn't your arm hurt?"

"My arm?" He smiled, confused and amused.

"From reaching over your shoulder to pat yourself on the back so much?"

He looked stunned for a moment, and then he laughed. "I repeat," he said. "I'm always right. I thought you were different. I just haven't figured out why yet." His eyes narrowed as if he was studying me scientifically. "It's like you're some kind of an observer here, above and beyond the din, like wiser or something. You seem to have more patience than other girls your age, too. I watch how you move. It's like . . . you're afraid you're going to step on a land mine or something."

"When are you watching me?" I asked, now not sure it had been smart to join him at his table. "And so closely?"

He looked away quickly. "Anytime I see you, I guess." He said it nonchalantly and then started eating again.

I ate some of my salad. He glanced at me as if he was waiting for me to respond. For any other girl, what he'd said would be quite flattering, but the idea that someone had been watching me so intently without my knowing it only made my nerves vibrate like piano strings.

"Well, now that you bring it up, everything you said about me also applies to you, and from what I hear, I'm far from the only one here who thinks so."

"Birds of a feather," he replied.

"I didn't say I accepted your analysis of me."

"Which only proves I'm right about you," he replied with a smug expression of self-satisfaction. "There's something wiser about you. You're more concerned with what you wear, how everything coordinates. You're just neater, better put together than the other girls here. Frankly, I think most of the boys are intimidated by you."

"What?"

"You challenge anything anyone says and take nothing at face value."

"How do you know all that so quickly? What are you, a mind reader or something?"

"Something," he said. "Maybe you'll tell me what I am." He suddenly sounded more depressed than witty. He looked down at his food and then sat back again and took on a more formal, stiffer posture. "What brought you to Littlefield? I mean, why this school?"

"You sound like a guidance counselor or . . ." I stopped myself from saying *therapist*.

"So? What would you tell a guidance counselor?"

"My father researched it and thought it was a good choice."

"You always do what your father wants you to do?" he asked, and immediately looked at his food again.

"I thought it looked good and was willing to try it. I'm not a puppet," I added, my building rage undisguised. Maybe Marcy was completely right about him, I thought.

He looked unscathed, not even blinking fast. "Where else did you go?" he asked.

"Public school. This is my first private school. Anything else?"

"Any conclusions yet?"

"Yes."

He looked up quickly.

"The open-faced turkey sandwich is very good," I replied.

His smile seemed to grow out of his eyes and trickle down to his lips. "What are you doing after dinner?"

"Nothing special. Writing some letters."

"Writing letters? You mean emails?"

"No, old-fashioned letters. There's still something about you in your handwriting."

"To old boyfriends?"

"I wouldn't write to more than one, would I?"

"Most of the girls here would. So it's a boyfriend?"

"No. I'm writing to my mother, if you have to know."

He nodded, sat forward, and ate some more. I did, too.

It did feel like some sort of fencing match, I thought, but strangely, as my surge of rage subsided, I realized that I liked it.

"How would you like to go for a ride first? I'll show you the neighborhood," he said, still looking at his food. "Nothing special, just a chance to get away for a while." He paused, like someone waiting to hear an explosion. I realized he was even holding his breath.

And I thought, *Here I go*. I felt like I was about to attempt a deep-sea dive.

"Okay," I said, and then, with caution still in control, added, "but not too far or for too long."

He went back to his dinner as if I weren't there.

"Are you shocked by my answer?" I asked.

He shook his head. "No, just hungry," he said. "And this is a good open-faced turkey sandwich."

Another girl might have felt taken for granted or something, but I felt just the opposite. It was a feeling I had practically disowned for the rest of my life when it came to being with a boy.

I was excited.

10

"What's it like living in Ridgeway?" Troy asked as we left Asper Hall and headed for the boys' dorm parking lot. One thing I had noticed about him immediately was that whenever he asked me anything even remotely personal, he avoided looking directly at me. The new amateur psychiatrist in me suggested he had been hurt deeply in some way and, like me, was nervous about getting too close to anyone. Lately, however, it seemed like I was diagnosing many people similarly, perhaps hoping to find kindred spirits. Misery truly loves company, which was probably why I got along so well with Claudia.

Maybe, I told myself, Troy really was just shy despite his great looks, his intelligence, and his obviously wealthy family. Shy people were too often mistaken for arrogant people. Perhaps all the girls in this school, including me, were unfairly judging him.

I had hardly gotten to know him, and here I was already looking for ways to rationalize being with him. However, I had seen the way the other girls had looked at us when we left the cafeteria, and I anticipated Marcy pouncing on me.

I walked with my arms folded over my breasts, my hands buried under them. Nights were cooler now, bordering on chilly. I hadn't chosen a warm enough jacket, only a light sweater over my blouse, but I didn't want to complain and have to return to my dorm. Troy had on a soft-looking black leather jacket, and as we walked, he began putting on black leather driving gloves.

He turned to me when I didn't answer his question. "You left lots of friends back there, I imagine."

"Some."

"They resent your going to a private school."

"Some," I said.

"Did you really want to come here, or were you pressured into it?"

"You mean you don't know all about me from watching me so closely?"

"I think you're like classified."

"Classified?"

"For national security. I overheard two dissectors discussing you outside room twenty-two the other day. One said, 'Getting Kaylee to talk about herself is like pulling teeth.' I wanted to turn around and ask her if she had ever pulled teeth. Sometimes it's not so hard to do. Apparently, not only don't you gossip about others, but you don't gossip about yourself. How do you expect to survive your teenage years?"

"Very funny. Naturally, I miss Ridgeway. I've lived there all my life," I said, in the tone of a captured soldier giving name, rank, and serial number. He wasn't too far off the mark. I was behaving as though most of my life were classified. Here at Littlefield, that wasn't far from the truth.

"One of the few places in the state I've never been to, so I can't comment. I like taking long rides. That's my car ahead, third from the end."

"I heard about it. A brand-new red Jaguar convertible."

"Birthday present when I turned seventeen in August. It was a bribe."

"A bribe? To get you to do what?"

"Turn eighteen," he said. He didn't smile or laugh.

He unlocked the passenger door and opened it for me. The interior was so new and pristine it was like no one had ridden in it yet. The leather still had that new-car scent. He closed the door and went around to get in. I waited until he was settled behind the steering wheel to ask about what he had just said.

"You're not serious about that bribe, right?"

"I said that's why they gave it to me, but I didn't say it was justified. My parents think I'm too . . ." He started the engine. "Dark," he said. "Seat belts," he added, clicking his own on and waiting for me to click mine. He backed out of the parking space.

"I can't imagine why your parents would think such a thing."

He gave me one of his rare direct and intense looks. "I hate being so right on my first impressions of someone all the time, but I sure was right about you."

"I know that's a compliment, but I'm not sure if you're complimenting me or yourself."

This time, he laughed. "I guess you're just going to have to wait and decide."

We drove out of the parking lot and down the drive to the school entrance. It would be my first time off the campus since I had arrived. It felt as if I had swum out too far in the sea. I hoped he couldn't see how nervous it made me. I had this recurring nightmare in which I went off campus with Marcy and the girls, and someone stopped us on the street in Carbondale and asked, "Aren't you that girl from Ridgeway who was abducted?"

If that really happened, I'd probably transfer out the following morning.

"So where are *you* from?" I asked Troy as he

turned right. Getting people to talk about themselves usually kept them from asking probing questions of me.

"Here. Carbondale," he said. "I'll drive past our house. It's kind of historic, once the home of a prominent coal mine owner who at one time employed most of the people living here. My mother wanted the house as a trophy, but she has this preoccupation with dust, as if the original owner came home covered in coal dust every day and it's embedded in the walls or something. She has air filters everywhere and has our two maids do a top-to-bottom cleaning practically every other day. Drives my father nuts. He claims their bedroom could be an OR."

"OR?"

"Operating room. It's that immaculate. Most of the year, my sister and I aren't there to make any sort of mess, not that we would. We've been brought up dabbing our mouths with a napkin after every bite."

"Where is your sister?"

"Jo, short for Jocasta, a name she hates, attends Merrywood, a private junior high school in Philadelphia. She's twelve."

"Interesting name, Jocasta."

"My mother was into Greek mythology. She was determined we'd be different. Jocasta is the mother of Oedipus."

"What about you? Troy? How is that mythological?"

"Helen of Troy, the city of Troy. Achilles and his heel . . . all of it."

"Your father went along with that?"

"My father chooses his priorities carefully," he said. "Which is another way of saying he didn't care as much as my mother did about our names. He wasn't into naming us after dead relatives or anything like that. He was into 'Get it over with. I've got a meeting.'"

I laughed, even though he didn't even smile when he said it.

Then he did smile. "I see you're someone who appreciates a dry but honest sense of humor. I like that."

"What's your father do that he has to have meetings?" I asked.

"He's the CEO of a major telecom company, Broadscan. It has international reach, so we've done some extensive traveling when my mother felt like going along. I've been to all the major European capitals, like Paris, Madrid, Rome. What's your father do?"

"Runs a software company. My parents are divorced," I added, hoping that would end the questions about family before they could really start.

"My parents should be divorced, but my mother is made of Teflon."

"Meaning?"

"The things other women would rage over just slide off her. I think she stayed married to my father just to get revenge."

"Revenge? For what? What's he done?"

"That's a list, arm's length," he said. "Besides, I don't like talking about parents, do you?"

"Sometimes," I said, "but most of my classmates would agree with you, I think. My roommate certainly would."

"Claudia, right?"

"If you come up with my social security number, I'm not going to be surprised."

This time, he really laughed. "I can see that there will be little or no pretending with you," he said, and was silent as he made one turn and then another. "About a minute more to the Dust Mansion."

"That's close by."

"I practically fell out of my bed to get here the first day."

"Are we going in?"

"Not tonight. My mother is not someone who tolerates surprise visits. Even by me alone," he added. "So how do you like this school, really?"

"I like it. I hope that's cool to say."

He shrugged. "I like most of my teachers. It's like anything else, I guess. It is what you make of it."

"I believe that, too."

He glanced at me to see if I was sincere or simply humoring him. "Do you really?"

"Yes, but beware. I'm not in the habit of agreeing with everything people say, especially people I meet for the first time. It gives the wrong impression."

"You sure you haven't taken fencing lessons?"

"I'm sure, but maybe I should."

"You'd be a natural."

Would I? I wondered. Is that what Haylee really did to me, made me forever defensive with any boy I'd ever meet? How much would any boy have to tolerate in order to develop a relationship with me? Would anyone think I was worth it, especially after he had learned the truth about me? Could I find someone with that sort of patience and sensitivity? Guys our age weren't exactly willing to overlook anything unpleasant. It was the snapshot generation. You could meet, fall in love, and break up the same day. There was little time for true compassion.

"Say," Troy said, "neither of us had any dessert. How about I take you to the place that makes the best ice cream sundaes in Pennsylvania?"

"With that description, how could I refuse?"

He sped up but didn't go over the speed limit. "Now, besides your favorite movie star, singer, color, fruit, and television show, what interests you?" he asked.

"What would you say if I said myself?"

He glanced at me. He didn't smile as much as his lips relaxed in the corners, and when an oncoming car's headlights washed us in a moment of illumination, his eyes seemed to glow with pleasure. I didn't want to be caught staring at him, but he was very good-looking, the way someone who was said to have a cinematic face was, and I felt like I was snapping pictures of him with my eyes. When he heard something that pleased him, his face lost its veil of gloom.

"I'd say you were one of most honest people I've met," he replied. "Everyone is interested mostly in himself, but I don't know many, actually any, who would admit it."

"I don't mean to sound self-centered. What I mean is I'm constantly wondering about my own thoughts and feelings, why I have them. So I guess I'm interested in psychology. When we read something in literature class, I'm usually intrigued with character motivation, like Iago in *Othello*. God, listen to me. I sound like some sort of intellectual snob."

He laughed a laugh that reeked of amusement and pleasure. "If you're an intellectual, most people, especially in our school, think you're automatically a snob. I doubt there have been too many conversations in your dorm room or at the cafeteria table about why Iago did what he did to Othello."

"No, but I'm fine with that. You do have to relax sometimes."

He was quiet so long I thought I had just turned him off me completely. Part of why I was afraid even to attempt any sort of relationship with a boy now was that he might think I was too serious all the time. Here I was telling Troy it was important to relax, but I didn't think I'd really had a single relaxing moment yet at Littlefield. I was too on guard, constantly distrustful, and worried that my story would emerge, break out like some horrible rash, and reveal every painful moment of my abduction and what my own sister had done to cause it. I'd be seen as some deeply wounded person, so scarred I might as well be an untouchable. There was no way to outlaw discrimination against my kind, victims.

"I think that's why you drew my interest," Troy said, and glanced at me.

"What?"

"Despite what you prescribe, you don't seem to relax. I don't relax, either," he quickly added, like someone who when criticizing someone had to admit he or she suffered from the same fault.

"You could tell that so fast?"

"As they say, it takes one to know one. I'm one. I'm sure you have your reasons. I know I have mine."

Now it was my turn to be silent. The obvious

question was *Why don't you relax?* I was afraid of the topic, afraid of how it would quickly lead to why I was not relaxed, so I avoided asking him his reason.

"There," he said after about thirty or forty seconds. "On the right."

I looked up at an enormous gray stone house at the top of the knoll. It was well lit and loomed over everything before it, rising higher and higher as we drew closer. It seemed to go on forever.

"What is it? The governor's home?"

"Almost. That's my house," he said, "or, more accurately, my mother's house."

He slowed down so I could get a better look at it. The driveway looked like it was made of glass with black marble beneath it. There were lampposts on both sides all the way up. The driveway wound around and disappeared behind the rise. Even in the darkness, I could see that the grounds were elaborate, with trees and bushes so perfect they looked like set pieces on a movie lot.

"It's so large."

"It's Georgian-style architecture," he said, coming to a stop. "Thirty-two thousand square feet on ten acres. It's one of the biggest houses in this area. We have seven bedrooms, a ballroom, a den with a pool table, a media center, my dad's home office, and two kitchens."

"Two? Why two?"

"One is solely for catered affairs like celebrations, business anniversaries. Sometimes my mother does a charity event. People pay five thousand dollars to attend and then bid on things donated, like a ten-day cruise or something. As I mentioned, we have two full-time maids, and we also have three regular grounds people. You can't see it from here, but there's a small building behind the house. The maids sleep there. It has a small kitchen, too. There's a pool off to the left, with a cabana and whirlpool, and to the right are a tennis court and my dad's putting green."

"It belonged to the owner of a coal mine?"

"Yes, but my mother redid the whole place, changed flooring, replaced all the furniture, and added some new windows and lots of new curtains. My father modernized much of the technology. Those driveway lamps are all solar. About five years ago, they added a wing to the house, too. It's mostly my father's home office and library, his sanctuary where he can smoke a cigar and have meetings at home."

He started to drive again. I looked back once.

"Very impressive," I said.

"It's like living in a museum, believe me," he said.

"No wonder your mother thinks your father is a nobleman. We have a big house, but that's really a mansion."

"Home sweet home," he muttered. "If you want, I'll give you a tour. You just have to take off your shoes, take a shower, change into a visitor's uniform, put a plastic cap over your hair, and put on a pair of surgical gloves before you touch anything."

"You're kidding, of course."

"Yes, but if you ever did meet my mother in that house, you'd understand that I'm not exaggerating as much as you think. Okay. We're coming to it, the best sundaes in North America, not just Pennsylvania."

He slowed down as we approached a strip mall with half its stores already closed. A few looked empty, out of business. The mall didn't look like anything special, so I was surprised when he pulled into the parking lot. There were very few cars.

"Here?" I asked. "The world's best sundaes?"

"It's a big secret. No one else at our school will know of it." He nodded to the right at a small shop whose sign advertised toys, magazines, and stationery goods. "The owners have an old-fashioned soda fountain. You'll see," he said, getting out. He moved around quickly to open my door and reach for my hand. "It's the proper way for a lady like you to get out of a royal carriage," he said.

For a moment after I stepped out, he continued to hold my hand and then suddenly realized he was doing it and let go.

As we drew closer, I saw the place was simply called George's.

"How did you find it?"

"I have this fountain pen my father's younger brother gave me for my sixteenth birthday, one of those two-hundred-dollar fountain pens. George Malen, the owner, special-orders the replacement ink tubes for me. He was quite impressed with the pen when I stopped by to see if he could get the tubes, and then I saw the soda fountain and ordered a sundae. His wife, Annie, works the fountain. I think they're both in their late sixties. This is a true mom-and-pop operation."

He opened the door for me, and we entered what looked like a very cluttered place. The shelves were stacked with a variety of notepads, envelopes, files, and other office supplies. There were desk lamps and office wastebaskets lined up under the shelves. Another set of shelves had board games and toys for very young children. Maybe the place had started out as a toy store. Smack in the middle of it all was a soda fountain with six well-worn black vinyl stools. The counter had displays of candy, and just to the right of that was a magazine rack and a rack of paperback books. It looked like a store that was frozen in time. I saw little of technology, computer supplies, and the like.

At first, I thought there was no one there, but then I saw a man with graying light brown hair shift in a rocking chair toward the rear and look up from the magazine he was reading. His face brightened instantly, and he stood. He was wearing black slacks and a white shirt with the sleeves rolled up to his elbows. He had muscular forearms and looked like someone who worked with his hands, rather than the owner of a small store.

"Hello, Troy," he said. "How you doin'?"

"Fine. Mr. Malen, this is my friend Kaylee. She attends Littlefield, too."

"How you doing, young lady?"

"Well, thank you."

"You out of ink tubes already?" he asked Troy.

"No. We came for sundaes," Troy said.

"Annie," Mr. Malen called, and a woman with stark white hair brushed and tied neatly in a bun at the back of her head emerged from a room at the rear of the store. She wore an apron over a midcalf-length floral-patterned dress. "Annie's the sundae expert," Mr. Malen told me.

"Troy," she said, smiling. Her nearly wrinkle-free face looked misplaced below her gray hair. "How is school?"

"Oh, it will survive," Troy said, and indicated which stool I should take.

Mrs. Malen went around the counter.

"This is Kaylee Fitzgerald," Troy said. "She attends Littlefield, too."

It was apparent that he wasn't simply an occasional customer. If he had been, he wouldn't find it necessary to introduce me, I thought.

Mr. Malen sat on the stool beside him. There were no other customers in the store. "Where are you from, young lady?" he asked me.

"Ridgeway."

"That's not far," Mrs. Malen said. "Your parents could visit often."

"Yes," I said, smiling.

"What's your flavor?" Troy asked me. "They have chocolate and vanilla and strawberry. You can have all three. It's a three-scoop sundae."

"Three? Okay," I said. "That sounds great."

"Two, please, Mrs. Malen," Troy said. "With the works."

"Coming up, two deluxe sundaes."

"Sounds overwhelming," I said.

"That's what he should do, overwhelm you," Mr. Malen said, moving closer. "Forty years ago, I overwhelmed Mrs. Malen, but not with sundaes." He winked at Troy.

"Oh, you did, did you? Seems to me it was the other way around," Mrs. Malen told him as she began cutting a banana. "He brags and blusters, but he was as easy to mold as this ice cream."

"Only because I wanted to be," he said. "The secret to a good marriage is letting your wife believe she is in charge."

Mrs. Malen tilted her head a bit and pressed her

lips together. "Wanted to be? You know how long it took him to ask me on a date? Two weeks. I nearly gave up on him after ten days and finally decided he needed a little more encouragement."

"I was doing my research," he pleaded.

"You were just shy."

Troy and I smiled at each other, and then he quickly looked away.

"What class are you in, Kaylee?" Mrs. Malen asked.

"Troy's," I said. "Senior."

"You just enter Littlefield? Or did it take him a few years to ask you out?" she followed, looking at Mr. Malen.

I glanced at Troy.

His cheeks reddened. "She just enrolled," he answered for me, and for himself. "But I don't just bring anyone for these sundaes. I do my research, too."

"He's picking up bad habits from you," Mrs. Malen told her husband. "And how is your sister doing?" she asked Troy.

"I guess okay. There have been no flares shot into the sky."

Mrs. Malen smiled. She smothered the ice cream balls in strawberries, adorned them with slices of banana and covered that with chocolate syrup before spreading the whipped cream over it all. She was neat about it, too.

"It's a work of art," I said when she placed mine before me. "I doubt I can finish it."

"Eat as much as you want," Troy said.

After she made Troy's sundae, she nodded at Mr. Malen, and they retreated to the rear of the store, clearly to leave us to ourselves. A customer for stationery came in, and then a woman and a young girl entered to shop for a board game, so they were occupied for a while.

"I guess you've been here quite often," I said.

"Yeah, sometimes I just hang out and talk to Mr. Malen. They had a son who was killed in Iraq, and they have a daughter who lives in New York City. She never got married. Works for a fashion designer. How's your sundae?"

"Unbelievable. I might just finish it," I said.

He nodded. "Thought so."

"But how come you hang out here? Are you related or something?"

"Something." He ate some more, staring ahead, looking lost in his own thoughts for a few moments. Then he turned back to me. "Let's just say we fill gaps for each other. I have no relationship with my grandparents and barely one with my father," he confessed. He leaned toward me so no one else would hear. "This is like an oasis in the desert I travel."

I didn't speak, because I had an intense urge to tell him I was traveling in a desert, too. Our conversation was in danger of becoming too heavy, and I knew where that might lead. I was happy when the Malens returned after their customers left and the conversation centered on what their youth was like. I think Troy and I circled their revelations and memories like two moths around a candle.

Mr. Malen was honest about how awkward he was when first courting Mrs. Malen, and whenever he tried to brag, she gently brought him back to "the way it really was." We were all laughing before we left, and on our way out, they both gave me a hug. Mrs. Malen hugged Troy. He didn't retreat from her affection. From the very little he had told me about his own family and home, I didn't imagine him getting many hugs like this one there.

"Come again," she said. "We're thinking of getting some pistachio ice cream. Mainly because George likes it."

"I love pistachio," I said.

"I knew you found the right girl to bring here," Mr. Malen told Troy. "About time."

Troy reddened a bit again, nodded, reached for my hand tentatively but held it tightly when I clasped his, and opened the door for me.

"That was fun," I said. "Of course, I'll have to walk ten miles to work off the calories."

"Thanks for going there with me. I know it's not exactly what you anticipated."

"No, it was fun. I really mean it."

He searched my face for sincerity and opened the car door for me. "It's not exactly the kind of thing your girlfriends would agree to do on a Friday night," he said as he got in.

"Stop apologizing. I enjoyed it, and I don't look to them for social guidance," I said.

"Who do you look to?"

Once, I thought, what seemed long ago now, I had looked to my twin sister, who was far more sophisticated than I was. Despite everything, that answer was still lined up ahead of anything else in my mind and ready to be spoken. But even suggesting it would crack open the dam that held all the horror I had endured. It would come rushing in and surely kill this budding relationship between Troy and me. Maybe for that reason more than any other, I slammed the door shut on even a hint of it. The sad thing I knew in my heart was that no relationship could flourish on a ground of lies and deceptions. Nothing could come of this. I was teasing myself and probably him.

"Myself," I replied.

I knew he wanted to talk more about himself and learn more about me, but I was too frightened to ask any more questions. Twice he tried to initiate a conversation about families, relatives, our early lives, but I didn't say much of anything. We were both silent all the way back. I was sure he was wondering if he had made a mistake asking me to take a drive.

After we parked and got out of the car, I realized it had gotten even colder. I hugged myself again, not looking forward to the long walk to my dorm.

"You're really cold," he said. "I guess you weren't planning on doing much tonight."

"No, but I'm all right."

"No, you're not." He took off his jacket. "Wear this. I'll walk you back."

"But won't *you* be cold?" I asked as I put on his jacket.

"I'll risk it, but let's move."

He reached for my hand. Then he started to jog. I laughed and kept up with him.

"Feels like it might snow tonight," I said.

"When it does, keep track of when the first flake hits your face. That's a lucky moment."

"Who told you that?"

"No one. I made it up."

There wasn't anyone outside my dorm when we arrived. We both shot into the entry and caught our breath in the pool of warmth. His face was red, and mine felt on fire, but in a good way.

"Got rid of some of those calories," he said.

I took off his jacket and handed it to him. "Thanks. Thanks for the sundae, too. I haven't gone for ice cream anywhere for a long time, probably not since I was a little girl. Now it's usually a cone of custard or frozen yogurt at the mall. And I don't do that often, either."

"Yeah, we grow up too fast these days. That's what George says. I mean Mr. Malen."

We stood there just looking at each other for a long moment.

"Well, I guess I'll put on some warm PJs and snuggle up with some English lit. My roommate went out on a double date tonight."

"Really? Then there's hope for me," he said. "How about I take you to get some pizza and go to a movie tomorrow?" he blurted, like someone who wanted to say it before he could think about it and hesitate.

"Okay." I said it without hesitation, but he could have no idea how difficult that was for me to say, despite the good time we'd just had.

"I'll come by for you at six."

"Okay."

He offered me his hand first, but when I took it, he pulled me closer. The memory of Anthony Cabot's face hovering over me while I was trapped in that basement bed flashed before my eyes. I couldn't stop it. I jerked back. Troy looked devastated for a moment and then quickly regained his composure. It was as if I had slapped him across the face. My heart raced with regret and residual fear.

"See you at six," he mumbled, then turned and hurried out.

I stood looking after him and feeling terrible. In a frightened moment, I had wiped away the warmth and happiness we had just enjoyed.

I can't do this, I thought. *Not yet. I'll call him tomorrow and cancel.* Feeling defeated, I lowered my head and walked to my room. Some of the girls were laughing in Terri's room, but I didn't stop by. I put on my desk lamp and then fell back onto my bed and looked up at the ceiling. I knew I was imagining it, but that didn't make it less devastating.

Haylee was looking down at me and smiling.

"You can't do this without me," she was saying. She had said it so many times. "We're the Mirror Sisters. We need each other."

I turned over and buried my face in the pillow to stop the tears from reaching my lips.

11

Marcy's loud laughter woke me hours later. It seemed to flow out of a dream. When I opened my eyes, I realized that I was still in my clothes. I was even still wearing my shoes. Both Marcy and Claudia came bursting in like runners charging the finish line. I glanced at the clock on my night table and saw they had just made curfew. Their faces looked flushed, but not from the cold night air.

"What's with you? Did you fall asleep in your clothes?" Marcy asked, catching her breath and grimacing.

Claudia stood beside her, gazing down at me. They both had dumb smiles on their faces, and I could smell the scented cloud of alcohol floating around them. In fact, Marcy wobbled a bit.

I sat up straighter and rubbed my cheeks. "Yes, I guess I did," I said.

"Have you been crying?" Marcy asked.

"Why do you ask that?"

"Your face looks blotchy, like tear-streaked or something."

"No," I said. "You two smell like a brewery or something," I added, to quickly put them on the defensive.

"I told you chewing gum doesn't make much difference," Claudia told Marcy.

"I guess we're lucky Platypus didn't inspect us," Marcy said. "The boys brought a little . . . what did you call it, Claudia? Libation? Claudia has a vocabulary I'd match against anyone here at Littlefield, even Mr. Edgewater."

"They were drinking and driving?" I asked.

"Oh, Grandma, relax. Ben drove, and he didn't drink."

"I wouldn't have gone in the car if he had," Claudia said.

"But Rob was already a little high when they picked us up," Marcy said, and laughed. "Both Claudia and I partook in the libation. We're all going to Fun City tomorrow. Want to be a fifth wheel?"

"Fun City? What's that?"

"An amusement park about an hour south of Carbondale. Ben suggested it. He comes from a little town nearby. So," she said, flopping onto Claudia's bed, "how was your institutional dinner? Anything exciting occur?"

The way she asked suggested she somehow knew already.

I looked from her to Claudia and back to her. Just like that, they had become closer friends? What happened to Claudia's hang-ups? What happened to Marcy thinking Claudia was a lead weight, especially on a date?

"It was fine," I said.

"Terri was practically waiting at the door for us," Claudia revealed, hoping to keep me from denying anything and looking foolish, I'm sure.

"What did she say?"

"That you went off with Troy Matzner," Claudia said.

"How could you go with Troy Matzner?" Marcy demanded, sobering quickly. "He's such a snob he won't even hang out with his own shadow."

They both stared at me, anticipating my regrets.

"He's just shy," I said. "Misunderstood."

Marcy's eyes widened as her mouth opened.

Claudia nodded as if she always believed it.

"Just shy? With a head like he has? I think his family is the richest at Littlefield, and he lets everyone know it. How could he be shy and drive a red Jaguar convertible?" Marcy asked.

"He could be," Claudia said. She looked like she was sobering up quickly. "Kaylee's right. People are too quick to make judgments about others."

It was clear to me from the way she glared at Marcy that Claudia was talking about how Marcy originally had perceived her. She went to her closet and began to undress.

"Whatever," Marcy said. "Arrogant or shy, it couldn't have been much fun being with him. The only thing you'd have to fight off is boredom. Speaking of which, where did he take you? To some foreign film or his favorite stop sign?"

"He took me for a nice ride past his family's mansion and then for an ice cream sundae," I said. "We had a very nice time."

Claudia smiled, but Marcy shook her head in pity.

"Nice time? An ice cream sundae? That was the best he could do? How exciting, and what an expensive date. Is that why you were crying? I don't blame you. I'm sure it was a big disappointment. If you would have listened to me and shown some interest in one of the other boys, you could have had a great time with us. First, we—"

"I said I wasn't crying, but I am tired. You can give your blow-by-blow description of your good time tomorrow. I'm going to the bathroom to wash up and brush my teeth." I rose and walked out.

"But I'm too juiced to go to sleep!" Marcy

called after me. "It's like leaving me on the brink of an orgasm!"

I kept walking. I felt like I had regressed to kindergarten. I had no tolerance for these games, these childish contests to see who was having a better social life. Drinking, getting high, all of it paled in comparison to the roller coaster I had lived through. And if one thing was certain, it was that I wasn't eager to toy with dangers or irresponsibility.

Claudia joined me in the bathroom before I was finished. "I sent her back to her room," she told me. "I'm sorry we were so boisterous."

"That's okay. I needed to be woken up to get to sleep."

She laughed and then looked very serious. "I had a good time with Ben. He's the shy one, not me. When we parked, he didn't put his arm around me until I said I was cold."

"You parked? You mean you guys went somewhere to make out in the car?"

"Sorta. I don't know what Marcy and Rob did. I avoided looking, but we mostly talked and kissed, the kisses almost like putting periods to sentences," she said. "As my father is fond of saying, 'nothing to break out the champagne over.' But I think Ben likes me, and I do like him."

"I'm happy for you, Claudia. And I was telling the truth back there. I did have a good time, too."

She smiled and started on her preparations for bed.

"See you in the room," I said.

"Don't worry. I'm tired, too. And I don't want to go over the night like some sociology report," she added. "Marcy will probably keep Terri up all night."

"Probably," I said.

Down the hall toward our room, Mrs. Rosewell was telling two other girls to lower their music. She stood in the doorway, giving them a lecture about the benefits of sleep.

"You girls are always so concerned about how you look. Well, don't you know that not getting enough sleep will age you faster?" she warned them. She glanced at me as I went by.

"Good night, Mrs. Rosewell," I said.

"Yes, good night. There's a good girl," she added for the benefit of the other two.

I hurried away. If there was one thing I didn't want to become here, it was a touchstone for the best behavior. I remembered how cruel Haylee could be ripping apart one of the girls in our school who refused to smoke a joint, drink, or talk openly about sex. Eventually, most of the girls would treat Haylee's target like a leper.

Curling up snugly in my bed, I thought about Troy. Something had made him extra cautious about whom he would share any personal or intimate things. In a way, he did remind me of myself. One thing was for sure. He had his secrets, and I had mine. Would that eventually drive us apart or bring us together?

"'Night," Claudia said when she returned.

"'Night. I'm glad you had a good time."

"Thank you. Actually, regardless of what Marcy wants to do, I don't want to talk about it. I'm afraid to admit I had a good time to too many people, afraid that if I do, it will disappear."

"One thing about good times, Claudia. They might end, but that doesn't take away what you had. That stays with you. No matter what, don't think you have to be as intense as Marcy. If it works, it works. If it doesn't, there's always tomorrow."

She didn't answer. I thought she had fallen asleep, and then she suddenly said, "Marcy is right about you."

"Oh? Right in what way?"

"Something has made you older and wiser."

Now it was my turn not to answer. She sensed it and didn't say another word. Sleep came not a moment too soon for her, probably because of the drinking, but it didn't come quickly for me. Instead, I tossed and turned, worrying that I was too obvious after all. Restraint was all right, but filtering every word I said through a strainer to be sure nothing would lead to a dreaded question was making me stand out. For most girls my age, calling someone older and wiser was a euphemism for boring. At a place like this especially, you want to feel like you left your mother and father home and all the promises to behave and be responsible along with them. Feeling independent and a little reckless was exciting.

Perhaps I should start making things up, I thought. Maybe I could create another persona for myself. And then it hit me like a snowball in the face. I already had another persona built in: Haylee. I wouldn't simply sit there like a mannequin when the other girls talked about their romances and experiences. I'd tell them what Haylee had done as if I had done it and take possession of it all. No one would call me Grandma then.

I snuggled with the plan, but then another voice spoke to me. *If you do that, it will simply be another victory for your sister. She always wanted to turn you into her.*

It was all so confusing, but why would it be anything else? I thought, and finally did fall asleep.

I was the first of the three of us up and dressed the following morning. When I rose, Claudia was still in a deep sleep. At the cafeteria, Terri told me Marcy was facedown, her arm dangling off the bed like the arm of a dead person.

"And she snored all night," she said. "I never heard her do that!"

My first impulse was to tell her and the other girls who were laughing about it that actions have consequences. I was about to say that when I stopped myself and started to talk about the worst hangovers I'd ever had, even though I personally had little reference for that. Instead, I recalled Haylee the first time we had gone to a party, where she not only drank vodka but also smoked pot. She was alert enough to know Mother would pounce and ground us for months if she realized it, so she pretended to be sick from something she had eaten, and I went along with it for her, claiming my stomach was upset, too. It was good enough for Mother, who lectured us on being more cautious when eating other people's food. Few, she said, would take the care to be sure whatever they made for us was nutritious and fresh.

Haylee slept until noon the next day. I tried to wake her, but she only groaned and chased me away. Consequently, I had to stay in bed as well, mimicking her symptoms. But it all worked, and she got away with it. She was right to predict that Mother would have forbidden us to go to another party, maybe even for the remainder of our school year, so I actually was lying for myself as well as Haylee. Afterward, as usual, Haylee made light of it all and complimented me on how well I went along with her plan. Fortunately, my father wasn't there. He would have seen right through us. Mother was still living in that bubble where she could be quite convinced we would never do anything so dreadful.

Troy wasn't in the cafeteria when I had gone in for breakfast, so I joined the girls. We had not made plans to meet, but I was hoping he would want me to join him. I was still worrying about my reaction to his attempt to kiss me good night. Would he have second thoughts and cancel our date tonight? Estelle Marcus noticed how I was watching the entrance. She nudged Jessie Paul, and they both smiled at me.

"What?" I asked, seeing their arrogant grins.

"You can stop waiting for him. Troy Matzner rarely comes to breakfast on weekends. He goes somewhere else," Estelle said.

"Some diner, I heard," Jessie said. "Didn't he tell you that?"

"Our daily routines didn't come up," I said.

"What *did*?" Toby Dickens asked. Pounced, I should say.

I looked at the girls and the way they were all looking back at me, anticipating. Simply saying he had taken me to get an ice cream sundae obviously hadn't impressed Marcy and wouldn't impress these girls, either. I didn't want to belittle our time together, but I suspected there wasn't anyone here who would have enjoyed it.

"Now, Toby, I was brought up never to kiss and tell," I said, with a wry smile that I saw lit each of them up with surprise, unleashing their own imaginations and fantasies. Haylee liked to tease our friends this way, too. She enjoyed toying with them, dangling the promise of some juicy sexual adventure.

"So you admit you kissed?" Estelle said.

"No one has gone on a date with him," Toby said. "He's good-looking, and he drives a cool car, but we all thought he might be . . ."

"Gay?"

"Whatever," Jessie said.

"You can put that theory in the garbage," I said. Then I gave them a Haylee Blossom Fitzgerald licentious smile. Surprise turned to fascination, just the way it would for Haylee.

"Did he take you to his house? I've seen the mansion from the road," Kim Bailey said.

"How come he brought you back so early?" Terri asked suspiciously.

"She was gone long enough to have a good time," Jessie told her.

"My mother told me the quiet ones are the ones to watch closely," Kim offered.

"How does he compare?" Toby asked, now growing more excited. "On a scale of one to ten?"

I sat back, thinking. Some of them were actually holding their breath. My instincts told me none of them was as experienced as they made themselves out to be. One thing was for sure, I thought: none of them would have lasted two days in Anthony Cabot's basement, not that it was an accomplishment I wanted to advertise. I widened my smile. I could see Haylee across from me, her eyes full of impish delight and sisterly pride, too.

"You don't judge someone on the first date," I declared, in the tone of someone who had vast romantic experience. "And besides, my mother told me," I said, leaning toward Kim, "that those who talk about it are usually full of what makes the grass grow greener."

Their faces collectively looked like a balloon losing air quickly.

Then Terri, who was a little smarter than the others, brightened with a thought. "Are you going to see him again?" she asked.

"Tonight," I said casually. "Which reminds me. I should get on that paper for Mr. Edgewater. See you in the library, maybe." I rose with my tray.

"On Saturday?" Jessie asked.

I shrugged. "As you all surely know, you never know how you'll be the day after," I said.

They all looked at a loss for words. I smiled, turned, and walked away. I knew it was crazy, but I imagined Haylee walking beside me and saying, "Very nice, sister dear."

Yes, she'd be proud of me, but flowing beneath that would be the rich green stream of jealousy. *You can learn from me*, she'd think, *but don't imagine you can get better at it than I am.*

Back at the dorm, Marcy and Claudia were sip-

ping what would be their only breakfast, some coffee they got from the machine in our lounge. They
had just risen and were both in bathrobes. Marcy
had come into our room and was sitting on my bed,
looking pale, her eyes still bloodshot.

"'Morning," Claudia said.

"Is it really morning?" Marcy asked.

"I can't imagine either of you having the energy
to go to a fun park or anything," I said.

"A shower is all we need," Marcy insisted, and
then closed her eyes and rubbed her temples. "So
what are you going to do today?"

"Work on the paper for Edgewater, and then
Troy is taking me to have pizza and see a movie." I
looked at Claudia. "You okay?"

"I'm fine," she said. "Oh. Your cell phone went
off, but I didn't answer it."

"Thanks."

I looked at it and saw there was a call from my
father. I put the phone in my bag.

"Why don't you get hold of Troy?" Marcy
asked, some life coming back into her face. "You
two could come with us."

"I'm fine, thanks. I don't want to leave this
paper for tomorrow. We've got a lot of math and
science, too."

"She's right," Claudia said. "We're not going to
have another night like last night."

"Don't you become Grandma, too," Marcy

warned. "I'm going to take a twenty-minute shower. We should dress warmly, Claudia. Terri the weather girl predicted the possibility of snow showers."

"I'll be right behind you," Claudia said.

I gathered the things I needed for the library.

"I hope you have a better time tonight," Marcy told me.

I realized Terri would be talking to her soon.

"Listen," I said. "I wasn't in the mood to be talkative last night, but I had a very good time. The sundae was just dessert."

"What's that mean?"

"Figure it out," I said, and walked out.

"You'd better tell me what that means!" Marcy shouted after me.

I kept walking. When I was outside, I went to one of the benches along the pathway to the library and called my father back. He answered quickly, which told me he hadn't called just to see how I was doing.

"I'm sorry I missed your call, Daddy. I left the phone in the room when I went to breakfast. Is anything wrong? Mother all right?"

"She's fine. Nothing has changed there yet, but it might soon."

"What's that mean?"

"Dr. Alexander has approved Haylee going home for Thanksgiving," he said.

"You mean she'll be there when I'm there?" I asked. I was actually trembling.

"It's part of what Dr. Alexander describes as taking baby steps toward a full recuperation, but Dr. Alexander wants to see you first before she puts her stamp of approval on the idea," my father said. "I told you I didn't want you ever to speak with her after she treated you like the bad one last time, but I'll tell her whatever you want anyway, Kaylee. Just think about it and let me know."

"When would I see her?"

"I'd bring you to her home office the weekend before Thanksgiving. Don't answer now. Think about it."

"Okay, Daddy."

"How are you doing there?"

"I like my teachers." I hesitated, and then I told him, "I became friendly with a boy who took me to have an ice cream sundae last night after dinner."

"Oh?"

"He's taking me for pizza and a movie tonight."

"That's very good, Kaylee. What's he like?"

"He's very good-looking and an honor student, but . . ."

"But what?"

"He's sort of a loner. The other girls think he's arrogant because his family is wealthy."

"What do you think?"

"I think . . . I think I have to get to know him a little more," I said. That seemed safe enough.

"That sounds very intelligent and mature of you, Kaylee."

"Maybe I'm just frightened, Daddy."

"You'll figure it out. Call me whenever you want, although I'm not the best authority when it comes to relationships."

"Yes, you are," I insisted. "'Bye, Daddy. I've got to go to the library."

"I'll call you after the weekend, okay?"

"Okay," I said.

I sat there for a few moments to let what my father had told me settle inside me. Haylee home for Thanksgiving? What would that be like? Would she gloat about how successful she was at deceiving Dr. Alexander and the staff at the institution? Would she continue to be unremorseful, even daring to ask me to give her the details of my abduction as if it were only an adventure?

On the other hand, what if she *had* changed? What if she begged for my forgiveness, using the spirit of the holiday and family to pressure me? Could she really believe I would simply shrug it all off? *Oh, well, you didn't really mean to get rid of me?*

And what about Mother? Whose side would she favor? Would she also try to persuade me to be forgiving and return the family to what it had been? Would I want to return to that? Would my resistance drive Mother back to the psych ward, and would everyone blame me?

Or would we all sit around the table and pretend nothing had happened? Not a word would be said, not a reference would be made to my abduction and Haylee's role in arranging it. Haylee would come into my room just as she used to and ask me questions about my new school, my new friends, and any boys I liked. She'd pepper me with questions just to keep me from saying or asking a single thing about what she had done. At the end, she might even kiss me good night and expect me to kiss her as well, just as we always had.

My father had clearly indicated that I might still stop all this. Dr. Alexander wanted something from me to convince her it would be all right to permit Haylee to go home for Thanksgiving. If I refused even to meet with her, that might be enough, but then how would I look, especially to Mother if she found out? Once again, Haylee would win. I could even imagine her gloating. She had proven I was worse. She was willing to try to redeem herself, but I wouldn't let it happen.

I rose and walked slowly toward the library. It did look like there would be at least snow showers today. The sky was almost completely overcast, and there was more of a chill in the air. Maybe the chill was really coming from inside me. I quickened my pace.

Right now, all I wanted to do was lose myself in my schoolwork and forget that I even had a family, not to mention Thanksgiving. After all, the things I'd be thankful for would give most girls my age endless nightmares.

12

Marcy and Claudia were gone by the time I returned from the library. I had dived so deeply into the assignments that I forgot to pause for lunch. Early in the afternoon, my stomach growled angrily at being ignored, and I came up for air. I stopped at the cafeteria to pick up a sandwich and a drink and returned to the dorm to eat in Claudia's and my room.

Most everyone else was out doing fun things. The snow showers came and went, and the winds blew holes in the overcast sky, revealing patches of blue that widened until it was partly cloudy, with enough sunshine to raise the temperature. I was sure Marcy, Claudia, and the boys were having a better time now, and for a moment, I was envious, but I had finished most of my weekend assignments. They'd all be cramming and moaning tomorrow, and Marcy would be begging me for my homework answers.

I looked over my clothes to choose something to wear on my date.

For most of Haylee's and my lives, even when we had entered high school, Mother would make it her business to choose what we should wear. When we were older, we had to have her approve of anything we had chosen for ourselves. Gradually, with Haylee in the lead, we had begun to dress differently, first in small ways, with different shoes and socks, different earrings and bracelets, and then with different blouses, skirts, and jeans. Haylee even packed things in her school bag to change into once we were out of Mother's sight.

For other girls our age, sisters or otherwise, making these kinds of choices for themselves was as natural as breathing. Who would understand how firmly Mother had imposed her will on us, stressing not independence but similarity always? She believed that as long as we were closely alike, down to the smallest of details, we were loving twins.

Our friends always questioned us about it or made fun of us, especially when we were younger, but gradually, they became used to it and were surprised and eager to point out the differences that especially Haylee created. We were like the puzzle in a magazine with two pictures of the same scene

side by side and you had to find the tiny differences. Haylee always enjoyed all this attention, but
I was embarrassed.

Once recently when Mother permitted herself
to speak about the horrible events surrounding my
abduction, she actually said it was her fault for not
being strict enough in forbidding us to seek out our
individuality.

"I saw you were drifting apart," she moaned,
her eyes filling with tears of regret, "and I didn't do
enough to stop it."

Long before all these terrible things had happened and Mother had been taken to a psychiatric
hospital for evaluation and therapy, Haylee would
tell me our mother was insane.

"She's not normal," she would whisper. "And
she will make us both crazy, too, if we don't do
something about it."

Of course, I knew how different she was from
other mothers, but for me, it was always easier to
humor Mother, to do what she asked, and whenever possible, as Haylee was doing, to change when
we were out from under her surveillance. Haylee
was far more defiant and even at the age of ten or
so would deliberately do something to challenge
Mother's wishes. She tried to sneak past her wearing a ring I wasn't wearing or different-colored
socks from mine. Most of the time, Mother spot-
ted what she had done and made her go back and

change. Haylee said Mother should work for the TSA, but pretty soon, she stopped joking about it. She complained more to my father than I ever did and in a real sense drove him into the arguments with Mother that laid the foundation for their eventual divorce. It was devastating to me, but Haylee seemed pleased.

"Now our father will be more on our side," she told me. She knew more about the ways children of divorce played one parent against the other. She was reluctant to be a good student, relying on me to help her or to do her homework, but she devoured any information about children of divorce after it looked inevitable that it would happen between our parents.

Now that I thought more about our past and all the little things I recalled Haylee doing, I realized I was the blind one in our home and deliberately so. I had more opportunity to see Haylee's real goals and intentions, but I wouldn't face up to it. Instead, I tried to placate her, do what she wanted us to do, and even tried to think about things the way she did. I wanted to keep the peace on a battlefield where there was no truce or any possibility of one.

In a real sense, then, I thought maybe Mother was right. I had caused it, too. I was in that conspiracy of silence she had described. Haylee might have been a victim of herself, but with my compromises and refusal to aggressively stop her, I had permitted her to do the terrible thing she had done. Turning a blind eye was exactly the wrong turn to make.

Thinking about all this now, I realized that there was no way I could refuse to see her psychiatrist. My father wanted me to decide after careful consideration, but there was nothing to consider. If I felt even the slightest responsibility for all this, I had to do what I could to bring about an end to the suffering we both endured, and even though she was the one incarcerated, I was imprisoned in a real way, too. I decided I would call my father in the morning and tell him to arrange the session with Dr. Alexander.

Meanwhile, for my date with Troy, I chose a pink long-sleeved blouse, a cream-colored sweater, and a pair of jeans. I had a black leather jacket with a white imitation-fur collar and a pair of black boots. I spent more time on my makeup than usual and decided to wear a black, fuzzy earflap beanie over my natural hair, which was still quite short but starting to look more fashionable. When I was ready, I went out to the entryway to wait for Troy. I wouldn't deny that I was nervous, even trembling a little. This was my first formal date since my abduction. Had all the therapy been enough? I was in such deep thought about it that I didn't even hear Jessie and Kim come up behind me. They were dressed for dates, too.

"Nice coat," Kim said.

"Thank you."

"What movie are you going to see?" Jessie asked.

I thought for a moment and then laughed. "I don't know. I never even asked him."

"Maybe he intends to take you to a movie in his house. I heard he's got an entertainment center with a big screen," Kim said. "Bobby Johnson's parents have been over to the Matzners' for a charity event."

"Maybe."

"You don't care where you go?" Jessie asked.

I saw Troy pulling into the parking lot and turned to them. "It's not the destination. It's the journey," I said. They both looked like someone had hit them in the face with a snowball. "Have a good time tonight," I added, and hurried out, smiling to myself. The goody-goody image was definitely washed off me now, I thought, but I couldn't help wondering if I might regret it.

Troy was getting out of his car when I appeared. "Hey," he said, "I was on my way to get you properly."

"Why put you through the inspection?" I said.

He looked back at the entrance and saw Kim and Jessie looking out at us, and then he opened the car door for me. "You look very nice," he said. "No," he added, putting his hand on my shoulder to keep me from getting in. "You look like you belong on the cover of a magazine."

"Better," I said, tilting my head as if I were really thinking about it. "But keep working on it."

He laughed harder than he had since I'd met him and closed the door after I got in. I saw that four more girls had joined Kim and Jessie, and both of them were talking at once, offering their opinions about me, I was sure. What sort of impression was I making? I was confident Marcy would tell me later.

"Am I out of my league dating you?" Troy asked after getting in. "I'd appreciate the warning."

"Too early to tell," I said.

He widened his smile and drove out of the lot.

I glanced back at the dorm. There were two more girls now, all watching us leave.

Troy looked into his rearview mirror. "We have an audience, all right. Have I brought you a little too much attention?"

"You do have a reputation," I said.

"Which is?"

"No reputation."

"Excuse me?"

"Apparently, from what I've been told by the dissectors, you haven't asked anyone here on a date for as long as you've been attending Littlefield."

"Is that good or bad?"

"Too early to tell."

He started to laugh and then stopped. "What exactly do they say about me?"

"Do you really care?"

He nodded and remained thoughtful for a while. I said nothing and wondered if maybe I was being too cute.

"I don't want to care," he said, "but I'd be a liar if I said I didn't, and for some reason, I'm not comfortable telling you lies."

I was afraid to feel the same way toward him. I needed my lies. "Some say you're arrogant. Some say you're gay. A few have these wild images of you seeing a much older woman."

"Really? Sort of like Benjamin Braddock in *The Graduate* with Mrs. Robinson?"

"Any of it true?"

"Too soon to confess," he replied.

Now it was my turn to laugh. "Where are we going?"

"There's this really special pizza place in a small town about twenty miles outside of Carbondale. Another mom-and-pop establishment. These people are authentic. Not only do they have a real pizza oven, but they had the stone shipped from Naples many years ago."

"How do you find these places?"

"I like to go off the beaten path. You know, like Frost . . . take the road less traveled. That's what I like about you."

"What?" I asked quickly, afraid he had somehow found out more about me than I wanted anyone here to know.

"You seem like someone who isn't afraid of turning down a side road."

I smiled. He knew nothing, really. If anything, I was someone who would be terrified of turning down side roads now. I wanted everywhere I went to be brightly lit and busy. Just the mention of the concept of a side road revived my memory of the road on which Anthony Cabot's family farmhouse was located. I could shout for help all day and night and be heard only by rabbits and squirrels. I couldn't even see the cars passing by, if there were any.

"You okay with this?" he asked when I was quiet for so long. "I mean, I could take you to downtown Carbondale or to a mall or . . ."

"No, I'm fine with it. I've never eaten pizza cooked on a stone from Napoli."

He smiled. "That's right. Napoli." He sped up and we did start taking dark side roads where houses were few and far between.

Drive down the dark voices clamoring to be heard like ghosts in a graveyard, I told myself. When would they be gone forever? How long would it take for the memories to fade until they seemed to be of things that happened to someone else?

"I've got about a dozen CDs in the glove compartment," Troy said. "Maybe there's something you like."

I took them out and began to sort through them. There were folk songs, jazz albums, and two recordings of Mozart. Under those was one by someone named Tom Waits.

"Tom Waits? Really someone with that name? What's he waiting for?"

"Try it," he said.

I inserted the CD. He glanced at me with that wry smile of his and watched for my reaction. The first song was "All the World Is Green."

"Well?" he asked halfway through it.

It had brought tears to my eyes, but I kept him from seeing it. All I could think of was the happy times in my life, when my father was still with us and Mother's passion for keeping us loving sisters was something to behold and not fear. Back then, all the world was green for us.

"It's beautiful. You're full of surprises," I said.

"I bet you are, too," he replied.

Don't find out, I prayed. *Please don't find out.* We drove on.

I shook my head in wonder when he parked in front of a restaurant that had no sign in its window and nothing written on the window either. There was just the word *MARIO'S* over the dimly lit front door. I could see the place was small and almost all the tables were occupied.

"Someone had to tell you about this place," I said. "Anyone would drive right by it."

"Naw, no one told me. I just have a nose for authenticity."

"It looks packed."

He shut off the engine. "Probably is, but I called Mario Carnesi, the owner, and he and his wife, Sophia, always manage to save the small table near the kitchen for me. Hope you're hungry. They have an antipasto to die for."

He got out and opened the door for me, reaching for my hand again. This time, when I stepped out, he held my hand firmly and for a beat kept us close. I thought he was going to try to kiss me again, but instead he just smiled and turned us toward the entrance. I breathed in relief, and I hated having to do it. How could you have any sort of relationship with someone if you freeze or retreat from a touch, a hug, and especially a kiss?

Even before he opened the door, the aroma of pasta and sauces and pizza swirled about me, churning up my appetite.

From the look of the small crowd, I saw that we were definitely the youngest customers. The chatter and laughter suggested most everyone here knew everyone else. A few people looked our way but not for long. The owner's wife stepped up to greet Troy, who introduced me. She led us to our table but was too busy to stay there and talk.

"They have a menu," he said, "but I can order it all. What would you like to drink, a soda, iced tea?"

"Iced tea, thanks."

I glanced around. The restaurant was cozy, with prints of the Amalfi Coast and small villages on walls that were painted deep red. The floor was hardwood. There was no bar. Toward the front, there was a couple who had brought along their small white dog, which sat obediently, hoping for crumbs to fall. Playing low, but not too low to hear over the chatter, was an Italian tenor singing "Nessun Dorma," a song Mother loved.

"It really feels like we should be in Italy," I said.

Troy smiled. "Authentic, as is the food."

"Did you ever bring anyone else here?" I asked.

"Ah, so now we begin to dig in our chest of secrets," he replied. "You want to know if I brought Mrs. Robinson?"

The waitress stepped up. She looked to be in her forties, her dark brown hair cut short, her light complexion flushed from rushing about in a room warmed by its customers and the stoves. She and Mrs. Carnesi were apparently the only waitresses. In one breath, Troy ordered everything for us, the antipasto and the pizza. She nodded, flashed a smile, and returned to something else she had to do.

"She's new," Troy said, looking after her. "Actually, I haven't been here for nearly a month. No," he continued. "I've never brought anyone else here, younger or older than myself, but now that you have started it, want to play truth or dare?"

"How does that work?"

"You never played it?"

"Maybe I'm from another country," I said. There were many times when I felt that way.

"You ask someone a question he or she has to answer or else take a dare. You want to go first? Actually, you did when you asked me to tell you if I had ever brought anyone else here, so technically I can go now. What do you say? Game for the game?"

Saying no would only lead to more probing questions. "Okay," I said, feeling like I was stepping out on thin ice.

The waitress brought our drinks.

"We'll keep it as innocent as possible. How old were you when you had your first kiss?"

"That's easy. A few hours."

"Very funny. I meant a kiss from a boy."

"You didn't specify that, so I go now. How old were you when you kissed the first girl unrelated to you or she kissed you?"

"Actually, that's perfect for this game. I was ten. My cousin Nora was sixteen, and she and her parents were visiting us, and Nora brought her friend Jenny. They started to play truth or dare in the room I was in, and when Jenny chose not to answer a question that had made her blush, my cousin Nora's dare was for her to kiss me like a lover. I was so frightened that I ran out of the room. Naturally, they were hysterical."

"Where was your sister?"

"Already sent to a private school."

"That young?"

"Yes," he said. His expression changed subtly, his eyes narrowing, his lips tightening. Then he quickly smiled again. "You just asked two questions. I go twice."

"That can't be fair."

"All's fair in love and war."

"Which is this?" I asked.

Before he could respond, the waitress brought our antipasto. It was enormous.

"No one goes hungry here," Troy said, seeing the way I was gaping at it. "They'll box whatever we don't eat, and you can bring it back to your dorm."

He served me some, and we began to eat.

"Okay, truth or dare. How old were you when you had your first boyfriend?"

"Fifteen," I said.

"How long did it last?"

"A few months."

"How old were you when you had your first?" I countered. "Truth or dare."

He looked at his watch, thought a moment, and then said, "Seventeen years, four months, three days, seventeen hours, and twenty minutes."

I stopped eating. "I'm your first girlfriend?"

"That's another question. You have to wait for mine. Did your boyfriend cheat on you and that's why you broke up?"

How do I answer this? I wondered. Yes, he had cheated on me, but he didn't know he was cheating on me. He was drugged and made love to Haylee, who had engineered the whole thing. Still, it was cheating, and I had been angry at him.

"Yes."

Our pizza came.

"This is as good as it gets in the United States," Troy declared, putting a piece on my plate for me.

"So you've introduced me to the best ice cream sundaes and now the best pizza. All within two days," I said.

"The best is yet to come," he replied.

Was it? I wondered. Not if we kept playing this truth or dare game, I thought.

When the pizza had cooled enough to eat, I had to confess that it was the best I ever had. He smiled with that self-confident, self-satisfied look that convinced everyone he was the king of snobs at Little-field. I should have changed the subject, but I didn't, partly because of my reaction to him. In some ways, his arrogance reminded me of Haylee, and I wanted to chase that ghost out as soon as I could.

"Truth or dare. Why didn't you have a girlfriend before me?"

He held his smile. "I'll take dare," he said.

I sat back. "Okay, then. I dare you to eat the rest of this pizza and antipasto yourself."

"Oh, come on. I can do it, but I'd be cheating you out of a great meal. Think of something else."

"It would be easier for you to just answer the question," I said, smiling.

He didn't. In fact, he looked suddenly very troubled, a darkness coming into his face. He lowered his gaze. All sorts of theories flashed through my mind. A girlfriend had hurt him very deeply. He was unsure of his own sexual interests, and I was a sort of test.

"Maybe we should wait to play any more. You're right. I'm hungry, and I don't want to give up the food," I offered as an escape.

That unfroze his face.

"Okay. I confess about the game. I was just being lazy trying to get to know you. Something tells me you're a challenge."

"Something tells me the same about you."

He smiled again. The tenseness of the moment passed, and he talked about safer subjects like the places he had been, the time he had been in Italy. I kept him busy answering questions about places.

"Doesn't sound like your family does much traveling," he said.

"My father's always been a workaholic, and my mother's not fond of traveling."

I wasn't surprised that he didn't ask me if I had any brothers or sisters. Claudia and Marcy, and therefore all the girls in my class and my dorm, believed I didn't. If he really was seeking information about me, which was what he revealed, he would just assume that was true, too.

"Are you really up for going to a movie?" he asked. He looked at his watch. "I'm afraid we might violate the curfew."

"That's okay. This was wonderful. Thank you."

"I'd like to show you something else, a sort of visual dessert."

"As long as I don't have to eat another thing," I said, looking down at my plate. "There's nothing to take back to the dorm."

"Didn't think there would be. No, nothing more to eat."

He signaled for the check. Mario, although still very busy, took a moment to say good night to us. I saw him give Troy the high sign about me and smiled to myself as we left.

Troy was unusually quiet when we were in his car and driving off.

"Thank you," I said again. "That was truly special."

"I'm glad you liked it. I was afraid it wasn't posh enough."

"Posh?"

"It's a British expression. It kind of means high-class. Comes from the cabins used by the upper class on voyages from England to India. The most expensive cabins were port side on the way out and starboard on the way home, Port Out Starboard Home, POSH."

"I bet you'd be great at trivia."

"*Au contraire, mon frére.* I hate anything trivial. So now you see that I am a bit of a snob."

"You're not a snob, Troy. You're just too serious," I said.

He looked at me quickly. I was sure I had made him angry, maybe angry enough to end our night. "Do you expect me to take that seriously?" he countered. I started to smile with relief when he added, "Especially from you? Remember? Birds of a feather?"

"You said that. I didn't."

"But you believe it."

"Oh, you're so self-confident."

"Does it bother you?"

I thought for a moment. "It's . . ."

"Too soon to tell. I know," he said, smiling and shaking his head.

He made another turn, and now we were on a road that really looked like the road not taken.

After a short while, the macadam disappeared, and it became a hard dirt road.

"Where are we going?" I couldn't hide the trembling in my voice.

"Just a minute more," he said, and we started up an incline.

It was so dark now, without even the weak illumination of a streetlight behind us. I struggled to hold back the hysteria building inside me.

"I don't like this," I said. "It's too out of the way. Please turn around."

He didn't answer. He jerked the car a little to the right, shifted gears, and climbed another small incline until we burst out on a flat piece of land and stopped. I had my head down and was embracing myself so tightly that I could barely breathe.

"Voilà," he said. "Hey, take a look."

Slowly, I raised my head and looked out. The lights of houses and buildings twinkled below. The night had cleared enough to reveal most of the twenty-five hundred stars visible to the human eye without any sort of telescope or binoculars, especially since there was no moonlight to drown out any. Two commercial jets were also twinkling, as though they were moving stars.

"I've never brought anyone up here," Troy said.

I hoped he didn't see me taking deep breaths. "How did you find it?"

"I overheard a meeting my father had with some real estate investors. Their plan is to develop the side road we took and create a housing development. My father makes so much money that he's always looking for different ways to invest. They raved about it, so I decided to make it one of my explorations. What do you think?"

"It's beautiful, and it didn't take us that long to get here."

"Now you're thinking like an investor."

We really couldn't see each other that well in the darkness, but I saw that he was sitting back, turned toward me, and looking at me not with a smile but with an intensity that, although I didn't want it to, frightened me. Best to keep talking, I thought.

"Why do you take so many rides by yourself, Troy? Don't you have any buddies?"

"Back to truth or dare?"

"No, just normal conversation."

"I guess I'm just too particular," he said.

"So why me?"

He sat up and leaned toward me. "I don't want to sound like a broken CD, but there's something about you that's different. You're not . . . obvious."

"I'm a challenge, is that it?"

"Exactly. You're a mystery."

"So are you."

He moved closer. "The very fact that you saw that rather than go with one of the labels your girlfriends assign to me convinced me you're head and shoulders above them. I just don't know why yet."

He reached out to touch my shoulder. He wasn't close enough to sense it, but I cringed.

"Maybe I'd rather not be solved," I said. "And something tells me neither would you."

He stopped moving toward me. "Maybe. Maybe we both would rather that wasn't true. It's all a matter of trust," he said, and leaned forward again. "It begins with something as simple as this." He brought his lips to mine, his hands gripping my shoulders firmly to hold me in place.

It wasn't a violent kiss. It wasn't even unexpected.

Any other girl would have simply kissed him back if she liked him or been indifferent enough to send a message that read simply *NO*.

But the feel of a man's lips on mine triggered an explosion of horrid visions.

Once again, Anthony Cabot's naked body was all over mine. Once again, I inhaled the smell of beer, an odor that seemed to spin my insides. Once again, I struggled to leave my own body and envision myself someplace safe. Once again, I felt the chain on my ankle. Once again, I screamed a scream unvoiced, a scream that echoed inside me. I was a child crying for her mother and father, a twin cursing her sister, a helpless girl about to lose everything that made her human.

My cry in Troy's car was a cry full of pain. He recoiled like someone who had felt an intense electric shock.

And all the stars looming before us seemed to fall out of the sky like diamond tears.

13

I could feel how shaken up Troy was. The air was that electric between us. The sound of my cry probably was echoing as loudly in his ears as it was in mine. Tears burned my cheeks. Gradually, the visions of terror receded and fell back into that dark place that was behind a door I had hoped was permanently sealed after all the therapy and the passage of time. The depth and intensity of my emotional wounds surprised me. I was ashamed and frightened again. All I wanted to do was curl up in a fetal position in some dark corner and disappear like Mother in the safety of her shadows.

"I'm . . . sorry," Troy said, although he had no idea why he had to say it. A little indignation stirred his pride when I didn't respond. "I thought we liked each other enough for a kiss."

"I do like you. I'm sorry. It's not your fault," I said, and wiped away the lingering tears. "I'm not . . . right yet. I shouldn't have gone out with you and given you reason to believe I was. Just take me back, Troy. I'm sorry. Really. Please."

He started the car and carefully turned it around. I curled up against the door.

"We're both not right yet," he said after a long silence. "But we've got to try, or at least want to try."

We were back on a road lit with streetlights and the windows of homes, but I didn't feel any less tense. The resurgence of the danger and pain I had suffered swirled about me like rings of fog. His words only resurrected the hours and hours of therapy and that repetitive warning my therapist practically chanted: *You've got to try.*

Of course, I had to try; I wanted to try to behave normally, to welcome affection, to trust someone enough to risk being disappointed, but all of it was as hard as walking up a hill made of ice. Right now, I wasn't in the mood to measure Troy's or anyone else's pain against mine.

"I'm not going to play 'you tell me your bad story and I tell you mine,'" I said. "I'm sorry."

I was really beginning to hate that word *sorry*, but I didn't know what would work better. I knew I sounded mean and angry, but right now, I couldn't find any other appropriate response. I was angrier at myself than I was at him for what had just happened, but I didn't think he'd understand the reasons, and I had no idea how to begin explaining.

The silence that followed felt like a widening dark crevice. I could see he was thinking long and hard. When he didn't speak, I concluded that this was it; my short-lived budding romance was over. I began to prepare myself for the myriad questions that would be tossed over me like a fisherman's net back at the dorm. Eventually, it would bring in the big catch, my recent history, and I would have to leave Littlefield, leave with the question of what was a good alternative now. Maybe I should join the army or the Peace Corps and go live in some third world country where no one would care who I was and what had happened to me.

"You don't have to tell me yours," Troy finally said through clenched teeth.

I didn't blame him for saying it. He had every right to be upset with me. "I understand how you feel," I said. I tried not to sound magnanimous. That would only make someone with his pride and ego angrier, but it was difficult not to sound like that.

"No, you don't understand," he said. He finally turned to look at me. "I lied to you that first night we met."

"What? What are you talking about? What lie?"

"When you had come outside to speak with your father, and I told you I was just taking my usual walk. I wasn't. I was actually hoping to see you, and when you came out, I lay back in the shadows listening, because I thought you might be talking to a boyfriend. I heard most of what you said."

The chill that had come over me turned into a surge of heat before it finished climbing up my neck. I was speechless, trying to remember what details I had revealed during that phone call. At a minimum, he certainly knew I had a sister.

"I heard enough to be more interested, and then I did some research on the Internet and found your story."

I didn't know whether to be angry or frightened. Perhaps I would be both. His confession churned up reasons for both.

"Don't worry about it," he quickly said. "I wouldn't tell anyone anything, especially at school."

I stared ahead silently. What was his next comment going to be? Would it be blackmail?

"Frankly, despite what happened back there just now, after reading about you, I anticipated you would be worse. For one thing, I didn't expect that you would go out with me so soon. Because of that, I assumed you had made more progress recuperating from it all."

"You should have told me," I said. "You shouldn't have lied."

"I was afraid to once I had done it. I didn't want to drive you away so quickly. I was selfish, and I was wrong, but I wasn't lying when I said we were birds of a feather. I wasn't abducted or raped or anything like that," he added quickly. "But you were right when you recognized that I had my secrets, too."

"I don't think I want to hear about them," I said petulantly.

"No. I don't blame you. Ironically, I've destroyed exactly what I was trying to win, your trust."

"Yes, you have," I said.

He sat back to drive and was quiet all the way back to Littlefield. When he pulled into my dorm parking lot, I told him not to bother getting out to open my door. He reached for my arm when I opened it.

"I meant everything else I said to you, Kaylee. You're not different simply because of what happened to you. You'd be head and shoulders above the other girls no matter what. I really like you, and I was wrong to lie to you. I know you feel . . ."

"Betrayed and embarrassed," I said. "Thanks for adding all that to the load I carry, but oh, thank you for the pizza, too."

"Kaylee," he said, but I shut the door before he could continue, and I didn't look back.

And thank you again, too, Haylee, I thought as I walked away. *Your actions will ripple into eternity.*

The dorm was quiet when I entered a good two hours earlier than our curfew on a Saturday night. I practically tiptoed to my and Claudia's room. Thankfully, she and Marcy were still out. I managed to get myself ready for bed without seeing any of the other girls. When I got into bed, I sat up with my arms folded across my breasts and thought about everything.

No, I thought, now defiant and raging with fury. I wouldn't do what my father wanted and agree to see Haylee's psychiatrist. I didn't for one moment believe what my father believed or hoped, that she was finally regretful and repentant. She was still conniving to get her way; she always would be. *I won't stop hating her; I won't.*

Thinking and even saying it aloud made me feel better, but only for a little while. Hating Haylee now was easy. Forgiving her was difficult, and loving her again seemed nearly impossible, despite what I had told Dr. Alexander. However, the realization did nothing to cheer me up or relieve any of the pain. I only fell into a deeper funk. I was tired of hating myself because of what I had become and even more tired of trying not to.

I glanced across the room at Claudia's dresser. I knew what she had put under her neatly folded socks in that drawer after she and Marcy had returned from their double date. I had pretended not to notice when they giggled and Marcy passed it to her, urging her to hide it.

I rose slowly, moving like someone in a trance, and opened her dresser drawer. I felt under the socks and found the packet of Ecstasy. After I took one pill out, I put it all back as neatly as I could and closed the drawer. I held the pill in my palm for a few moments and debated with myself. I could be expelled for this, and what a mess that would create. It would reinforce the belief that I was contaminated, that I had been so violated there was no possibility of any recuperation.

But I couldn't stand this disappointment and depression that made me feel like I had swallowed dark shadows. Taking one of these pills was definitely something Haylee would do, but I wasn't going to get to sleep anyway, and if there was one thing I didn't want the moment the girls returned, it was the two of them seeing me upset. I just wasn't ready to answer questions. I'd never be ready.

I downed the pill with the glass of water on my night table and returned to bed, sitting up just the way I had been. I remained there, defiantly expecting relief, waiting and watching the clock. I felt no different after ten minutes and only a lot more restless after twenty. This was disappointing. It wasn't changing my mood the way others my age had claimed it did and the way I had seen it change

Haylee's. Probably a weak dose, I thought, and rose quickly to return to Claudia's drawer. I took out the packet and plucked another pill, not putting it back as neatly as I had previously. I didn't even close the drawer all the way, but I didn't notice at first and then thought, what difference did it make? No one was going to complain about my stealing her pills.

I swallowed the second one and went back to my position on the bed. I was starting to feel warmer. I was even sweating a little. I couldn't continue simply to sit. I got up and began walking about the room. I paused when I thought there was someone at the window. It was Troy, I decided. He'd come back to spy on me or something. I rushed to the window and threw it open. The cold air was like a splash of ice water over my face and breasts. Nevertheless, I leaned out and looked left and right.

"Are you out here in the shadows again?" I screamed. "Listening for another phone call?"

I saw a car pull up to the dorm. The headlights washed the side of the building. There wasn't anyone standing there. I heard laughter coming from the car and quickly stepped back and shut the window. Shortly after, there was noise in the hallway and more laughter, Marcy's laughter. I went to the door to listen and heard Mrs. Rosewell telling them to be quieter.

"There are girls who didn't go out and are

asleep," she said. "We must respect others, or they won't respect us."

Nothing could sound sillier to me at the moment. *Respect others, or they won't respect us?* I opened the door and leaned out.

"Will you stop being so quiet!" I screamed. Marcy and Claudia froze. Mrs. Rosewell gaped at me. "Sorry," I said. "I was trying to stay awake."

Marcy's face practically exploded with laughter, and the two of them hurried down the hall, promising Mrs. Rosewell that they would be quiet, we'd all be quiet. She remained there watching suspiciously. Marcy pushed me back, and Claudia followed, closing the door behind her.

I started to laugh again and slapped my palms over my face to muffle the sound. The expressions on their faces made me laugh harder.

"What's going on?" Marcy asked. She brightened with the realization. "What are you on?"

"On? On the earth," I said.

Everything I said and everything they did made me laugh. The two of them practically smothered me and forced me back onto my bed.

"Check it out," Marcy told Claudia.

Claudia opened the door slightly and peered out.

"She's gone," she said.

"Great. Kaylee, what did you take? What's going on? And don't start laughing."

"He was in the shadows," I said.

"What? Who?"

"Never mind. Never mind anything. Never."

Claudia's suspicious eyes turned from me, and her gaze went to her dresser.

"She was in our Ecstasy," she announced, and rushed over to the drawer. She held up the packet for Marcy to see.

"You? You took Ecstasy now? Why now? You're supposed to take it when you go out, stupid, not when you're going to sleep. Oh, pickles," she moaned. "When did you take it? How many?"

Claudia had emptied the packet onto her bed and counted the pills. "She took two," she declared.

"When, Kaylee?" Marcy shook me, but that only made me laugh.

"You're tickling me," I said.

"Where's her robe?"

Claudia found it, and they got me into it. Claudia opened the door slightly again and looked back at us. Marcy had her arm firmly around my waist. Claudia nodded, and they both rushed me out and to the bathroom. Once there, Marcy brought me to a toilet and then stuck her fingers in my mouth. I gagged and wiggled to get free, but they were both holding on to me now, and Marcy pinched my face with her fingers and the thumb of her left hand so that I kept my mouth open while she pressed the fingers of her right hand over my tongue. I gagged and struggled, but she kept it up until I started to vomit. Vomiting made me vomit more and more, until I practically collapsed on the floor.

"You idiot," Marcy said. "Why did you do this? You could have gotten us all in big trouble, Kaylee. We don't do that in the dorm. The Iron Lady would throw us out for sure."

I wasn't listening now. I was feeling sick and even chilly. Claudia checked the hallways again, and they practically carried me back to our room and got me into bed. My skin felt like it was on fire. I tried to get up, but they held me down.

"You're going to feel like hell tomorrow," Marcy predicted when I started to laugh again. She made me drink some water, and then they loosened their grips on me, but sat beside me on my bed.

"What should we do?" Claudia asked.

"What do you think? We'll take turns keeping her in bed. Two of those aren't that much."

"According to Rob, that is. He's not exactly a good source of information, Marcy."

"Let's hope he is this time," she said.

I listened to them both, moving my head from one to the other in short, exaggerated motions that eventually made them both laugh.

"How are we going to keep her quiet?" Claudia asked.

"I could lie over her," Marcy facetiously suggested, "and smother her."

Suddenly, I felt achy and tired and closed my eyes. My body relaxed.

"The vomiting helped," I heard Claudia say.

"I'll go get out of my clothes and come back," Marcy told her. "Stay right beside her."

I had short stabs of energy for a while and laughed, but then my head began to ache, and I closed my eyes.

"Watch the window," I told Claudia. "He's out there."

"Who?"

"Secrets," I said. Then I laughed, closed my eyes, and drifted off, but not for long. Marcy was back when I woke again and sat next to me for a while before lying down beside me. Claudia went to the bathroom, returned, and got into her pajamas, too. The three of us eventually all fell asleep on my bed, Claudia sprawled across the bottom and Marcy curled up at my side. Sometime during the night, Claudia went to sleep in her own bed. I woke many times, but I did not get up. I couldn't remember why Marcy was there, but I chose to fall back asleep rather than think about it.

When I woke again, Marcy was dressed in jeans and a school sweater, sipping a cup of coffee and looking down at me. Claudia was still asleep.

"Here," Marcy said. "Drink a little of this."

I groaned, sat up, and sipped. I thought it tasted putrid.

"This is going to feel like the worst day of your life," she predicted.

I shook my head. "I've already had that day," I said.

But she was right. My mood swings went from episodes of energy to dark depression. I had no appetite and ate a minuscule amount for breakfast. Once Claudia was up, she and Marcy took turns watching me take short naps and then keeping me from going out to run across campus every time I threatened to do so. I felt that energetic at times. Finally, late in the afternoon, I began to settle down.

Marcy brought me some oatmeal and toast and more coffee.

"You should take a good long shower now," she advised. "You'll sleep tonight."

"Thanks." I ate most of what she brought.

Claudia returned and shook her head when Marcy looked to her with some expectation. She had gone out to see if anyone knew anything about what I had done the night before, I thought. They were careful not to attract any attention. Most of the girls were busy doing their homework anyway.

"What happened, Kaylee? Why did you come back here and take the Ecstasy? Did something bad happen between you and Troy Matzner?" Marcy asked.

"I don't remember. Troy who?"

She looked at Claudia. "Okay. I warned you about him, Kaylee. I'm not surprised."

"Fools rush in where angels fear to tread," I muttered.

"What?"

"She's quoting Alexander Pope again," Claudia said.

"Great." Marcy's eyes widened with a new thought. "Did you do all the science and history homework before you went out with him?"

"Yes," I said.

She smiled. "At least something went right yesterday."

I wanted to laugh but closed my eyes instead. After another nap, I rose, took the long shower Marcy had prescribed, and tried to get myself organized for tomorrow's classes. The prospect of going to dinner still seemed enormous. Claudia told me she would bring back a sandwich and a drink for me.

"We'll tell everyone something you ate for dinner last night upset your stomach. Don't worry about it."

"Thanks."

I tried to do a little reading, but my eyes were just too heavy, and the words seemed to liquefy on the page, running into one another. How long would this last? I wondered. And why would anyone want to go through it?

I did eat the entire sandwich Claudia brought me. She sat watching me and then described her and Marcy's date at Fun City and afterward and how much more she liked Ben. I couldn't help thinking that I had concluded too quickly that she was going to be the loser here and I would have to work at keeping her stable and happy. The irony of the reversed roles wasn't lost on me, and from the way Marcy talked about their good time, it wasn't lost on her, either.

They repeatedly tried to get me to tell them about my date, but I just said it was okay and refused to give them any details. Claudia said Troy wasn't in the cafeteria for dinner.

"At least tell us if you're going to see him again," Marcy pleaded.

"I'll see him," I said.

"What's that mean?"

"Let's just leave it at that," I said.

They looked at each other, shrugged, and went on to talk about their date and their boyfriends.

Maybe this was my fate, I thought, to listen to everyone else's good time and think about happiness the way we thought about a distant star. It looked beautiful, but you could do nothing more than gaze at it and dream.

I did see Troy the next day, of course. He didn't come to breakfast, but I saw him in the halls and classrooms. He avoided looking at me, and I avoided looking at him. Both Claudia and Marcy picked up the negative vibes.

"If you don't tell us what happened, I'll ask him," Marcy threatened at lunch.

I was confident he would say nothing. He sat alone at his usual table and read, avoiding conversations with anyone. As usual, no one seemed to care. Strangely, I felt sorry for him. I had a right to be angry, but that didn't mean I was totally disinterested in him and what were the secrets that gave him the idea he and I were birds of a feather.

For a few seconds at the end of the day, I caught him looking at me before he started for his dorm. I looked away quickly, and when I looked back, he was walking with his head down. I had the urge to run after him and almost did when Marcy came up behind me.

"You can't keep secrets forever," she warned. "Especially here."

My worst fear was that she was right.

"Thanks for helping me Saturday night," I replied.

"Yeah, well, it wasn't entirely unselfish. I told Rob, and he admitted the pills were stronger doses than he first described. Both he and Ben were terrified you'd do or say something."

"I doubt that, but you're crazy to play roulette with drugs, Marcy. Eventually, you'll make a mistake like I did, and a lot of people will suffer.

I know that sounds goody-goody, but that's what reality is, goody-goody."

She was silent. I glanced back and saw that Troy had gotten into his car and was driving away, probably for one of his frequent solo rides accompanied only by loneliness.

Just before dinner, my father called. I was alone, so I took it in our room.

"Hey, sweetheart, how are you doing?"

"Okay," I said, hoping he wasn't as perceptive as Mother, who could pick up an irregular note in our voices and pounce with questions.

"Good. So have you given thought to what I told you? We could come up Saturday. It's the weekend before your Thanksgiving break, and we'll take you to see Dr. Alexander. She'll see you on Saturday at her home office, like I said."

"We?"

"I'll bring Dana along to meet you. She's very excited about it. Before you ask, she knows why I'm coming to get you, so there'll be no awkward moments."

"Of course there will. For me," I said. He was quiet. "But I'll get over it," I said.

"Dana's very bright, sensitive, and compassionate."

"I don't know, Daddy. I don't know if I'm ready for this . . . Haylee coming home."

"Well, as I told you, that's part of what Dr.

Alexander wants to know. If anything, she doesn't want to create new problems or set back the progress both you and Haylee are making."

"Progress," I said. He was quiet again. I was tempted to tell him how terrible my first date since my abduction had gone and how much it had reinforced my rage, but he would probably tell me that was more reason to want to see Dr. Alexander. Who else could better understand?

Maybe that was true. Maybe I'd only be hurting myself by refusing to go along with the plan.

"I know this is hard," he said, "but . . ."

"I'll go," I said. "What time will you be here?"

"Is ten too early? You, Dana, and I can have a little lunch before you visit with Dr. Alexander."

"No, that's fine."

"Great. We'll see you then," he said. I didn't miss the way he said *we*. There was a new *we* in his life. Would there ever be one in mine?

I dove into my homework. Both Marcy and Claudia had remained at school to watch Rob and Ben at basketball practice. They grew bored with it after a while and returned to the dorm. I knew they were not going to give up on finding out what exactly happened between Troy Matzner and me. I began to dream up some possible scenarios that would satisfy them, but everything was so false, and I had this unexplainable need not to denigrate him. I was still quite angry about his spying on me and deceiving me, but he wasn't wrong about calling us birds of a feather. Something had brought him great emotional pain, so great that, like what happened to me, it had changed his life, changed the way he saw the world, and changed whatever dreams he had for his future.

Maybe it was time not to think first of myself, I thought. Maybe that was the only door out of the darkness.

I wondered if he would come to the cafeteria for dinner or stay on his drive and stop at one of his out-of-the-way discoveries. On our way over, I couldn't help but be very nervous. I did my best to hide it, expecting that it would only revive Claudia and Marcy's curiosity about my Saturday night.

When we first entered, Troy wasn't there. Despite all I had gone through, I was disappointed. We got our food and sat with the other girls, who were still giving reviews of their weekends. I kept anticipating questions about mine, but Marcy or Claudia had probably warned them not to ask anything. I was nearly finished with my meal when Troy came in, got his food, and went to his usual table. He sat, opened a book, and began eating without looking my way. I could feel everyone's attention on me.

Suddenly, I lost the little appetite I had. My stomach was still sore from the roller-coaster ride I had given it. I stopped eating and sat back.

"You all right?" Kim asked.

"Yes. I shouldn't have eaten such a big lunch," I said. Nobody believed it. "I think I'm just nervous about the science test, too." I looked at Claudia. "See you back in the dorm," I told her, and stood with my tray. No one spoke.

I avoided their eyes and walked off to place my dishes, glass, and silverware in the return bins. While I was doing that, I glanced at Troy. He was looking up now, looking at me. I saw more than apology in his face. I saw deep regret and sadness. For a moment, it was as if there was no one else in the cafeteria. The clamor and chatter were gone. I started toward him, running solely on instincts and avoiding any warnings or logic. He sat back, antici-pating more rage.

"I'm not apologizing. I was hurt," I said. "But I was wrong to get involved with you, with anyone, so soon. That was unfair. I share some of the blame. I shouldn't have used you like that, like some sort of test."

Before he could respond, I turned and walked away. I heard him call to me, but I didn't stop walking. Out of the corner of my eye, I saw my girlfriends all watching, frozen with fascination. It made me walk faster.

When I stepped outside, I felt like running to the safety of our dorm room, sheltering myself with science information to study, and avoiding thoughts about anything else. I was well on my way before he caught up with me. He put his hand on my shoulder, and I stopped and turned to him.

"Why do you think I kept your secret and wanted to be with you anyway, knowing how hard it could be? I really believed the pain we shared would be a bridge bringing us back to the so-called normal world. Together."

"Maybe it would be too much like therapy for both of us," I said. "I've had enough of that."

"I haven't had any, formally, but I doubt any therapist you could have would feel what I feel for you. It's worth the risk," he said. "At least, I think so."

I looked toward the dorm. *Walk away*, a voice inside me was saying. *Don't listen to him.*

I was going to do just that, but another voice said, *That's the Haylee in you talking. Don't listen to her. She doesn't want you coming up for air.*

"Take me for a ride," I said.

Troy smiled and reached for my hand. "Sure. Where?"

"I want to see those lights and stars again."

14

We drove most of the way in silence. I thought we were both afraid of saying the wrong thing and causing us to turn around and return to the campus. Despite my father's assurances when he first enrolled me in Littlefield, I never truly believed that no one would discover my recent horror and Haylee's involvement. Whenever anyone looked at me too long or whenever I saw people whispering behind my back, I braced myself for the inevitable questions and shock.

As soon as Troy and I drove off, I decided that if he asked me any questions, I would stick to the truth, despite where that truth might lead. Running from it did not make any of it disappear. It was always there, an undercurrent woven and streaming along under the thin crust of deceptions

and half-truths. I was tired of being afraid, tired of
anticipating someone approaching me and smiling
like someone who had discovered something no
one else knew, someone who enjoyed the sense of
power over me, and someone who might even say,
"I'll keep your secret." The implication would be
clear. *From now on, be afraid of me, and never contradict me. Never refuse a favor I ask, and glorify
me with compliments.*

"My father and his girlfriend are coming on Saturday to take me to see my sister's doctor," I said.

"Why?"

"According to what my father and the doctor
believe, my sister has made great progress toward
redemption. She, Dr. Alexander, wants to let her
go home for Thanksgiving, when I will be there, of
course. She wants to see if I will cooperate, accept
it. She wants to explain it to me and, I'm sure, get
me to believe that Haylee is sincere and I should try
to mend what's been broken between us."

"That's a lot to put on you, considering what
you went through," Troy said. "I can't imagine any
apology washing away the memories." He made
the turns and started us down the dark road that
turned into gravel.

"Neither can I."

"What are you going to do?"

"Listen to what she has to say. Maybe try."

"So you still want to forgive your sister?"

"When someone has hurt you, you only give them more power when you remain vengeful and angry."

"Who told you that?"

"My therapist," I said.

"Maybe that's why I've stayed away from them."

He drove up the incline, stopped, and turned off the engine. It wasn't as perfect a night sky as it had been the first time, but there still were enough flickering stars to make it special. The lights of buildings and homes twinkled, and we were high enough and distant enough to make it look like a toy world. Smoke from fireplaces looked limp, like chiffon scars drifting toward the heavens, and headlights of cars were pinpoints as they wove over the streets. It was easy to feel we were above the day-to-day conflicts and troubles that confronted us. We could be safe here; we could reveal our pain.

"Okay," I said. "I'm wearing my emotional armor. Tell me why you would even need a therapist."

He was quiet so long that I thought he was not going to answer. I remembered how my therapist would avoid pushing me to reveal my feelings and thoughts. *When you're ready* was her favorite expression. It put more pressure on me. How would I really know when I was ready? She was the doctor; why wasn't she the one to decide when I was ready?

But there did come a time when what was inside you had built up so strongly that it threatened to explode, to tear you apart until you were no good to anyone else and especially to yourself. It was just like steam. You did need some sort of release, and that did help you to feel better. In the end, despite our reluctance, we realized we all needed someone we could trust. Loneliness was far more painful and unbearable. For some, I saw the only solution was to invent imaginary friends, but ghosts were impossible to hug, and their kisses were nothing but a slight breeze, barely felt and never remembered.

"Five years ago, when my sister, Jo, was only seven, I was walking past her room. Her door was slightly open. My mother was on some shopping expedition with friends in Philadelphia," he began.

His voice was thin, like the voice of someone fighting back the urge to cry. I said nothing. I didn't move. I don't think I even breathed.

"I heard my father talking and paused. As far as I knew, he was rarely in Jo's room. Whenever my mother had a question about something for or about Jo—furniture, clothes, anything—his stock reply was always, 'Women know more about girls. You decide.'

"What drew my attention was the way he was talking to her. He was speaking in a loud whisper, his voice so different that I almost didn't recognize it and thought there was some stranger in the house.

I inched up to the door and opened it just a little more to look in on them."

Troy paused to lay his head back on the seat and take deep breaths. In the dim starlight, I could see some tears glistening at the edges of his eyes. I reached for his hand and held it. He sat forward again, but he didn't look at me.

"She was naked on the bed. He was on his knees beside her and looking her over. His left hand was on her left leg and moving up slowly as he whispered to her, telling her she had to be aware of this part of her body and how, as she grew older, there would be more and more nice feelings to enjoy there as well as here, he said, touching her nipples. She wasn't moving or crying or saying anything.

"His fingers moved up her leg, and he started to touch her, stroke her, and then leaned all the way down to kiss her there. I had just had some chocolate and a peach, and suddenly, it all wanted to come up my throat. I gagged as he started to turn toward the door. I ran down the hall, down the stairs, and out of the house. I just kept running until I was out of breath. The more I ran, the better I felt, and I kept from throwing up.

"But I collapsed on the grass, and without even knowing why, I started to cry. Then I lay down and remained crunched in a fetal position for hours, I think. My heart was pounding for so long I thought I would die right there on the grass."

He lowered his head. I waited for a few moments. No one had to tell me how difficult that was for him to reveal. I was crying for him, too. He took another deep breath and looked up again, but not at me.

"I didn't think he had seen me in the doorway, but I couldn't be sure. I was afraid more than anything else. For a while, I didn't say anything. I couldn't look at him without thinking about it, though, and I thought he realized why. He couldn't ask me, of course. He didn't mention anything when he saw me right afterward, but there was a look in his eyes now when he saw me, and whenever he looked at me that way, I always turned away like I was the guilty one. I hated that feeling.

"Finally, one day when both our parents were out, I went to Jo's room and sat on the floor with her. She had beautiful furniture in her room, but she also had this thick, fluffy pink rug and liked sitting on the floor while she read one of her books or listened to music on her earphones.

"I rarely went into her room to play something with her or talk to her. I was a macho guy who wanted to be like his macho father. No girlie stuff for me. Imagine how that image shattered. What I didn't want to do was frighten her or make her cry. I was smart enough to speak casually, making it seem like I was only curious and not making her feel guilty or upset.

" 'Father doesn't talk to me about myself,' I began. 'I have to learn everything from my friends or from books. Does he ever talk to you about yourself?' I asked, making it seem like I was jealous. She nodded. 'Well, when he talks to you, does he show you stuff, like touch you or something?' She nodded again. 'Did he do that more than once?' I asked her, and she nodded. Then I held up my hands and started to show fingers to count how many times. She indicated it was seven. 'Did you ever tell Mommy?' She shook her head.

" 'Father says not to,' she told me. 'He says Mommy wants to be the one to tell me things about myself and would be mad at him for doing it. He made me promise not to tell her,' she said.

"I nodded and then started to fiddle with her iPad and pretend that none of what she had told me was important. Of course, I felt like it was thundering in my head. He had done it multiple times and most likely wasn't going to stop. Nevertheless, it still took me weeks to get up the courage to tell my mother. My father was on one of his international business trips at the time, which probably boosted my courage. Luckily, she hadn't wanted to go with him.

"I went to her room. She was having one of her migraine headaches and was lying there with a warm wet cloth over her eyes and didn't even hear me come in. She didn't realize I was there until I sat on her bed. She looked up, surprised, of course. She realized from the look on my face, I guess, that this was no ordinary moment. I wasn't there to ask to do something or invite someone over for the weekend.

" 'What?' she demanded. Going to her while she was having a migraine wasn't the smartest thing, but when the courage finally came to me, I wanted to do it quickly and get it finished. After I told it all practically in one breath, I thought the look on her face was more frightening than what I had seen my father doing. Without asking me anything or saying anything at all, she rose and went to Jo's room. I went to mine and tried to do some homework. Finally, I just lay on my bed and stared up at the ceiling. In anticipation, my heart had been pounding the whole time, just as it had that day.

"Whatever Jo told her was enough to overpower her migraine. She came to me and told me never, never, ever to speak of what I had seen. She said she would handle it.

"Her way of handling it was to immediately enroll Jo in a private school where she would be sleeping. A friend of hers had placed her children there, and she and my mother were always arguing about where children would get the best education these days.

"I never knew exactly what she told my father when he returned, but life changed dramatically in our house. He never confronted me about it, but whenever he did look at me after she had spoken to him, he lowered his eyes first. The following semester, I was enrolled in a private junior high affiliated with Littlefield, and then when I was in senior high, I came here."

"So he never said anything to you or you to him?" I asked.

"No. My mother preferred that we pretend it never happened. Embarrassment and losing face in the social world were always more important. My father spoiled me with gifts in a pathetic attempt to win back my respect for him.

"The funny thing about all this was that my mother wanted me out of the house, too. I think whenever she saw me, she recalled the day, the moment, I revealed it all to her. You know that old saying *Don't shoot the messenger*? Sophocles in *Antigone*: 'No one loves the messenger who brings bad news.' Well, that was me. It's like a stain my mother sees on my face, even to this day, I think. She knows that what I know will never be forgotten. I have nightmares about it. I used to wake up and run to the mirror to see if there was actually a stain there.

"Anyway, I didn't need a therapist to tell me where my introversion and other complexes were born. Once, my mother toyed with the idea of my seeing one because of how much of a loner I became, but the humiliation I'm sure she imagined potentially coming from my revelations swallowed up that idea quickly. *You're on your own for a good reason, Matzner*, I told myself. *Get used to it.*"

"I'm sorry," I said, and hated saying it immediately, because it was something I hated anyone saying to me.

He nodded. "There are all sorts of ramifications from what I witnessed and knew. I've gotten so I hate my name, Matzner. Someday I'll change it." He sighed and sat back.

I looked down but kept my hand in his.

"You know what frightens me the most, Kaylee? Thinking I might be like my father. I was afraid to look at little girls, and that fear kind of expanded, I guess, to older girls."

"You're not going to be like him," I said.

"And you know this how, Dr. Fitzgerald?"

"Instinct. I've looked into the face of ugliness. I know it too well now."

"I bet. Well, sorry to have laid all that on you, especially you. You certainly don't need someone like me around. You've got enough on your plate to stuff any hungry masochist."

Finally, I could laugh.

He smiled, too. "Here we are, gazing at the indifferent universe, the two of us, the psychologically wounded."

"But not beaten," I said. What happened then

came to me like a gust of desire. I leaned in to do what I had fled from before and kissed him very gently, very quickly, on the lips.

"Am I still a frog?" he asked.

"Not to me."

He leaned toward me to kiss me again. Neither of us showed the least resistance. *It can be different*, I thought. *With him especially, it can be different.*

"You're the first girl I've kissed like that since the eighth grade, and when I did it then, the static electricity frightened us both so we didn't do it again."

I laughed. "Shocking," I said.

He reached out to touch my lips. "You're so beautiful, Kaylee. You're going to be fine."

"So are you."

"I never thought so until I met you," he said. He glanced at his watch. "I don't want to, but I think we'd better head back."

"Okay, but we're not heading back, Troy. We're moving forward," I said.

He liked that very much, and so did I.

We kissed one more time before he started the engine and turned around to drive back to Little-field. This time, neither of us let a second of silence come between us. It was as if a dam had broken. He rattled off social plans we would follow after the Thanksgiving break. And then he asked me if I thought I might be up to going to his house on Friday night. After what he had told me, the thought of meeting his parents, especially his father, made me very nervous. He knew immediately why I was hesitating.

"Oh, my father's not going to be there, and as it turns out, my mother has an event to attend as well. My father's in New York City for a convention."

"Just us, then?"

"Yes. My sister doesn't come home until next Wednesday. The maids will be around but out of sight, I'm sure. I'll order in some salads and pizza for us. It won't be as good as Mario's, but it will be fine."

I was still hesitating.

"Am I moving too fast?"

"No," I said, turning to him and smiling. "I'm moving too slowly."

"Well, we're a work in progress. No worries," he said.

He drove to my dorm parking lot. After he stopped, I reached for his hand again.

"Thanks for trusting me, Troy. I wish I'd had the courage to trust you after we went out the first time."

"It would have made me even more ashamed of deceiving you," he said. He got out to open my door and then walked me to the dorm entrance. "I imagine your girlfriends are going to be slightly confused."

"Their natural state," I said.

He kissed me again. "Sweet dreams."

"Might be the first time in a long time that I've had any," I said.

"Me, too."

He started for his car. I watched him for a moment and then entered the dorm. I had no doubt that if Haylee had heard his story or knew I had heard it, she would say Troy and I didn't like each other as much as we pitied each other. *Pathetic*, she would add.

But maybe that was the old Haylee. Maybe all she had gone through—the drugs, the shock therapy, and the months of counseling—had changed her. Couldn't I hope for that?

Next, you'll hope there really is a Santa Claus, I told that part of myself that wanted sunshine and stars, smiles and laughter, and nights without nightmares.

Thanks to Terri Stone, who had come out of the cafeteria just as I walked away with Troy, everyone knew I had gone off with him. Marcy and Claudia were ready to pounce the moment I entered the room. I saw they were attempting to do homework but obviously waiting anxiously for my return.

Marcy practically leaped off the bed. "Where have you been? Where did you go?"

"For a ride," I said casually, and took off my

jacket. I picked up my books and started to thumb through the history text.

"Oh, no, you don't," she said. "Don't think you're going to leave us hanging."

"Excuse me?"

"We both decided that since we saved you from being expelled, we deserved to know what happened and why you went for a ride with him now after having had a miserable enough time to want to take our drugs and then ignoring him as if he was Jack the Ripper. It's only fair," she whined.

In the time it took for me to walk from the entryway to Claudia's and my room, I had begun to work on explanations. Telling them it was none of their business was out of the question. I'd lose their friendship very quickly, and I did like them. No one was perfect, least of all me, but I was far from ready to share the truth with anyone else. Weaving an answer they'd accept from half-truths was all I could manage right now. I'd been schooled by an expert in doing that: my sister.

"Despite how everyone sees him, I like Troy," I began, and sat on my bed facing them. "Yes, he's movie-star handsome, but when you get to know him, he's very interesting and very funny, too."

"When you get to know him," Marcy said, raising her eyes to the ceiling. "So?"

"So what?"

"If that's all true, why did you stop seeing him, and why did that drive you to take Ecstasy and avoid even looking at him the next day?"

"It's embarrassing."

"Oh, and taking too much Ecstasy before you go to sleep is not embarrassing?" Marcy said.

I looked at Claudia, who seemed even more interested now.

"I'm still a virgin," I said.

Marcy flopped back onto Claudia's bed as if I had just confessed to murder.

"I know I give the impression I'm not. Right, Claudia?"

Marcy looked at her. Claudia nodded.

"What information did you two share?" Marcy asked her.

Claudia shrugged. "That I didn't enjoy it," she said.

"Holy baked beans. You're not a virgin? You never told me that. I feel like I'm just meeting you two. Anyway, what's this have to do with Troy Matzner?"

"He had the same impression of me. I just wasn't ready, and then I thought I was too hung up on it, too uptight, and even a little afraid of sex. I wasn't any different in public school, and the more I thought about it, thought about how my friends back then thought about me, I was depressed about myself. I thought I would always have disappointing dates, and the word about me would spread here quickly, too. No one would ask me out."

"Probably not," Marcy said. "So? What happened tonight? Are you over your lily-white self-image?"

"We'll see."

"And sex?" She looked at Claudia and then at me. "Are you going to join the club?"

"Probably. I just want to feel like I'm ready. Troy's more understanding, but we'll see."

Marcy looked at Claudia again and then back at me. "That's it? That's your whole story?"

I shrugged. "You think I'm wrong?"

"No. Yes. I don't know. Claudia?"

"It's a personal decision. I don't give my father credit for much, but he did say something very wise once."

"What?" Marcy asked, grimacing.

"The more precious things we reduce to the ordinary, the less we become."

"What? Oh, please, you two. I'm drowning in morality!" Marcy cried, reaching up as if she had to be saved.

"I've got to finish my homework," I said. "Drown quietly, please." I turned to my books, smiling to myself.

Now bored, Marcy left, and Claudia went to her homework as well. Even though it was small, it was another crisis passed. Was this the way I would spend the rest of my life, twisting and turning to avoid being known as a victim, to avoid pity rather than honest affection, and to hide what I really thought about myself in order to avoid days of tears and sorrow? Would my only real friends be those who, like Troy, had some emotional pain? Birds of a feather?

For the remainder of the week, Troy and I were together as much as we could be. My father called Thursday night to reconfirm our arrangements. I could hear the worry in his voice, worrying not only that I would back out but that it would backfire somehow on all of us, including Mother. Being with Troy more, talking about our lives, and really just getting to know each other better filled me with new optimism. My father heard it in my voice, and it boosted his hopes, I knew. Before the conversation ended, he told me more about Dana and some of the things they had done together, including trips to Philadelphia to see shows.

I bore down hard on my schoolwork the remainder of the week and tried very hard not to think about what was coming up with Dr. Alexander during Thanksgiving. I was very excited on Friday because of my date with Troy. To keep their confidence and win their trust, I revealed to Marcy and Claudia that I was going to Troy's house.

"Tonight might be the night, then?" Marcy

asked. Then she smirked and said, "Like you'll tell us."

"I might," I said. "Or you might see it in my face."

"If it's that obvious, you'd better avoid Mrs. Rosewell," Claudia said.

"Don't worry. I'm sure she wouldn't know what it was," Marcy told her. Then she looked at me and grimaced as if she were going to cry.

"What's wrong?" I asked.

"We're just going to the movies," she said, her romantic excitement deflating. "We don't have a house to go to afterward like some people we know, especially that house."

"Oh. I see. Beware of jealousy. It's the green-eyed monster which doth mock the meat it feeds on," I said, waving my finger at her.

"What?"

"*Othello*," Claudia said. "We read it last week."

"Oh, save me!" Marcy cried. "I'll end up being an A student because of you two."

The three of us laughed as we prepared for our dates in Claudia's and my room.

"Maybe you can talk him into having a party at his house one night," Marcy suggested.

"Maybe," I said, even though I doubted that would ever happen. It was better to leave possibilities dangling.

I had done a little of that verbal fencing Troy

had accused me of when we first began to speak to each other, but when I walked out to get into his car, I wondered myself if this would be the night. Was I capable of it? Could it bring anything to me besides the horrid visions of what had happened to me in that basement?

Two things occurred to me. First, I was thinking of it as if it were an experiment and not the result of a romantic evening during which we both felt so strongly about each other that it was simply a natural outcome.

And second, I wanted it to happen because it was another way in which I could defeat Haylee.

I wondered what was more important and what would win out in the end.

15

We were both nervous. Twice we started to talk at the same time and laughed.

"Okay. You go first," I said.

"I was just going to say that I've avoided going home so long that I feel like a stranger to the place, too," he said.

"Weren't you home during the summer?"

"Just for a few days. I attended a seminar in international politics at Antioch University in New Hampshire. Actually, I chose it for the ride. I spent three days on the road enjoying the trip. I had just gotten this car. But I am interested in the subject, and it was a great place to be. There were students from a number of states and two from the U.K. Both were attending Oxford. We've stayed in touch. They're both guys," he added for my benefit.

"Did you tell your mother you were going to be at the house tonight?"

"Sorta." He smiled. "I said I would drop in to get some things I need and might hang out. She just told me she would be out until eleven or so and not to leave a mess. She refuses to acknowledge the mess has been there for years, only it's not dust or smudges on the windows."

"I think I'm just as nervous about going to your house as I'm going to be about returning to mine," I said.

"Relax. My house is a mind blower. You won't have time to be nervous. You'll be busy gobbling up everything with your eyes."

When we arrived at the large, scrolled black iron gate and it opened slowly to reveal the long, winding driveway, I couldn't help but agree about that. As we went up, the house was more and more impressive. It seemed to rise higher and higher. Beside it, something I couldn't see from the road below, was a four-car garage. Windows were lit above the garage in what Troy explained was the house manager's apartment.

"House manager?"

"Dean Wagner. He was here before we bought the house, and my father kept him working for us. Lucky he did. My father is barely capable of changing a lightbulb, not because it's too difficult, but he doesn't have the patience for anything mechanical, and there is a lot of technology equipment involved with this house and the grounds. The sprinkler system for the lawns is as elaborate as the ones on most golf courses, and there are literally three hundred different lightbulbs to change inside the house and on the outside of the property. Dean takes care of the pool as well. Of course, he has a half dozen on his staff. He's a tough boss, and any one of them is lucky to last six months."

"He was here before? How old is he?"

"I think Dean's about seventy, although you'd never know it looking at him. He's not a weight lifter or anything; he's naturally strong. I've seen him lift stuff that would take two or three men to budge. He keeps to himself. All I really know about him is that he was married, but his wife died before their second wedding anniversary, and as my father once told me, he stepped out of the world and married the property. He'd be lost without it."

He parked in front of the large, short but wide tiled stairway that led to the front entrance. Two deliberately weathered-looking sconces were hung on both sides. The arched brass doorway was at least nine or ten feet tall.

"Dean doesn't respect my father," Troy added. "He obeys him only because he respects the property."

"How do you know that?"

"I can tell by the way he looks at him. I could

practically write his thoughts. Dean thinks that a man who can't tighten a screw is worthless, regardless of how much money he's earned. It's funny," he continued, still not moving to get out of the car, "but when I was growing up, I wanted to prove myself to Dean more than I did to my father, and that was even before the incident I witnessed. I would fix anything I could just to impress him."

He turned to me. "I suppose that's sad, a young boy looking up to an employee more than to his own father."

"I don't know, Troy. I love my father, and I suppose I respect him, but he did disappoint me when he chose to flee rather than stay and fight for us. I know he's trying to make up for it. I guess we have to start thinking of them as people flawed as much as anyone and not heroes."

He smiled. "When I'm right about someone, I'm right," he said. "And I'm right about you. C'mon. Let me show you Kublai Khan's Xanadu."

He came around to open my door and led me up the steps. Instead of a key for the lock, there was a box with numbers on it. He punched in the code, and the door clicked open.

"Magic," he said. "Otherwise, you can be sure my mother would have a butler." He opened the door for me.

The foyer was half as big as most homes I knew. The black marble floor glistened. Immediately on the right was a shelf for shoes and what looked like the slippers worn by nurses and doctors during surgeries.

"What is all this?"

"My mother insists that anyone who doesn't take off his or her shoes wear them. See why I compared the house to an operating room?"

He handed me a pair. We sat on the black leather settee and took off our shoes.

"She'd know if we didn't," he said, nodding at a security camera in the corner of the ceiling.

The foyer opened to a large living room on the right, with a fieldstone fireplace that took up most of the center wall and ran as high as the tall ceiling. I felt like I was looking at a room in a museum because of the statuary and the large paintings, most of which I recognized as realist art popular in the second half of the nineteenth century. There were even some woodcuts capturing country scenes. All the oversized furniture, tables, and rugs on the dark hardwood floor looked just delivered.

"It's beautiful. Magnificent. But does anyone use this room?" I asked.

He laughed. "In the mornings, my mother goes in there with a white cotton cloth and checks the tops of tables and sofas, searching for evidence of dust. If you listen carefully, you'll hear the hum of air filters."

"Should I breathe?"

"I don't," he said, then took my hand and turned me toward the grand dual stairway. I had never seen one like it.

"Wow. Why two? Ascending and descending? And the way they arch, the work in those balustrades. I half-expect the queen of England to come walking down."

"You're not far off. The concept is known as an imperial staircase. It was originally designed for the flow of guests arriving and departing in palaces and theaters and such, but ours only leads to the bedrooms in this house, only my father or I could see my mother or the maids descending. But what's a grand mansion without one of these?" he said. "Coal barons were like kings once."

He led me left to the dining room, which had a gilded white marble-topped table that could seat eighteen, a mirrored wall, and an impressive Persian rug that nearly covered the whole room. On the other wall was a painting of a stern-looking man, appearing regal as he stood with a mountain range behind him.

"Who's that?"

"Madison Morley, the original owner of the mansion. My mother thinks it makes the house more grand to keep him up there. I think he looks like someone who's surprised he had blood in his veins. My mother gets angry when I ridicule him. C'mon," he said, and we walked through the kitchen to a small dinette in the rear. Every place I looked and everything I saw sparkled and shone. Nothing was out of place. In fact, it looked more like a model home than a home in which people lived.

"It's like growing up in a bubble," I said, without thinking.

"Exactly. In many more ways than one. That was also the main reason I didn't have many friends over. I was actually embarrassed. Before she was shipped off, Jo had friends over occasionally, but the maids were instructed to pounce the moment they left. My father claims one of the maids has been ordered to enter his bedroom when he gets up to go to the bathroom and remake his bed before he returns."

"His bedroom?"

"As long as I remember, they've had his-and-hers bedrooms with adjoining doors. I think the door adjoining theirs these days has been cemented."

"I wondered about that. I mean, since . . ."

"I never thought of my parents as a lovey-dovey couple. Sometimes I think theirs was an arranged marriage. You know, like royals used to have."

"Oh," I said, seeing that the smaller dinette table was already set with salad plates, main plates, water glasses, silverware, and, at the center, a stand for pizza like the ones in restaurants.

"Who did all this?"

"I emailed Martha, the head housekeeper. The pizza was delivered and is in the oven being kept warm. The salad is in a large bowl in the refrigerator. I asked that we be permitted to serve ourselves. Shall we?" he asked, and pulled a chair out for me. "I'll show you the rest of the house afterward. Did I mention that we have an indoor pool?"

"No," I said. "How could you forget to mention that?"

He shook his head. "We filthy rich take so much for granted."

He brought out the salad bowl and placed it beside me.

"Help yourself," he said. He returned to the refrigerator and brought out a bottle of Chianti. "My father gets this by the case." He opened it and poured us each a glass. Then he took some salad for himself. "Let's toast to something before I take out the pizza."

"What?"

"Tomorrow," he said after a moment. "As long as you're in it."

I smiled. We touched glasses and sipped, looking directly into each other's eyes. Then he took out the pizza and put it on the stand.

"Wait," he said after slicing it. He went to a console on the wall by the refrigerator and pressed a button. "We've got to have some Italian music to make this authentic."

Almost immediately, I heard the famous Three Tenors.

"I can play this through the whole house," he said. "There's a remote in practically every room, too, and video security in each. Everything is on Wi-Fi."

"Despite everything, I think you really like this place, Troy."

"Never as much as I do right now," he replied. He poured us some more wine. "It's Xanadu. How can we not like it? Everything unpleasant has been left outside the walls. There is only us in the here and now. We'll make our own magic. At least for a night. Agreed?"

"Agreed," I said, not sure what I was agreeing to but nevertheless happy to do it.

I wanted to help clean up after we had eaten, but he said Martha was waiting in the wings.

"No matter how well we did, it wouldn't be good enough. Martha knows my mother. She'll check everything with a magnifying glass. Not even Sherlock Holmes would be able to tell we had eaten here."

"She sounds obsessive-compulsive," I said.

He shrugged. "She's something, but the truth is, I've never blamed her for being who she is. Everything is a defense mechanism when you're married to my father. Maybe the best thing that could have happened for both Jo and myself was being sent to spend most of our lives at school and away from . . . from all this. You can imagine what our Thanksgiving is like."

"Not any more intimidating than what mine looks like it might be," I said.

"We've got to stop talking about family," he said. "It's like reliving the sinking of the *Titanic* or something. Let me show you the rest of the house."

He took my hand, and we walked out another doorway from the dinette. He showed me the entertainment center, with a wide-screen television that looked as big as some small movie theaters. Instead of sofas and settees, there were large black leather theater seats. He pointed out the sophisticated sound equipment.

"This is impressive," I said.

"Impressive waste is what it is. We don't use it very much. Much of this house is for show."

His father's office was literally as large as our living room. As was every room in the house, the office was spotless, every book and paper neatly placed on desks and shelves. There was a conference table, settees, and some office equipment. There were the same realistic paintings, and to the right of the desk was a picture of a jet plane.

"My father is partners with some other guy on the plane," he said, nodding at it.

"You don't know who?"

"He bought it recently. I have yet to take a ride on it. I don't ask him about his business. I don't ask him about much of anything anymore," he added.

I noticed that he didn't really enter the office. He just stood in the doorway with me and pointed things out. Then he took my hand and led me farther into the house and to the right. We arrived at double bone-white doors within a gilded frame.

"The spa," he announced, and opened the doors. The heat flowed out over us.

Directly before us was an oval indoor pool in light blue tile. There were chaise lounges to the right with towels rolled neatly on them. He played with some switches on the right, and the room darkened a bit, but the pool light came on.

"There's a steam room over there and a sauna beside it. Another room has a massage table. My father, when he's home, has a personal masseuse. Of course, there are showers and toilets. It's as good as what you'll find in any five-star hotel, believe me. When we were here most of the time, Jo and I used this. She had friends over. I didn't. In fact, you're the first person I've brought here."

"I'm sorry. You could have had a lot of fun with friends here. You certainly would have been very popular."

"But mostly because of this," he said sharply. "Maybe that's why I didn't even mention it to my classmates."

I stepped forward and knelt to put my hand in the water. "It's warm."

"Always," he said. "Want to go in?"

"Really? But I don't have a bathing suit."

He shrugged and went back to the light panel. He turned off the pool lights as well as the lights illuminating the room. There were only emergency lights on over the doors, casting a dim orange glow.

Like bad food I'd eaten, my memory of being naked in the basement began to rise from the dark depths of my innermost fears. Troy turned up the music a little. He moved to the other side of the pool and began to undress.

"We can keep the water between us," he said. When he was naked, he slipped into the pool smoothly. "You know, I just realized that I haven't been in this pool for more than a year, a year and a half."

He swam a little, then paused and bounced up and down. He began to sing with the Three Tenors. The flow of my terrible images began to slow. I laughed, and then, my fingers fumbling, I began to undress. He swam again, deliberately ignoring me so I wouldn't change my mind, I'm sure. The moment I was naked, I slipped over the edge and into the pool.

"How's it feel?" he asked.

"Delightful. It's hard to believe how cold it is outside."

"Don't think about that, or you'll start to shiver."

I swam a lap and stopped. We were both in the shallower end.

"I know that took a lot of courage," he said, stepping closer. "Was it me or the pool?"

"I'd be lying if I didn't say both."

He lowered himself and glided to my left, then behind me and to my right, each circle he made drawing him closer. Finally, he reached out, and I took his hand. Neither of us spoke as he gently pulled me toward him.

"Troy," I said when we were inches apart.

"Don't speak. I'm afraid I'll wake up in bed and realize this was a dream."

I was going to say I wasn't ready, but he kissed me with our bodies softly pressed against each other. Then he lifted me unexpectedly and tossed me into the water.

"You creep!" I cried, and splashed him. He splashed me back, and I swam away. He dog-paddled up to me, spurting water like a whale, and when I tried to swim away again, he seized my ankle and drew me back to him.

"Right now, this is my birthday and Christmas wrapped into one moment," he said, and kissed me again. This time, I was really kissing him back and welcoming his hands on my waist and up and over my breasts. He whispered my name and said,

"Nothing has ever happened to us before this moment." Then he lifted me in his arms, carrying me through the water to the steps. He brought me to a chaise lounge and immediately began to dry me with one of the thick terry towels, meticulously moving between my toes and over my legs. I reached for another towel and began to dry him.

We laughed, kissed, and held each other.

"Comfortable?"

"Yes," I said.

He stepped to the side and brought back a thin blanket. Then he put his arm around me, and we lay there listening to the music.

"Can you forget enough to welcome me into your heart?" he asked.

"I think so. I'm trying."

"Maybe we should pretend to be Adam and Eve, just created."

"Yes, maybe."

"God wants me to discover you, realize your beauty. He wants us to enjoy each other. They had to have some time like this before the snake came."

"Maybe."

His lips were moving over my neck and down over my breasts, gently lifting them with his cheeks and pressing his lips to my nipples. I felt his hardness when he moved against me. Memories flashed like hot sparks. I drove them back into the darkness by kissing Troy even harder, even longer.

"I am like Adam, and this is the first day," he whispered.

"And I am Eve," I said.

"Then you'll believe me when I say I love you more than anyone in the world."

I was able to laugh. I was able to be naked beside him, to feel his sex, to let him touch me and kiss me anywhere he wanted and not scream or cringe. This wasn't simply two people making love. For me, it was a true rebirth. I wanted it more than he could. My legs relaxed and opened to him.

"Wait," he said, and stepped off the chaise lounge. He was back in moments. I heard him tearing the wrapper. "I don't want to tell you how long I've had this."

"I hope it's still good."

"Oh, it is, and so am I," he said, returning to me.

Was I too easy? Was I too eager? Was this simply part of an experiment to see if I could have a normal relationship, fall in love, marry, have children, and never think of what had happened to me years ago?

Perhaps.

But I did feel something deeper for him. He was vulnerable, too. He was looking for the same answers about himself, really. We were two explorers, discovering ourselves again. How could this be wrong?

Both of us feared that lovemaking would never work for us. We'd be afraid of the feelings and terrified of failing. I could hear that fear in every moan and cry, feel it in every long kiss. I was clinging to him as if he were a parachute and I was falling and falling, until the moment came, the moment of pleasure I feared I would never have. I cried out in both delight and relief, and afterward, we lay there holding on to each other as if we were afraid that if we let go, all of this, including ourselves, would disappear.

He turned onto his back and lay there beside me, smiling.

"You have a smug smile on your face," I said.

"Yes, yes, I do. I'm an arrogant, confident, and happy bastard." He turned to me. "And it's all your fault for being so beautiful and intelligent and loving."

I laughed, and I didn't want to come down from the high I had reached. "You used a multimillion-dollar estate to seduce me," I said.

"Guilty."

"And wine and pizza and beautiful music."

"Guilty."

"But I'm not satisfied."

"What?"

"I want something more."

"You do?" He sat up and looked down at me. "What else?"

"Laugh if you like, but I want the best sundae in the world."

He was silent for a moment and then broke into real laughter. "I don't know if we can make it before they close. Let's give it a shot. Everything you need is in the bathroom—hair dryer, body lotion, whatever. Wait."

He rose and brought back a pink silk bathrobe for me. Then he went for his clothes. I got mine, went into the bathroom, and got myself ready in record time, I'm sure.

"I called. They promised they'd stay open for us," he said when I came out.

We hurried through the house, put our shoes on in the foyer, and got into his car, laughing most of the way. I felt like I was on one of those rafts navigating river rapids, incapable now of changing direction but screaming with glee at the dangers. Troy's face was glowing, as I had seen mine was. Nothing now seemed too difficult to do, even having Thanksgiving dinner with my sister.

Later, when he finally brought me back to my dorm, we were still laughing and talking a mile a minute, as if everything that had bound and restricted our thoughts and dreams had been broken. For a moment after he had parked, we sat looking at each other. Neither of us wanted the night to end. We were clinging to every final second.

"Happy?"

"Very," I said.

"As a rule, I don't believe in luck. Coincidence,

yes, but good and bad luck, no. But tonight, I have to thank some lucky stars that you were brought here. I suppose that's selfish. I should think of why you were brought here."

"Why stop now?" I asked.

"Stop what?"

"Being selfish."

He laughed. "I can see my tombstone now: 'Here lies Troy Matzner, teased to death.'"

We laughed and kissed, and then he nodded and grew serious.

"I'll be thinking about you tomorrow," he said, "but I'm confident you'll be fine. Just say and do what you think is right."

"I feel like my good and bad angels are wrestling. A part of me wants to lead Dr. Alexander to believe that permitting Haylee to go home for Thanksgiving will be a disaster because I'm not ready for it."

"And a part of you wants to give her a chance?"

"Yes. Most of our lives, I've been the one who gives in. Especially during our early years, Mother wouldn't let us do something if one of us didn't want to do it. We had to like the same things. Haylee would always promise to like something I liked, even if she didn't, as long as I gave in to her sometimes, but she had a way of showing her displeasure subtly, and Mother usually wouldn't let us do what I wanted or get what I wanted. I used to believe, and now probably more than ever, believe that Haylee would get Mother to reject something I wanted just to prove she had more power than I did. There were lots of little things Haylee did to me when we were growing up, things I couldn't think of doing to her."

"Maybe you didn't share the DNA the way you were told you did. Maybe you got most of the conscience DNA."

I laughed, but this wasn't the first time I had heard that. I had heard myself think it often.

"How do I look?" I asked him, thinking now of meeting someone in the dorm, especially Marcy and Claudia.

"As close to perfect as anyone I know."

"No different?"

"Oh. Maybe a little more blossomed. And me?"

"Maybe a little more arrogant."

He laughed and leaned over to kiss me, then opened my door and walked me to the dorm entrance.

"Call me when you get back," he said.

"I will."

We kissed again, and I went inside, pausing to glance at my reflection in one of the windows.

Here I go, I thought, feeling like someone who had been ordered to run barefoot over hot coals. Maybe I was always this way; maybe I was always afraid of revealing anything intimate. I didn't have

Haylee's indifference and self-confidence. Humility was weakness to her.

My test was postponed for a while. Again, neither Claudia nor Marcy had returned yet. They'd push the curfew to the final seconds. I went about preparing for bed, and when they came into our room, they both stood there gaping at me. I was just pulling back the blanket.

"What?" I asked, my heart starting to pound. Was it true? Did I have a different look now? Was I like a blossomed flower? Was it simply impossible to hide what I had done, where I had gone, who I had become?

They looked at each other and nodded.

"You don't have to say anything," Marcy said. "We see it in your face."

They didn't look that sure.

"You're just saying that to get me to admit it."

They both laughed.

"And what's so funny about that?"

"You just did," Claudia declared.

I threw my pillow at them. Funnily enough, I felt relieved. I didn't want to add any more deception to our relationships, and I didn't want to constantly deny, deny, and deny. Besides, I was far from ashamed.

We stayed up well into the early hours, talking about ourselves, our feelings, and our fears. Sharing confidential innermost thoughts and actions with close girlfriends was another thing I had believed I would never do. I would always be the outsider, different, cold, and doomed only to observe, never to share.

But that had changed.

Maybe, I thought, *just maybe, I've really defeated Haylee this time.*

16

I was surprised my father was alone when he came for me. I'd thought he was bringing Dana with him. He had called before he set out and then called when he was close, so I went out to the lobby to wait for him. I had told Marcy and Claudia that my father was taking me to lunch and spending most of the day with me. Both went on about their own fathers and how the visits they would get were clearly "guilt" visits. I avoided giving them as much detail about my parents' breakup as I could, leaving it cloaked in the typical generality: "They couldn't get along. They had developed different tastes and just lost that magical thing that had first brought them together." I could truthfully add that *compromise* was not in my mother's vocabulary.

That set them off talking more about their own parents. Even though Claudia's had not divorced, she still had stories that rivaled Marcy's, describing what it had been like living in a war zone. They both made it sound as if they had to navigate thunder and lightning from the moment they woke up in the morning to the moment they fell asleep at night. The most I would say was "Yes, it was something like that before my parents divorced." It seemed to be enough, at least for now, but it made me wonder just how shocked they would be if they knew the truth about me. The world I had woven around me here was as thin as the membrane of a chicken egg.

I rushed out to my father when he pulled in and got into the car before he could get out to hug me. He looked surprised but leaned over to kiss me hello.

"Everything all right?" he asked. "You look like you want to make a getaway or something."

"Yes, I'm fine. I just didn't want you to have to deal with some of the busybodies. I thought Dana was coming, too," I said.

"I'm picking her up while you're in with Dr. Alexander. As it turns out, she's not far away. We'll be taking you to lunch after that. I didn't think you'd want to talk about it with her yet, and I didn't want you to be any more uncomfortable. But she knows everything," he quickly added.

"She's been a great person to bounce things off. You'll like her for sure."

"Does Mother know I'm doing this?"

"Oh, no," he said, starting out of the parking lot. "The less detail she knows about the entire situation, the better for her right now."

"But does she know that Haylee might come home for Thanksgiving?"

"Dr. Alexander advised me not to say anything until after you and she meet," he replied, and looked at me. "It's seriously in your hands, Kaylee. Without your okay, I won't permit it."

"What about Haylee? Does she know it might happen?"

"I'm not sure, actually. Probably not," he added. "I would understand if Dr. Alexander believed that promising something that might not happen would result in a setback."

"Setback? Then you really believe she has made progress, changed, and accepted responsibility?"

"She's different," he said.

"How?" I pursued, forcing him to convince me.

"I would never have used this word for her, even before the terrible thing she did to you, but I'd say she's *meek*. I won't say *meeker*, because she's never been even slightly humble. I saw it in you, this milder, modest side, but never in her, and when I mentioned that to your mother once, she nearly bit my head off. To her, it was impossible that there would be such a dramatic personality difference between the two of you. All she would agree to was that you might be a little better at hiding what she called 'super confidence' than Haylee was, but it was a difference only she could see. Even I couldn't see it. I was simply not around the two of you enough. That was always her argument."

I was silent. Mother wasn't far from the truth when it came to that, but I thought his not being around enough was her fault. My father wanted to avoid the confrontations that would inevitably be there. In her eyes, he was bound always to make a mistake in the way he treated Haylee and me. No matter how slight an error, it was still a serious issue for Mother. Forget to kiss one of us hello, forget to ask one of us the same question about school, or forget to give one of us a similar compliment, and she would pounce like a wildcat. Who could blame him for trying to slip in and out of our lives as unnoticed as possible, especially when we were very young?

"What does Dr. Alexander want to hear from me?"

"I honestly don't know, Kaylee. You know how this psychiatrist, therapist, or whatever she calls herself can be. She wouldn't confide even in me for fear I'd have you prepared or something," he said. "If I hadn't seen changes in Haylee myself,

I'd continue to call it all voodoo." He smiled. "Let's not dwell on it. You'll know soon enough. Tell me about this boy you're seeing."

"His name is Troy Matzner. His father is the CEO of a major telecom company, Broadscan."

"I know it. Powerful company, international. That's a big job."

"They live in a mansion once owned by a coal baron here. It's like the estate of a king or something."

"So you've been there? What is the family like? Brothers, sisters?"

I swallowed down all that I normally would want to tell him, but I was afraid that he wouldn't want me to associate with someone who was also suffering from deep psychological wounds. The whole reason he had arranged for me to be at Littlefield was to be around healthier teenagers who led what we could call a "normal life." That way, I'd have less time to remember and relive my own miserable events.

"His father was away on a business trip, and his mother had a previous engagement, so I didn't meet his parents. He has a younger sister, but she's in a private school, too."

"Oh. Nice house?"

"Over-the-top nice." I was comfortable talking about the house, the paintings, the dual stairway, and Troy's father's office, but I skipped mentioning the indoor pool. Just thinking about it made me blush.

It was at times like this when I missed having a mother or even Haylee when we were close and could honestly share things. I wasn't what anyone would call a feminist, probably, but for me, it was true that women had things they were comfortable sharing only with other women. Even a daughter, no matter how close to her father, couldn't bring him into that territory.

I wondered how fathers, even in this day and age, centuries in time and thought from the Victorian era, reacted to realizing that their daughters were no longer virgins. Was the first reaction always disappointment, sadness? For fathers especially, it was a double standard, I thought. If I was a son instead, I could imagine him smiling, recalling his own first time, and then quickly warning me to be careful.

But how would he view the girl his son had been with? Would she drop seriously in his estimation and respect? Would he believe, even hope, that she was temporary? And if they did go on together and eventually get engaged and married, would he always harbor that little disrespect he had felt for her? Would he rather have had his son come to him for advice, asking him if he should remain with a girl who wouldn't do it? What advice would he have given? *If she doesn't think of you as special enough to do it, drop her now?* Or would he say, *She sounds very special, son. Cherish her?*

We were always worrying about what our girlfriends would think of us. We knew our mothers would be concerned and stress protection, but we avoided thinking about our fathers' reactions. Was it simply out of embarrassment, or were we truly ashamed? For so many girls I knew, having their fathers' respect was of primary importance, even more important than having their mothers respect them.

"Sounds like quite a house," my father said. "But you're not really telling me much about him. Troy?"

"Yes. His sister's real name is Jocasta. His mother was into Greek mythology or something."

"No kidding? That's . . . different."

"He's very bright, a four-point-oh student. He's very interested in international politics."

"Better-looking than me?"

"Oh, it's neck-and-neck," I said, and he laughed. Then he turned serious, and I knew what was coming. "Have you said anything, confide—"

Here we go, I thought. There was no skimming the truth here.

"He overheard me talking to you one night and checked me out on his own."

"Oh?"

"But he wasn't discouraged, and he's not the type to spread stories. Actually, he's a bit of a loner, a very serious person."

My father nodded. He didn't have to say it. I could hear him thinking it: *If he knows your story and is still interested in you, he's either quite the young man or quite strange.*

"Hopefully, I'll meet him next time I come up here. Maybe I'll take you two to lunch or something."

"Maybe. Tell me about Mother," I said, hoping to change the topic. "I've called often. When she gets on the phone, she gives me monosyllabic answers to everything, and she still doesn't ask me much about Littlefield."

"I stop by periodically. Irene tells me she's doing better. She looks better. She is caring for herself more and has more energy."

"Good."

He looked at me with that expression that said, *There is a little more to it.*

"What's wrong, Daddy?"

"To tell you the truth, Kaylee, it's a little eerie."

"Why?"

"She seems to be preparing for Haylee's imminent return. You'll find she's done some work on her room."

"Haylee's?"

"Yes. She's changed the decor, the bedding.

There are new curtains, and yesterday she had a new rug installed."

"Different from mine?"

He nodded.

We were both silent.

"That's good, Daddy," I said, after considering what it meant.

He smiled. "I think so, too, and so does Dr. Jaffe. For whatever reasons, she's letting go of her obsession with the two of you. Actually," he said, turning to me, "I think she's accepted some of the responsibility. It only took nearly eighteen years."

"It took more than just time," I said.

He dropped his smile. "Yes, of course."

"Now, you tell me more about Dana," I ordered. "And tell me how serious it's become."

He saluted. "Yes, boss," he said, and began.

I listened, but my mind clung to thoughts about my mother. Was she really ready to accept the differences between Haylee and me? If only she had done so years ago, none of the terrible things might have happened. How easy it would be for me to hate her, but how warm and hopeful it made me feel to learn of the changes coming over her.

I did pick up enough from my father's descriptions of Dana to realize he had been developing a wonderful relationship with her. She sounded unselfish and sensitive but, as he wanted to be sure to point out, fun to be with. Sometimes, I thought, if you were willing to share your vulnerabilities with someone, you could find someone you could be happy with. You wouldn't be alone anymore. No matter how many friends you had or how popular you were, if you locked up that troubled part of yourself, you would always be alone. I knew that few girls my age would be this wise. The journey I was forced to make to come to this point was not one I'd wish on my worst enemy, but nevertheless, it was there: something good from something so horribly bad.

"Almost there," my father said about an hour later.

I was prepared to see another impressive house. After all, Dr. Alexander was an important psychiatrist at the correctional facility. I had never asked my father much about her personally, but now, when we turned down a side road and passed one modest home after another, I wondered about her. Was she married? Did she have children? I asked my father.

"To be honest, I never inquired about her, Kaylee. None of that seemed important."

I nodded, but I disagreed. I didn't care how professional she was or how many degrees she could list after her name. If she was someone with a family, her view of what had happened to us had to be different from that of someone who lived alone, who maybe never had a serious romantic relationship, and who had only professional relationships with young people. Everything doesn't come out of a book or a laboratory.

When the GPS announced we had arrived, I thought I had some answers. Her home was a single-level with a nice stone front, but it looked small to me and had only a single-car garage. We pulled into the driveway and sat for a moment. Outside, there were no signs of young children, no playthings. The lawn was well kept, with unpretentiously arranged bushes and flowers. She lived alone, I thought. I looked at my father and imagined he was coming to similar conclusions.

"It's the sort of house someone might have inherited," he decided. "Could be a starter home, very young family. She's not that old."

"I don't remember her wearing a wedding ring."

"Whatever. She's the one who wields the sword," he said, and opened his door. "I'll just get you started and then go for Dana, okay?"

"Okay," I said, and got out.

She had obviously been keeping an eye out for us. The front door opened before we reached it over the short but neatly tiled walkway. Unlike the way she dressed at the institution, she was wearing a forest-green waffle-knit sweater and dark green jeans with a pair of navy wool boat shoes similar to a pair Marcy had. Her hair was down around her shoulders. She looked relaxed but still had that smart, fashionable, and attractive look. My mind raced. Why wasn't she married? Or had she been? What was it like for a psychiatrist who fails in a marriage? Was that like a fat physical trainer or something?

"Hi," she said. "Right on time. Thank you for bringing her here," she said to my father.

"The miracle of GPS."

"I know." She smiled at me. "You look well, Kaylee. Come in. Please."

"I'm going to leave her with you," my father said. "I have to pick someone up. What do you figure, an hour?"

"At least. I have some nice cookies and some great tea or whatever you like," she told me.

I looked at my father and raised my eyes toward the sky. Cookies?

"I'm okay," I told him. He nodded.

"See you then," he said, and started away.

Dr. Alexander stepped back for me to enter. The simplicity of the outside was reflected in the interior as well. Nothing in her small living room appeared particularly expensive. The pictures on the wall were all prints that looked chosen more for decor than for art. In fact, I thought they were quite bland depictions of country scenes, nature. The house was well kept but not nearly with the obsession Troy's mother enforced. I saw she had a book turned over on a side table and a cup and saucer beside it. There were magazines on the coffee table, and a jacket had been thrown over the back of a large cushioned chair across from the sofa. She moved quickly to pick it up.

"Something to drink?" she asked. "Soda? Tea?"

"I'm fine."

"Please," she said, pointing to the chair. She hung the jacket on a hook in the small entryway and returned to sit on the sofa. "So, all is going well at your new school?"

"Yes, I like it very much."

"Very wise decision to change schools," she said.

I really didn't want to talk about myself. I had done enough of that with my own therapist and my father. I also was afraid I had become one of those special cases for psychiatrists, one that would be cited in textbooks or something.

"Does anyone you treat ever really get better?" I asked aggressively, to make it clear that I wasn't here for myself.

I could see that her training enabled her to deflect the slings and arrows in my tone and question.

She shrugged. "I think it's a matter of degree rather than stamping someone with approval and saying he or she has been completely cured. Some are like cancer patients and go into remission. We hope it will last, but there is a high percentage of regression, too."

"And where does my sister fit into that analysis?"

She smiled. I was forcing her to get right down to it. No dilly-dallying here.

"There are, and I suspect always have been, significant differences between the two of you, no matter how you were raised and what you were told. Your sister is nowhere near as direct, for one," she said, and leaned forward. "She subtle, she's conniving, and she's very clever. She has an excellent eye for reading the situation and adjusting it to her benefit. But," she said, sitting back again, "I suspect you knew all this."

"It doesn't sound like you think she's improved."

"Honestly, I'm not completely sold one way or the other, which is why I think you're important in this now. I can observe and confront her in therapy forever and not have the insight you have when it comes to her and, I imagine, she has when it comes to you. That much about the two of you I will grant your mother."

"You're going to blame her, too?"

"I don't think it's of any real value to us now to assign blame. I always found guilt to be a tricky thing. Nothing is really black-and-white when it comes to that." She smiled. "It doesn't help to say 'the devil made me do it,' either. I think the thing about our relationships is how much we share in creating them and the results that follow. When they're negative, the relief we experience comes only from being honest with ourselves, first and foremost. If Eve wasn't vain, she never would have listened to the snake."

"But who made her vain?"

"So we continue to spread the guilt around, look for ways to escape the truth about ourselves. To get to the point, I think your sister has cut back on that. I'm not saying completely, but maybe enough to face and accept responsibility. With that could come regret, and with regret comes a desperate need for forgiveness."

"Forgiveness?"

"Which brings us to you."

"And what you want to know from this visit is if I am capable of forgiving her?"

"Something like that. You have to want to, of course. You're in control, Kaylee. What you want and what you do will determine how this eventually goes for yourself but also for Haylee and your parents."

"So no matter what I suffered, the pressure shifts to me? I'll receive either compliments or blame?"

"Isn't that always true? In the end, the victim either decides to go on hating, seeking revenge, or he or she lets go. The victim has to accept that society has dealt justice, but to continue wanting more only keeps the violence and abuse done to him or her alive. Don't you want to bury it, too?"

I looked down. I was determined to be hard and reluctant, no matter what, but the reasonableness of what she was saying was too overpowering.

"She has to be sorry," I said. "To be really sorry."

"Oh, I agree with that. And no matter what tests I put her through and what the opinions of my associates, to my way of thinking, especially in this case, only you can decide if she is. What I will tell you is that she has suffered, too. The catatonic condition you witnessed was triggered by her inability to face the truth, the responsibility."

"I thought she was angry that I didn't look as devastated as she'd hoped," I said.

"That, too, but whatever the main cause, it was a form of escape. We had to treat it, and it didn't last. All the self-deprecating things she has done while in the institution only reinforced my diagnosis," she said.

She paused. I looked away. Strangely, I wanted and didn't want to hear all this at the same time.

"Sure you don't want something to drink?" she asked.

"Maybe just some water."

She went to the kitchen. I looked around the living room more closely and saw a picture of people who had to be her parents. I didn't see pictures of any brother or sister.

She returned with a glass of water.

"Thank you."

She waited for me to drink. "I think Haylee has made a turn in the journey," she continued. "How far and how strong a turn is something we'll have to see, you'll have to see. What I want to stress here is that your opinion will matter most to me, Kaylee. Before you return to school, your father will bring you back to see me. I'd rather we met here again. Is that okay?"

"Sure."

"But first we have to decide if you're willing to have this happen."

"I think my mother is anticipating it."

"What do *you* want?" she insisted.

"I want to return to being five years old," I said.

She smiled.

"Okay," I said. "I won't deny that I'm curious about her."

"Would you, could you, accept her apology and welcome her remorse?"

"If it's true, yes," I said.

She leaned back again. "You're both quite remarkable, despite how you were raised, but even though you were the one who truly suffered a life-affecting experience of horrid proportions, I think you're going to be fine, outstanding, and more successful. Any visions of what you'd like to do?"

"Maybe what you're doing," I said. Her eyes widened as she smiled with surprise. "Now, you tell me something about yourself. What brought you here, to the place you're at?"

Her smile didn't fade as much as it was replaced with a look of vulnerability that only someone much, much younger might have.

"I was one of those children who never stopped asking why from the first day I could. Most of us have this quiet acceptance. Things happen, and we go on, but doing that never satisfied me. I was particularly aggressive in school. Most of my teachers actually tried to avoid me. My hand was always up after they said something. I was once sent to the principal because I was too disruptive with my demands to know the reasons behind rules. So it seemed natural for me to go into psychiatry."

"I don't suppose that made you popular with girlfriends and especially boys."

She laughed. "No, it didn't, but I learned how to control my inquisitiveness."

"You were never married?"

"I was engaged once, but my fiancé collapsed under the scrutiny."

"You caught him cheating on you," I said.

"Something like that. You are going to do well,"

she added. "I'm impressed. How is your social life at this new school, since we're getting personal?"

"It's good. I've met someone."

For a moment, I wondered if I might not tell her everything about Troy. She was a psychiatrist, after all. Maybe she could offer some advice, but then I thought that would be a kind of betrayal. Troy was keeping my horrible experience secret. How could I not keep his?

"That's great," she said. "Again, I'm impressed. Dr. Sacks has done well with you. Well, I don't know about you, but I would like to sample the cookies I made. I followed my mother's recipe for oatmeal chocolate chip. How about it?"

"Maybe one . . . or two," I said. "Where are your parents?"

"My mother passed away a little more than two years ago. Cancer. My father works on a cargo vessel, and since my mother's death, he takes every assignment he can. He says travel keeps the lid on grief. This was their house. He signed it over to me, and for now it's enough."

"Life's not easy, is it?"

"No," she said, smiling. "But neither is the other option. C'mon," she urged. "Let's have some tea or coffee and talk about your school a little more. You're more interesting."

"Classic avoidance," I said.

"Yes," she confessed, smiling. "C'mon." She reached for my hand, and I rose.

When my father arrived, he found us both laughing and sampling cookies in the living room. The look of shock changed quickly to a smile of relief.

"You can come to pick up Haylee anytime Thursday morning," Dr. Alexander told him.

"Okay."

"Bring her back on Friday morning. I've only been able to manage the one-day pass for now."

"Fine," my father said.

"Let's give Kaylee a chance to think through the experience. You can bring her back here on your way to her school on Sunday. I'll be here all day," she said.

He nodded and looked to me.

"Thank you," I told Dr. Alexander. "Your mother had a great cookie recipe."

She nodded, and my father and I left. Dana was in the car. I got into the backseat quickly. Dr. Alexander waved, and my father backed out.

"Hi, Kaylee," Dana said. "I'm Dana Cartwell."

I didn't shake her hand so much as grasp it and smile.

"Well, I guess that went well," my father said.

"Yes," I said.

The momentary silence that followed hammered home that I didn't want to discuss it in front of Dana. She was still a stranger to me, despite how well he and she were getting along.

For most of the time after my father had left the house and gone through with the divorce, I didn't like to think of him being with someone else. It didn't bother Haylee. She saw that it did bother me, so she teased me a lot, imagining him going around with "probably a much younger woman." She said men were like that, especially during a divorce. Their egos needed to be stroked. When I asked her how she was so sure of it, she answered the way she usually did: "I just know."

The implication was clear. Haylee believed she had better instincts than I had and was far wiser when it came to male-female relationships. Maybe she was wiser, but I didn't have to believe her or think about my father and another woman if I didn't want to. Now I had no choice.

At lunch, I relaxed a bit and revealed more about my visit with Dr. Alexander. Dana mostly listened and spoke only to reinforce something my father said. But afterward, when we had left the restaurant and I happened to glance into the front window of a clothing store and saw an attractive sweater, she picked up on it faster than my father and suggested that we take a look at it. Fortunately, the store had a chair and some magazines so he could be occupied while Dana and I sifted through some unique fashions. I couldn't help myself from fighting against liking her, but she was very relaxed with me, and I found that the effect of female company, doing things a mother and a daughter should be doing, was stronger than my instinctive resentment of anyone taking some of my father's affections.

She actually persuaded me to buy a different sweater and then plucked a matching cap off the shelf and convinced my father it was absolutely necessary. He wasn't really going to resist anything anyway.

On the way back to Littlefield, Dana talked more openly about herself, her youth and school. She and my father joked about people at the company, and for a solid hour, I thought nothing about why I had made this trip and what was soon to follow.

They both hugged me when we parted in the dorm parking lot.

"I'll get up here by eleven on Wednesday," my father said. "I'll pick up Haylee early on Thursday and let her see her new room and settle in before Thanksgiving dinner."

"Okay."

He gave me another hug and kiss. "I'm really so proud of you," he said.

I tried desperately to keep from crying, and he knew the best way to help me do that was to leave quickly. I waved to them and then hurried into the dorm. Thankfully, neither Marcy nor Claudia was there.

The first thing I did was call Troy.

"I've been waiting like an expectant father," he said.

"Give me forty-five minutes to shower and change, and then come get me."

"And? What happened?"

"The new baby's coming. Whether she's good or evil remains to be seen."

17

From the first questions he asked, I saw immediately that what interested Troy the most was how I arrived at agreeing to consider forgiving my sister. Troubling him for years was a similar question. Could he ever forgive his father? How do you get to that place? How do you overcome the anger and, yes, the fear in order to even give it a chance?

Hating is so much easier than loving, and hating someone you're supposed to love or you have loved is often more painful for you than it is for them. Like me, whose memory was filled with happier times Haylee and I spent together, before his incident with his father, Troy also had his mind crowded with good memories of him. Little, seemingly insignificant things—like the time his father let him steer the car or when he gave him a tennis lesson or when he carried him on his shoulders on a beach or simply when Troy stood beside him and saw the respect his father commanded from other people—all made it harder to despise him. How he wished he had just walked by his sister's room that day. But of course, there was his sister to be concerned about, and that was impossible to ignore.

When he picked me up, we went for a drive with no specific destination. We simply wanted to be off campus to talk. Even if we sat in a corner in one of the lounges or lobbies, we'd feel the eyes of the other students studying us, and if Marcy, Claudia, or some of the other girls saw us, they wouldn't hesitate to barge in, hoping to fish out something they could pass on like breaking news reporters.

"It wasn't as if Dr. Alexander cornered me into feeling guilty if I didn't agree," I began. "I believe she means it when she says she is looking forward to my opinion of Haylee. And she made me consider what good it will do now to continue hating my sister."

Troy nodded. "I don't know if she really came up with this," he said. "But a quote attributed to Marilyn Monroe that I like is 'If you can't handle me at my worst, then you sure as hell don't deserve me at my best.'"

"My sister should get a T-shirt with that on the front."

"Maybe she doesn't need it; maybe it's there but

invisible to most. Anyway, I'm not saying you did wrong by agreeing to celebrate Thanksgiving with her at home. Actually, I'm jealous that you have the strength to make that choice after all you've gone through."

I sat back and wondered myself where I had found the strength. "You'll find your way through it, too, Troy."

"Will I? Maybe with you as my copilot."

He sat forward when a turn was approaching.

"Hey, there's a pretty good old-fashioned diner about half an hour ahead. Nothing fancy, just good food, and I like their music. It's as if they're stuck in the fifties and sixties. But I warn you, the youngest customers are in their fifties and sixties."

"Sounds fine with me. For now," I added.

"What do you mean, for now?" he asked, turning to me because he sensed something critical in my tone.

"You can't keep running away from today, Troy. I love every place you've taken me and the people, too, but you have to find your way to face reality and fully experience what's out there for today."

"Oh. That. Rejoin society? Become a card-carrying member of the human race again?"

"Joke about it, but yes. That's what I'm hoping to do. What I've been trying to do and what I want you to try to do, too," I added, and reached for his hand.

He held mine for a few moments and drove quietly in deep thought for a while. Had I said too much? Was I pushing him too far? Did my session with Dr. Alexander make me arrogant, an overnight expert on psychological trauma? Who was I to take on someone else's burdens while I still carried so many of my own?

"It's not something I haven't thought about," he said, releasing my hand. "I've watched everyone else enjoying what I should be enjoying for too long. I'll admit it, but it's that first step that's the hardest. Maybe I should be seeing a therapist, too, after all."

"Maybe. What about your sister?"

"What about her?"

"Besides that day when you questioned her, have you ever spoken about it with her?"

"No."

"How is she?"

He looked at me, clearly deciding whether he wanted to continue the conversation. "Wounded," he said. "Like me."

"Then maybe it's time you had another talk with her. You have to look out for each other, and you can only do that by ending the see-no-evil, hear-no-evil syndrome."

"Is that what you're doing?" he asked, a stream of tormenting rage bubbling beneath his words, not directed at me as much as at himself, at the place in his life he wanted to escape.

"Maybe," I said.

"Don't take on too much, Kaylee, and don't let any of the guilt shift to you. That's the way my mother made me feel the day I told her about my father."

"I won't," I said, but it did sound more like a hope than a commitment.

We dropped the subject, and when we arrived at the diner, which was everything he had described, we talked about everything but family. On the way back to Littlefield, however, he revealed that his mother knew he had brought me to the house.

"Was she mad?"

"No. She surprised me, actually. She told me to bring you around for dinner before the Christmas holiday break. She wants to check your fingernails to see if there's any dirt under them."

"You idiot," I said, punching him playfully. "Now I'm nervous about it."

"Good. Then you'll be just like me," he said.

He turned up the radio, and we sang along with an early holiday tune that we both remembered growing up. Even as I sang, I wondered, was it too dangerous to be happy and to hope? Disappointment for us both, especially for me right now, would be like a nuclear disaster.

What should I recite before I go to sleep tonight? *Fools rush in where angels fear to tread?* Or *To err is human, to forgive divine? Tread on in, Kaylee Blossom Fitzgerald, tread on in.* I didn't have much longer to wait to find out which quote fit better.

It was a long and hopeful kiss good night at my dorm. Troy would have as hard a time falling asleep as I would. The sun in the morning would struggle with us to light up our smiles.

However, the excitement at Littlefield before a holiday break wasn't much different from the excitement Haylee and I used to experience at our public school. The air was electric with it. There was more laughter, louder conversations in the cafeteria, and more genuine grins of anticipation on everyone's face, especially our teachers'.

Both Troy and I worked hard at controlling the nervousness that bubbled just beneath the surface of our own smiles and laughter, hiding it as best we could even from ourselves, until that Wednesday morning when classes broke at ten and parents began arriving to pick up their children. Seniors with cars drove off, beating on their horns as they exited the parking lots, as if we were celebrating the end of a war or something. Troy lingered, waiting with me for my father. They had yet to meet, of course.

Marcy was all right about going home. She was going to have two Thanksgiving dinners, one with her mother on Thursday and then one with her father on Friday. We talked about it Tuesday night.

She said she was also looking forward to reconnecting with some old friends she knew when she was attending public school.

"What about you?" she asked me. "Reconnecting with anyone?" she sang, her eyes widening. I knew she meant an old boyfriend.

"Not really," I said. "I'll be going to a dinner with my father and his girlfriend Friday night, though."

"Your father's girlfriend. How that sounds when I say it, too. Sisters of divorce," she said. "That's who we are."

We turned to Claudia, who had fallen into a funk that was more pronounced than when she had first arrived.

"What's wrong with you?" Marcy asked her.

"Thanksgiving."

"C'mon. It won't be that bad," Marcy told her.

Claudia smirked. "My mother is a lousy cook," she said, which made us laugh. "My father won't take Friday off. It'll be just another weekend at the Lukases' except for cranberry sauce from a can." Then she surprised us with a smile. "But Ben might show up on Saturday."

"You creeps!" Marcy cried. "When did you plan that? Rob never even suggested it."

That cheered Claudia. She loved being special. Then they both turned to me.

"You're the one with the boyfriend who could easily drive over to see you," Marcy said.

"He might." It was actually an idea neither of us had considered.

But now, as we sat in the lobby waiting for my father to arrive, I toyed with the idea of suggesting it.

"How do you think you will spend the long weekend?" I asked him.

"We'll go out to dinner rather than have one at home on Thursday like most families. We'll probably go out Friday, too. My father will work on Friday in his home office." He hesitated for a moment and then added, "I think I'll have that conversation with Jo. I don't know how it will go or what we'll do after that."

"My sister will be gone on Friday. I have no plans for Saturday."

"Oh," he said. "Why don't I come by and spend Saturday with you? I'll take you to dinner, too."

"I'll call you," I said. "That might be very good." I saw my father arrive.

Troy carried my small suitcase out to the parking lot. My father stepped out of his car and watched us approach.

"This is Troy Matzner," I said. I nearly laughed at the way they looked each other over. They reminded me of gunfighters in an old western, only the two of them waiting to see who would reach for his handshake first. Troy, more nervous than I had ever seen him with anyone, offered his hand quickly.

"Happy to meet you, Mr. Fitzgerald."

"Glad to meet you, too," my father said, shaking his hand. He glanced at me. "Heard a little about you."

"A little is enough," Troy quipped.

My father smiled. "When are you heading home?"

"About ten minutes after you leave," Troy said. "We're nearby, so I don't have to rush."

"I heard. I know your dad's company well." He glanced at me and then picked up my suitcase. "Have a great holiday," he told Troy, and busied himself with putting my suitcase in the trunk so Troy and I could say a quick good-bye, with a quick kiss, too.

"Should be good weather the whole weekend from what I hear," my father said, gazing around.

"Good," Troy said. "Maybe I'll take a ride."

My father nodded. "Ready, Kaylee?"

"Yes. I'll call you, and we can plan your visit," I told Troy, and got into the car.

He stood there watching us back out and drive off.

"My imagination, or was that boy really sad to see you leave?" my father asked.

"Maybe a little of both."

He laughed. "When would he visit?" he asked, more concerned about that. We both knew why.

"Not until Saturday, maybe. Let's wait and see," I said.

"Very good idea. Wait and see," he repeated. "In the meantime, Irene tells me your mother has been working hard on the Thanksgiving dinner. She went out with her to buy all the food and has the dining room looking beautiful. She even put up some old decorations."

"She wants to forget everything as quickly as she can," I said. My father nodded.

"How does that make you feel?" he asked.

"Playing therapist?" I regretted how quickly I had come back at him. I saw the sting in his eyes. "I don't blame you," I said. "I know you're worried."

"I just want what's best for you right now, Kaylee. That's my priority." He turned to me with that intense gaze he could draw up instantly. "I mean it."

"I know, Daddy. Thanks," I said.

The little ball of tension and anxiety that had begun rolling around inside me the moment we left Littlefield grew bigger and bigger as we drew closer to my home, and by the time we arrived, it felt like a bowling ball.

"Your mother gave me a dress, shoes, and a jacket for Haylee to wear out of the institution," my father said before we got out of the car. "I brought it there yesterday, but I didn't see her. I made a point of telling your mother not to expect you to be wearing the same outfit and not to lay it out for you. I warned her that I would bring Haylee right back to the institution if she pulled any of that stuff."

"What did she say?"

"She said the two of you should make those decisions yourselves now."

"I hope she meant it."

"I'll be a phone call away. Dana and I are having a small dinner at her place Thursday night. Her brother, who lives in Philadelphia, is coming with his wife. They have a ten-year-old boy and an eight-year-old girl."

"Don't you feel funny being with another family? Doesn't it make you unhappy remembering our Thanksgivings?" I asked. Maybe it was really rubbing off on me, Dr. Alexander's direct and incisive questioning. Maybe I was asking him because it still made me angry that he had left us. Maybe I wanted to see how sorry he was about us, too.

"I just want everyone around me happy. I'll think about myself tomorrow." He smiled. "Just call me Scarlett O'Hara."

"You and Troy with your old movie quotes," I said.

"Oh, yeah? Sounds like a boy I would like."

We got out of the car. My father got my suitcase, and we walked to the front door. He still had the key.

Mother was waiting eagerly for me in our small foyer. I could see how different she was from the woman I had left the day my father took me to Littlefield. She looked more like the mother I remembered before all this had happened. For one thing, she was back to wearing bright colors and had on an orange Calvin Klein fit-and-flare cable-knit dress I recalled. She looked like she had put weight back on, too. She had always had a figure her girlfriends envied. I saw she'd had her hair recently styled in her familiar textured bob, a little longer than usual and with longer bangs. She was wearing light makeup, and her complexion looked as rosy as it had been.

I had anticipated Irene greeting us at the door, but she was nowhere in sight. My father carried in my suitcase and paused to smile at my mother.

"You look very nice, Keri," he said.

"Thank you," she quipped, like someone dismissing a pest. "Kaylee, you look like you've grown another inch or something. Maybe I just forgot how tall you are. Come in, come in," she urged. "I've made some changes in the house I want you to see, and then we'll have some lunch, and you can tell me all about your school. I sent Irene out to get us fresh bagels and that cheese you and Haylee love."

It was weird now hearing references to the two of us. No one at school but Troy knew yet that I had a twin sister.

My father gave me the look that asked if I was going to be all right.

"I'll take my suitcase, Daddy. Thank you."

"If either of you need me for anything, I'm a phone call away," he said, handing it to me.

My mother's all-too-familiar look of disdain invaded her revived look of happiness. "Right. A phone call away," she said dryly. "How lucky we are."

I hugged my father and watched him leave. I couldn't shake the feeling that I was out on a ledge a thousand feet above the ground and had nothing to grasp but myself. The moment the front door closed behind my father, however, my mother seized my hand.

"Come on," she said excitedly. "I have so much to show you before Haylee comes."

I followed behind her, glancing at the dining-room table and seeing how beautifully it was set for tomorrow night. She paused when she saw where my gaze had gone.

"I found all those Thanksgiving decorations we had stored in the pantry," she said. "Remember how you and Haylee helped me put them up, both of you making sure everything was pinned just right? What a team we three were back then."

If we were going to remember good times, I thought, were we going to remember the bad ones? Should I even suggest why Haylee wasn't here?

"Wait until you see what I've done to Haylee's room," she said. She started up the stairs.

Why, I wondered, if she was going to change a room or improve it, would she choose to do Haylee's and not mine? Wasn't that like rewarding Haylee?

Not a thing had been changed in my room. Every single thing was exactly where I had left it. I put my suitcase down. She was waiting impatiently in the doorway. *Stay calm*, I told myself. *Don't be too quick to judge.* I followed her to Haylee's room.

Daddy hadn't mentioned how much brighter Mother had made it. With pink polka-dot curtains, pink floral bedding, and a light pink rug, all new, it smelled like a room in a newly constructed home. Three of our rag dolls looked like they had been washed, or maybe they were even new, duplicated. All three were dressed in multicolored outfits. She had them on the oversize pillows, looking at us. There was a vase with a rainbow of artificial flowers on Haylee's desk, too. I stared at it. It was on the computer desk where Haylee had arranged for my abduction. At least there was no computer there, new or otherwise.

"Isn't it beautiful?" Mother asked. "I had a decorator, you know."

"Yes," I said, but I really had doubts that Haylee was going to like this. It seemed to explode with color. If a room could be exaggerated, this was it. Mother was trying too hard to wash away the past. It was a room for a much younger girl.

My subdued reaction annoyed her. She stepped forward to straighten one of the framed rock-star posters hanging on the right wall. I hadn't noticed it.

"I think this singer was one of your favorites, right?"

"More Haylee's," I said. If I had said that a year ago, she would have ripped it off the wall.

"Well, it will be more of a homecoming for her, then, won't it?"

"I wouldn't think of this as a homecoming. She hasn't exactly been in school or something like that, Mother."

"It's a school," she said. "Just a different kind."

"No, it's a punishment, or it was supposed to be. You never went there, did you?"

My question made her face ripple with tension. Her smile, which I thought was so forced that it resembled a mask, dissolved into her more familiar motherly expression of concern.

"No. I was told it wouldn't do either of us any good, and besides, I hope that's all coming to an end. It will do us no good to talk about it, Kaylee," she added, with that definitiveness we had heard many times when we were told we couldn't do something.

I used to think my mother would make a good

undertaker. She could slam our dreams and aspirations shut in a coffin and bury them forever whenever she refused a request Haylee or I made that violated her main principle: *Nothing different for either of you, ever.*

Her smile flickered back on like a neon light. "Besides, I want you to come down to lunch now in the kitchenette and tell me all about your new school. I want to know everything, your teachers, your subjects, how you're doing, the dorm you're in, friends you've made, all of it. It will take us all night to catch up, I'm sure. Come, come." She beckoned and started away.

I glanced back at Haylee's new room. Actually, I was looking forward to seeing the expression on her face when she first confronted it. Then I hurried after my mother. As we descended, we heard Irene coming in with the groceries.

"Perfect timing!" Mother cried. "Look at Kaylee. Doesn't she look like she's grown?"

"She looks older, yes," Irene said. "Hello, Kaylee."

"You'll have lunch with us and hear all about her new school," Mother commanded.

"I look forward to that. Let me get everything together for you. Go on and relax," she fired back at Mother with just as much authority.

"Right, right," Mother said, surprisingly obedient. "Let's go into the living room, Kaylee."

I looked at Irene, who raised her eyebrows and smiled. She was obviously pleased with the progress Mother had made.

Mother sat on the settee and smiled up at me. I sat across from her. Haylee and I always sat across from her on the matching settee.

"Don't sit so far apart from each other," she might tell us. Or "Kaylee's not crossing her legs like that. Why are you?"

All our lives, we were made conscious of what the other was doing. As little girls, we knew that if one of us folded her hands in her lap, the other should, too. We were keen on pleasing Mother. She took such delight in our seemingly unconscious mimicking of each other. It wasn't much of a stretch for anyone now to imagine which one of us was the first to work at being different.

"Your father tells me you have a roommate. What is she like?"

"She's very bright, especially in math. We get along very well. I think she's enjoying this school."

Mother's eyes didn't blink. There was a colder glint in them. "What did you tell her about our family?"

"Daddy and my therapist, Dr. Sacks, both believed it would be best for me to say that I was an only child. That way, I wouldn't have to explain anything nasty."

She didn't respond. She held her cold gaze.

"It was easier for me to do what they suggested. I had to try to recuperate, Mother."

"Exactly," she said, smiling. It surprised me. I was anticipating her anger, even her ranting against my father and my doctor.

"You understand?"

"Of course I do, Kaylee. As should you."

"Understand what, Mother?"

"When I tell you that your sister is coming home from her school tomorrow." She held her smile. "I'm trying to recuperate, too," she said.

As Mother and I went into the kitchenette for the lunch Irene prepared, I considered what she had said. In my mother's mind, there was no such thing as forgiveness; there was only forgetting or pretending that the bad thing had not happened. She was telling me how she would survive all this.

Was she telling me to do the same?

Although Irene asked a lot of questions about Littlefield, Mother asked many, too. She was so much like her former self that I decided not to challenge her way of dealing with the horrible thing Haylee had done, not only to me but to all of us.

Afterward, Irene pulled me aside to tell me my mother had made enough of an improvement for her to consider cutting back to only a weekly visit.

"Her doctor agrees," she said. She didn't mean to suggest it, but I realized all the pressure was on me now not to spoil the recovery. If I expressed any anger in front of Mother when Haylee was here or if I was in any way mean to her, this fragile reconstruction of Mother's life might crumble.

Irene had Mother take a rest before dinner, and I went to my room. I had some homework to do over the holiday, and I thought it would provide the best way to avoid thinking about the challenge that lay ahead.

My father called to see how things were going. "I see her feisty self has returned," he began.

I told him a little about the way she was behaving and how she was coping.

"Well, that might be for the best, but don't you permit anyone there to make you uncomfortable, Kaylee," he warned. "I won't stand for you enduring an unpleasant second. Understand? You call me, and this whole thing is called to a halt. Your sister is going to hear the same from me."

"I know, Daddy. Thank you. I'll be fine."

Just before I went down to dinner, Troy called. He told me his sister had just arrived, but his father was not home yet. I told him how it was going for me.

"Do you think I should speak to my sister before Thanksgiving dinner or after?" he asked.

"I'd do it after, just so you don't make her uncomfortable for the evening."

"That was my thinking, too. It's great to have

someone bright enough to bounce ideas off of," he said.

"I wish that was all I was."

"I'll call you Friday," he said. "Right now, I'm going to the indoor pool to relive a memory."

"Glad you can't see through the phone," I said, and he laughed.

"Kaylee," he said, then paused.

"I know," I said. "Me, too."

I had this eerie feeling after I hung up. Anticipating words, feeling similar about things, was, after all, what had made Haylee and me the Mirror Sisters.

18

In anticipation of Haylee's arrival, Mother was up before either Irene or me; she was even up before the sun. I heard her moving through the house, but I remained in bed. It had taken me longer than usual to fall asleep.

I had done as much as I could to occupy myself the night before. After Irene suggested that Mother go to bed so she would be fresh for tomorrow, Mother had kissed me good night, something she always hesitated to do because Haylee wasn't here to get a kiss as well. But now I saw the excitement in her eyes. It was on the tip of my tongue to warn her not to expect everything to return to what it was, but at this point, I was even afraid to look worried or pessimistic.

A song by Charlie Chaplin that Haylee and I

would play on our pianos together flowed through my thoughts: *Smile . . . Hide every trace of sadness . . . Smile, what's the use of crying.*

"You go to sleep, too, Kaylee. It's a big day tomorrow," Mother had said.

"I will," I promised.

Irene had escorted her up, assuring her that everything was set for Thanksgiving dinner. I heard their chatter die away and then sat and stared at the two pianos, remembering Haylee when we were only eight, beaming with pride at how well we sounded together. Perhaps she was only proud of herself.

Now, when I rose in the morning, showered, and fixed my hair, I pondered what to wear when I greeted Haylee. When my father had taken me to visit her, I had deliberately chosen that sexy dress. Dr. Alexander had picked up on it immediately. She knew I wanted not only to rub my survival in Haylee's face but also to emphasize that I looked better than she could look at the moment. I wanted her to be jealous of me. I wanted her to hate herself.

I had no intention of doing that now. In fact, I chose one of the dresses Mother had bought for us that Haylee thought did nothing for our figures. She even hated the color, a shade of beige that she claimed was blah. I put on no makeup or jewelry, either. Then I slipped into the plain-looking low-heeled beige shoes Mother had bought to go with our dresses and went down to breakfast.

Irene was at the kitchenette table having coffee alone. Before I could ask where Mother was, Irene nodded toward the dining room. I looked in and saw Mother intently studying the table settings like a champion chess player, adjusting a fork a little to the right, a knife a little to the left.

"Good morning, Mother," I said.

She looked up with an odd expression for a moment and then smiled. "Oh, I'm glad you're up. I was thinking of having the two of you sit together rather than across from each other as usual," she said.

"It's only the four of us, right?"

"Yes."

"Then it won't matter, Mother. The table looks picture-perfect. It could be in a magazine, especially with all the holiday decorations."

"Could it? It's so important that everything goes well, Kaylee."

"It will. Let's have some breakfast. Daddy's picking her up in an hour."

"I hope he doesn't start lecturing her and getting her in a terrible mood before she arrives," she said, looking like she was going to growl.

"It will all be fine, Mother. Don't worry. Let's join Irene."

"Yes. I'm so happy you feel that way," she said.

I turned and walked away. Seeing her smile,

hearing her words and the way she wanted to sugarcoat everything that had happened, churned my stomach. I had all I could do just to eat a bit of cereal and a slice of toast and jelly. Mother was so energetic this morning that she insisted on doing everything, clearing the table and rinsing off the dishes and silverware before putting them in the dishwasher, something she always had insisted Haylee and I do. She returned to wipe down the kitchenette table. Irene and I looked at each other, neither wanting to say anything that might put a hole in Mother's balloon of happiness. Irene winked at me, and I retreated.

A little more than two hours later, I was in the living room reading one of our assigned novels for literature class when I heard the front door open and knew she was here. Was that the sound of my heart pounding or their footsteps?

I heard my father talking to my mother about the weather. I expected that he was waiting for me to appear before he would leave, waiting to see my reaction to Haylee and her reaction to me. I hated that I might appear nervous or afraid. With my head high and my shoulders back, I took a deep breath and stepped into the foyer.

Anyone, even the best detective, would have had to employ a microscope to see any evidence of Haylee being nervous. She burst into a smile of glee the moment she set her eyes on me.

"Oh, I love the way your hair has come back! Mine, too, don't you think?" She turned around, like someone modeling a new style. She had made it sound as if both of us had gone through chemotherapy or something. Of course, it was on the tip of my tongue to say, *I didn't want mine to be cut*, but I swallowed back the words. I would gobble down my feelings and thoughts all day and night, for sure.

"Very pretty," Mother said. "Both of you."

Haylee glanced at her, flashed a smile, and then picked up her overnight bag and hurried over to me. "Let's go upstairs. I have a lot to tell you," she said, seizing my left hand.

"Wait. I didn't introduce you properly to Irene," Mother moaned.

Haylee looked back at her, then at my father, and began to apologize vociferously. "Oh, I'm just so excited to be here. I'm sorry. I didn't even notice you. Your name is . . ."

"Irene Granford, dear," Irene said. I could see from the look of amusement on her face that she immediately recognized Haylee's insincerity but at the same time was amused at her performance. She was also seeing us together for the first time, and like everyone else who did, she was quite astonished by the mirrored faces. It was as if the turmoil, tension, and agony we both had endured were equally damaging.

"I want to know all about you," Haylee said.

I fought back a laugh. Since when did she ever care more about listening to someone else's story than she did about reciting her own? But it was the perfect thing to say. Mother's smile brightened. My father looked sufficiently skeptical and cautious. He glanced at me, and I gave him a small nod so he would understand I was fine.

"We'll have much to talk about at our Thanksgiving dinner," Irene said. "We've planned it for three o'clock. Is that all right?"

"Absolutely," Haylee said. "I'm going bonkers. I haven't had a home-cooked meal for ages. Did you make your famous pumpkin pie, Mother?"

"Of course," Mother said.

"With gobs and gobs of whipped cream on top," Haylee reminded me. "I've been dreaming about it."

"Yes," I said. "It's practically all I've been dreaming about."

I said it as dryly as I could without sounding sarcastic. Mother clapped her hands and brought them to her chin as if she were about to give a Hindu greeting. To Hindus, it meant, "I bow to the divine in you," and I had no doubt she meant that, too, when it came to us.

She turned to my father with that *See? They are still so alike* look.

A wave of pessimism swept across his worried expression.

"We have to think about what to wear to dinner," Irene told me. She looked back at Mother, expecting to hear her dictate our clothing down to the very socks.

"Oh, go up and choose whatever you wish," Mother said. "Surprise us."

Haylee raised her eyebrows and looked to me for some confirmation.

"Yes, why don't we do that?" I said.

"Thank you for bringing me home, Daddy," Haylee said.

"I'll be here at ten tomorrow morning," he reminded her sternly.

"Why so short a visit?" Mother asked, her face wrinkling with displeasure.

"Baby steps," my father said. "That's how her psychiatrist, Dr. Alexander, described it, Keri. Let's not do anything to sabotage the efforts." That warning carried many different meanings, the primary one being *Don't return to the way things were.*

Mother nodded quickly and turned to Irene. "We have so much to do," she said.

My father gave me one more look to assure me he would stay on high alert in case I needed him.

"C'mon," I told Haylee, and we started for the stairs.

I heard my father leave. We walked up quickly. I was most eager to see Haylee's reaction to her room.

The moment she saw it, she dropped her bag and stood in the doorway, astonished. "What the hell . . . Is this some sort of punishment?" she asked me.

"Don't ask Mother that. She thinks it's beautiful and perfect. She had the help of a professional decorator."

"Did she do this to your room, too?"

"Oh, no. Mother's been in therapy, remember? She's trying to be different, treat us differently."

"It looks like a room made of candy. How am I going to fall asleep in here? I'd be ashamed to bring anyone to it. Maybe when I'm back, I can get it changed."

"Maybe," I said, shrugging.

"You like that she did this to me, don't you?" she asked, her whole demeanor changing, returning to what I expected it to be.

"She's doing her best, I guess. Just wear sunglasses," I added.

She stared at me a moment and then burst into laughter. "Very good. You *are* different. You've got to tell me everything about your new school, the girls there, and the boys, of course. Did you meet anyone? I mean a boy, of course."

She entered the room and dropped her bag at the foot of her closet.

"Before you start, I'll tell you why my life has changed, and it has nothing to do with the dumb treatments or Dr. Alexander, either."

"Really? What changed it, then?"

"I met someone I really like," she said, her eyes wide. She ripped the comforter back and flopped onto the bed. "I know I've said that many times before, but this time I really, really mean it, Kaylee. But let's make a pact first, just the way we used to. A pinkie promise," she said, holding up her hand. I looked at it suspiciously. "You can break the promise if you just can't stand keeping it."

I moved slowly to the bedside and entwined my pinkie with hers.

"I promise not to talk about the terrible thing I did to you, and you promise not to talk about what it was like or how you suffered."

"No wonder you came up with that one. That's all good for you," I said.

"No, no. You must have been told, just as I've been, that reliving the past, the gruesome past, does neither of us any good now. I'll just say I'm sorry. I was stupid and selfish and never realized how serious it was. It started out as a joke and just exploded into something so terrible I was terrified of anyone discovering that I was responsible. And when they did, I went a little nuts. That's an explanation, not an excuse," she added.

"Whether I believe you or not is another thing."

"Okay. Let's leave it at that. You'll decide, but in the meantime, let's be sisters again."

I didn't speak.

"For Mother, if not for ourselves," she said. She was holding my pinkie tightly in hers. I hated to think it and certainly wasn't going to say it, but to get through this dinner and this night, she was right. I shook our pinkies, and she let go of mine.

"Now, let me tell you all about it," she said, pulling her legs up so she was in a lotus position, the way we sat whenever we were talking intimately with each other in her room or mine. She patted the bed, and I sat. "There's this boy in the nuthouse. We both call it that. Neither of us cares how it makes us look, which was one of the first things that attracted me to him. His name is Cedar Thomas. Can you imagine anyone naming their son after a tree?

"He's half Cherokee, and it comes from one of their legends describing how God created night and day. The people first asked that there be no night, but that got them exhausted, so they asked for no day, and that caused them to starve, from lack of crops. Many died. So then they said it was all a mistake, and God created night and day. He felt bad about the dead, so he created the cedar tree and put the spirits of all the dead in it. So when they smell a cedar, they smell their ancestors. That's pretty neat, right?"

"Yes," I said, impressed. "But why is he there?"

"He tried to kill his little brother because he thought he saw an evil spirit in him," she said with stunning nonchalance.

"Saw an evil spirit in him? How?"

"Cedar was into some crazy stuff like peyote. But he's so sexy-looking. He has these onyx-black eyes and a kind of olive complexion, with ebony hair he keeps long, down to his shoulders. They wouldn't dare cut it. He's very proud of his Indian heritage and keeps himself in great shape. He talks a lot about the aura around people. He says an ancient medicine man taught him how to see it. Fascinating, right? We spend every free hour together. It's hard to do much more than talk, because everyone's watching you breathe," she said, her voice full of frustration. "He hates one of the attendants because he calls him Chief. We play around and plan how we'd like to kill him. Just kidding," she added quickly. "But remember, it's better to release your aggression in nonviolent ways. He pumps iron. I've done some great work in arts and crafts.

"He couldn't go home for Thanksgiving," she concluded. "That's why I'm not so terribly upset about going right back. Don't tell Mother any of this." She paused, but before I could say a word, she added, "You look good. You look . . . older. You have something to tell me, too, don't you?"

"I like the school. It's called Littlefield."

"Yes, Daddy told me. Not too snobby?"

"I get along with the girls I want to get along with."

"And? Come on. I told you my secret. Tell me something no one knows."

"It's not a secret. I've been seeing one boy."

"Good. Let's hear about that. He's not coming here for Thanksgiving, is he? I mean, I hope he is."

"No. He has a family, Haylee."

"Right." She shrugged. "Some other time, maybe. So? Don't just sit there like Buddha, Kaylee. Talk."

How much should I tell her? I wondered. My memory of our sharing secrets and dreams was somewhere inside a fog. Too much had happened for me simply to return to the comfort we'd once had when we revealed intimate thoughts to each other.

"I didn't get into any social life for a while, Haylee. It wasn't easy getting used to being away."

"Tell me about it."

"Anyway," I said, ignoring her, "we've gone out only a few times, so there's not much to say other than I like him. He's very bright, witty, and—"

"Good-looking, I hope."

"Yes."

"What's his name? You know that by now, right?" she asked, smirking.

"Very funny. Troy."

"Troy." She sat back and repeated it as if she were trying it on for size. "I like it. I hate boys with ordinary names. It shows that their parents have no imagination. At least Mother came up with interesting names for us. Everyone says so. What kind of dates did you have?"

"Rides, pizza."

"And?"

"I've been to his home."

"And?"

"That's it," I said firmly.

Her eyes pooled with disappointment, but a new thought brightened them. "What do you know about Daddy's girlfriend? Are they living together? He didn't talk much when he brought me over here. He could have been a limo driver. So?"

"She's very nice, witty, and funny."

"Can't you come up with more? Witty. What's witty, anyway?"

"Someone with interesting conversation, insights. Not boring to talk to," I explained. "Loquacious."

"Very funny. Always the English teacher." She looked down. "I've probably fallen so far behind in school. They have classes, but they're run by teachers who look terrified most of the time. And so many in my classes are so backward that most of the time is spent on remedial work. Anyway," she said, getting off the bed, "I don't want to think about it. Let's just think about what to wear at dinner. Who's going to be here? Not Daddy and his girlfriend, so who?"

"Just us, Mother, and Irene."

"Who is this Irene? She looks like she belongs where I am."

"She's very nice, Haylee, and has done Mother a lot of good. She's a psychiatric nurse."

"I knew it. More analysis and eyes full of microscopes. Okay. We'll make the best of it." She opened her closet. "What to wear, what to wear. I haven't had that to think about for some time, although Cedar said it wouldn't matter, I'd look great in a sack. That's where he would like to get me, by the way. We're working on it."

"Why don't we each choose something and then see what we've picked?" I suggested.

"Testing? You expect we'll miraculously choose the same thing? Want to see if we still would?"

"Maybe," I said nonchalantly.

"You are different." Her eyes narrowed. "And you're not telling me everything, but you will," she said. "You will."

She hadn't lost her self-confidence. That was certain.

"I forgot what I had in this closet. And these colors Mother chose for my room are making me nuts. Maybe I'll sleep with you tonight."

"That would really hurt Mother. Not a wise thing to do, Haylee."

"I suppose you're right. Pretend, pretend, pretend. I thought those days were gone. You're actually very lucky to be living away from this place."

"I had no choice," I said. She was bordering on forcing me to break our pinkie promise, and she knew it.

"Well, I'm taking a shower and doing my fingers and toenails, something I haven't done since I don't know when. I want to put on some makeup, too. We're not permitted to do that. We're lucky to be able to brush our teeth."

I stood there waiting to see just how much she was going to tell me about her treatment and life in the institution.

She glanced at me and seemed to snap back into the present. "Oh, I forgot those black suede booties. Remember when I talked Mother into buying them for us? She practically measured the heels on each pair to the tenth of a millimeter to be sure they were exact."

"I'd better go and consider my wardrobe, or I'll be influenced about what to choose," I said.

The truth was that this initial confronting of her and the way she was behaving were making me a little sick inside. I wasn't sure exactly what I'd been hoping for, but I knew it had something to do with some sign of remorse. She was more like Mother, sweeping the recent past under the rug and finding blame with anyone who made the slightest reference to it. To survive simply meant to forget. Shelve the nightmares and bury the anger, unless you wanted to live with hate and vengeance alive and well at your side. Haylee's psychiatrist and my therapist were on the same page when it came to moving forward. Maybe my father was right the first time. Therapy and psychoanalysis were all voodoo. No one was guilty. Everything was the fault of some twisted psychological issue. Right and wrong had meaning only on final school exams.

Haylee had said she was sorry, but she had also rationalized it well. I was sure she had used those excuses from the day she was caught and probably believed them all herself now. What point was there in expecting anything more?

I did like those booties Haylee had mentioned, but I also liked my tan suede-tasseled ankle boots with the zippered sides. They had only one-inch heels. I had worn them just once and had not taken them with me to Littlefield. I selected the camel-colored dress to wear with them. It had a tan belt. I decided not to wear any makeup. I was consciously trying to be different from Haylee now. The novelty of miraculously choosing the same things to wear whenever we were left to do it was gone.

Were the Mirror Sisters gone?

Haylee was still working on her makeup when I stepped out to go downstairs. She was sitting at her vanity table in her bra and panties and didn't see me look into her room. I stepped away quickly.

"I'll be downstairs," I called, and hurried away

before she could ask to see what I had chosen to wear.

Mother and Irene were changing by now, too. I could smell all the wonderful foods they had prepared and glanced into the oven to see how the turkey was coming along. In the refrigerator, I saw the homemade cranberry sauce. Mother had worked so hard on this dinner. It was as if she believed one meal could work miracles.

Irene was the next to appear. She complimented me on how nice I looked. With both Mother and Haylee still getting ready, I had a chance to talk more frankly to Mother's caretaker.

"Do you really think she's ready to live on her own? I won't be here, and my guess is neither will Haylee for a while," I said.

"The last few weeks, I've deliberately faded into the background to see how she would do. She keeps busy. She has plans to do much more redecorating. I think she believes that if she changes the physical surroundings, she will wash away the bad memories. It's not unusual. The other day, she met one of her friends, Melissa Clark, in the supermarket, and they talked for quite a while. I heard them make plans to get together in the near future. She's learned how to handle the questions and the sympathy well. There's a point where if you don't get her away from being dependent, she never will be independent. Everyone will check on her. She'll be fine."

Her words cheered me. Maybe we could have something close to a nice Thanksgiving after all, I thought. When Mother appeared, she did look beautiful. She wore diamond-studded earrings with her diamond necklace, something my father had given her on their tenth anniversary. It was a good sign that she could handle those memories and not cast out the evidence of what had once been a happier time. Her turquoise pleated A-line dress brought out her healthier complexion. She was always good at being subtle with her makeup.

"You look beautiful, Mother," I said.

"Thank you, dear. So do you. Where's Haylee?"

"Coming," I said. "What can I do to help?"

"Irene and I decided you'd both be our guests today. Just enjoy," she told me.

"Ta-da!" we heard Haylee sing and looked at the stairway as she descended.

We couldn't have been more different. She wore a short, silky black dress sprinkled with blue, peach, and red dots over a white turtleneck and a pair of black tights. And of course, her black booties. Her makeup was a little heavy, but she wasn't unattractive. She paused halfway down and pointed at me.

"Surprised?"

"No," I said. "You look very nice, Haylee," I added quickly.

"Very nice," Mother said. "Both of you. Go

wait in the living room," she ordered. "We'll ring the dinner bell."

"I just had to wear this," she said, hurrying to join me when I turned toward the living room. "I wish there was a way to sneak it back. Cedar would love me in this. You don't have to wear a school uniform or anything at that place, do you?"

"No, but there are strict rules about what you can and can't wear."

"Won't it be nice when we're both somewhere where there are no rules?" she asked.

I sat on the settee. She walked around the living room, gazing at everything as if it were the first time she was here.

"There's no such place," I said.

"We can hope, can't we?" She smiled and ran her hand over her piano and then tapped on a few keys. "Seems so long ago," she said.

"It's not the time that's passed; it's what happens in the time that's passed. That's why some days seem longer than others."

"Who taught you that?"

"My therapist," I said.

I watched her standing there and thinking. If there was ever a pregnant pause, this was it. She snapped around, and with a grin unlike any I had seen on her face or my own, she asked, "Do you think you'll ever stop hating me?"

"Do you think you'll ever truly be sorry?"

"I said I was."

I saw no point in telling her that what she had said was more rationalization than apology. "I stopped hating you a while back," I said. "The bigger question is, will you stop hating yourself?"

She laughed. "Don't you remember what Mother taught us? If we hate each other, we hate ourselves. If you don't hate me, I won't hate myself."

Irene appeared in the doorway. "Your mother says she's ringing the dinner bell," she announced.

"Oh, good. I'm absolutely starving!" Haylee cried. I rose and followed her to the dining room. "This table is absolutely a work of art, Mother," she said when she entered ahead of me.

Mother stood by her chair, beaming. "Take your usual seats," she said.

Haylee moved quickly to hers. We were sitting across from each other. Mother now sat where my father used to sit, and Irene sat in Mother's usual place.

"Before we begin," Mother said, still standing, "I'd like to give thanks. I am thankful that my daughters are safe now and that once again, they are sitting together in our dining room. I am thankful that we will all get a second chance at happiness, and I am thankful that I had such support from people like Irene." She took her seat.

"I am thankful, too, Mother," Haylee said. "I

am thankful that I am here and we are enjoying your wonderful dinner."

Mother nodded and looked at me.

"I am as well, Mother."

"Well, then. Let's pass everything around, and don't forget, girls, leave room for pumpkin pie."

We began eating. Haylee was quickly back to her old clever self, asking Irene questions and showing how interested she was to know about her. I wondered if Irene bought into how fascinated Haylee was in her life story, how she'd had to earn money for herself and her mother and how she'd worked to get her education.

"I swear," Haylee said, "after seeing how spoiled some people are, it's refreshing to hear someone describe how she achieved so much with so little."

Mother was obviously delighted at how well Haylee spoke and how humble she sounded. Haylee then turned to me and asked questions about Littlefield, the facilities, and my teachers. I had to admit that Mother heard more about my school then and there than she had ever heard before. Despite her warnings, both Haylee and I ate more than we should, but everything was truly delicious. When I volunteered Haylee and myself to clean up, Mother refused.

"I'd rather the two of you go into the living room and prepare one of your piano duets for us.

I've been telling Irene for months how wonderful you both play. Now, don't make me look like a liar. Go on. Rehearse," she ordered. "After that, we'll have our dessert."

"I'm a little rusty. How about you?" Haylee asked me.

"The last time we played here together was my last time, too."

"Then we'd better do as Mother asks and rehearse," she said.

If the food hadn't been so wonderful, I might have heaved right there at the table, but I smiled instead, rose, and followed her to the living room.

When we sat at the pianos, Haylee looked at me and said, "Let's make her happy, Kaylee. Who knows when we will have a chance to do it again?"

I should have paid more attention to that, but I was thinking about the music.

19

Despite what she had said, Haylee played the piano as well as I did. I began to suspect she had been rehearsing at the institution. We worked on two of Mother's favorite holiday songs, and then Haylee surprised me after we had played them for Mother and Irene by beginning Gershwin's Prelude No 1. It was, as I recalled, the last duet we had done together before she staged my abduction. She looked at me, challenging. I saw how pleased Mother was, and then I started to play, too.

"You rehearsed," I accused as soon as we finished.

Haylee shrugged. "When something is so special to you, you can't forget it," she said.

For Mother, that was like spreading warm butter on toast. She clapped, and Irene joined her. "Aren't they simply special?" Mother asked.

"They are," Irene said. "I've never seen two like them."

Haylee glowed so brightly with pride that my smile of appreciation paled. I felt like a candle next to a spotlight on the stage, which was what every room in this house had been for us. Even when there was no one but our parents here, we were performing. We thought we had to in order to keep Mother's love. The moment we woke in the morning, the curtain was raised.

After our duets, we all returned to the dining room to enjoy our pumpkin pie. Haylee acted as if a dam of frustration had been broken. She was behaving now like someone who had been kept in solitary confinement for months and months. She talked a regular blue streak, describing the food they had and the institution facilities, the recreational activities she enjoyed, what she was reading, and, yes, she confessed that she had been practicing on the piano.

"I wanted it to be a surprise," she declared.

"That it was," I said.

"Kaylee was always a little better than I was, so I was confident she would be able to get right into it," she explained to Irene.

Then we both looked at Mother to see if she would be as adamant as she had been in the past about not giving one of us more credit than the other. She just smiled.

Maybe it was over, I thought. Maybe I should relax and think only of my own future. We went back to the living room, where Irene, now more comfortable with the three of us, talked more about her own youth. Haylee was suddenly her best audience. I watched with amusement as she wrapped herself around Irene's memories, appearing sincerely interested and amazed by some of it.

Mother then insisted we watch some of the videos of us when we were younger. Haylee volunteered to set things up so we could watch on our big television screen. To me, it was painful to see the four of us when we were still a happy family, a family with no inkling of what would become of us.

"They're absolutely interchangeable at that age," Irene said. She had seen these videos before, but now that she was sitting with both of us, glancing at us and then at the screen, she was even more impressed. "Their gestures, expressions, amazing."

She told us about other twins she had known, something she had told Mother, I was sure, but made the point that there was indeed something unique about us. That set Mother off telling anecdotes about some of the things we had done naturally, things that had impressed her friends.

"They were so good at anticipating what the other wanted and what she would do. I think they still are," she added, looking at us.

Never before had that comment saddened me as much. If that were true, I would have anticipated and avoided the abduction Haylee had so cleverly arranged by weaving a thick web around me and that horrible man. How did Mother process that when she thought of all this tonight?

"Well," Irene said, after looking at me and perhaps seeing the sadness in my face, "I think everyone's a bit tired. I know I am."

"It's going to take me forever to go to sleep anyway," Haylee said. "It's been exciting and wonderful, one of the happiest times of my life. Thank you, Mother. And thank you, Irene. Thank you for taking such good care of our mother." She looked at me with that smug, self-satisfied expression she kept well hidden from anyone else.

"Ditto," I said, and Haylee laughed.

"Everything could have been so much easier to do if we had thought of 'ditto,'" she said.

Even Irene, who really had no idea what she meant, laughed.

"I hope you enjoy your new bedroom tonight," Mother told Haylee.

"It's fantastic. I feel like I'm on a cloud, a pink cloud. Thank you, Mother."

Haylee rose and looked at me, expecting me to mimic her every move. As usual, she led. I stood, and then we both approached Mother the way we had all our lives, me kissing her on the right cheek and Haylee kissing her on the left. Mother held our hands, the tears streaming down her face. I couldn't keep my own eyes from tearing up, too. Haylee just smiled. She turned to give Irene a hug.

"Have a good night," Irene said.

"Thank you. You, too," Haylee told her.

I hugged her as well.

"It's going to be fine," Irene whispered. I wanted to believe her, but the darkness in my heart grew thicker. I said nothing and followed Haylee up the stairway.

"I'll be sleeping with the sheet over my head," she said. "Pink cloud."

"You'll survive."

"Thanks. At least come into the cloud and spend a few more minutes with me," she said when I looked like I was just going to head for my own room.

She slipped off her booties and lay back on her pillows.

"Well, sister mine, how did I do?"

"I think you know."

She smiled. "Are you jealous or happy?"

"For Mother's sake, I'm happy," I said. "It wasn't as bad as I feared."

"I thought it went rather well. Make sure you tell Daddy. He absolutely hates the air I breathe. It's all right. I know. Don't try to deny it."

"Daddy will make his own decisions about you,

no matter what I tell him. If it's important to you, you'll work on winning back his love," I said.

"Oh, you're so wise, Kaylee, but then again, you always were."

"I think I'm really tired. I'll see you in the morning," I said, and started to turn away.

"You didn't tell me much about Troy. It's not fair," she whined.

"There's nothing much to tell you yet. We're just getting to know each other."

"So you're still a virgin?"

I stared at her. She wanted her vision of me to be true; it still made her feel superior.

"No," I said. "But that's all I'm going to say."

She laughed. "I knew it!" she cried as I started out. "Help! I'm sinking in a pink cloud."

I left her laughter behind me and hurried to my room. When I closed the door, I realized how exhausted I was. The emotional tension for hours had drained me. However, before I went to sleep, I called Troy.

"I hope it's not too late," I said.

"No. I was waiting and hoping for your call. You first. How was it?"

"Actually, it went better than I thought. My mother is doing much better. From the way everyone behaved, you'd think nothing had happened. I don't trust Haylee, of course, but I'm tired of it. She'll be who she is, no matter what."

"She didn't seem sorry at all?"

"She did, but she's mastered how to live with it now, how to rationalize and diminish it. I think she's learned how to work us all, even her own psychiatrist, but Haylee was always a quick study when it came to manipulating people to do what she wanted, when she wanted."

"You were hoping to see her in more pain?"

"I guess so, but I hate that I was."

"What are you going to tell her doctor when you see her?"

"I'm not sure. I'm happy I have a little time to think about it."

"You'll make the right decision," he said.

"What about your Thanksgiving?"

"What Thanksgiving? It was the same as any other dinner out. My father brought a guest, a young man he's mentoring in the business. Most of the time, he talked with him. My mother was busy with some of her girlfriends who sat at tables near ours, so Jo and I were almost forgotten."

He paused, and I waited.

"Before we went to bed, I told Jo she and I have to talk tomorrow. She knew why."

"And?"

"She nodded, but she looked terrified. Maybe I'm not the one who should be talking to her. My mother won't, but maybe Jo should see a therapist. She's nowhere near as happy as other girls her age."

"You're probably right. What you should do is get her to agree to it first and then demand it."

"That's exactly my plan. Maybe you're my twin, too."

I laughed. "Believe me, Troy, one is enough." I told him I would call him in the late afternoon tomorrow to let him know if he should come to see me. The answer to that was forming as I slept.

Once again, Mother was up earlier than any of us. I heard her moving about and listened for Haylee. She was rarely up ahead of me anytime. I tried to sleep longer, but anticipating my father arriving to take Haylee back and Mother's reaction to it kept me from even closing my eyes. I knew how sad Mother would be, and I worried that it would set her back. I showered and dressed and went down for breakfast.

Irene was up with Mother, and they were at the kitchenette table having some coffee and toast and jelly.

"Is your sister up, too?" Mother asked immediately.

"Her door was closed, so I didn't bother her," I said.

"Yes, well, I'm sure it was exhausting, all the excitement of being home again." She looked at Irene, who nodded. "Irene's leaving today, you know," Mother said.

"Oh, today? I thought you were leaving Sunday."

"No, dear. I have to catch up on some things, and then I'm thinking I'll take a bit of a vacation." She smiled at Mother. "My first in quite a while. I'm going to visit my older sister in Tampa, Florida. She's a widow, and her only child, a daughter, lives in Hong Kong. She married an Asian businessman."

I got myself some coffee and sat at the table.

"Do you want some eggs?" Mother asked.

"I'm going to have to work up an appetite after all I ate last night," I said.

Mother nodded, but I saw her attention was fixed on listening for signs of Haylee getting up. "It doesn't seem fair or even sensible to let that girl come home for only one night," she said. "Maybe it will do more damage than good."

"They have a protocol they have to follow," Irene said. "Things will progress faster from this, I'm sure." She patted Mother's hand.

"Well, at least I can make a turkey sandwich for her to take," Mother said, standing up. "Maybe you should go check on her, Kaylee. If she's still sleeping, let her be. She might be up but so sad she has to leave that she's delaying it."

I nodded and rose. "Why don't you and I go to dinner tonight, Mother?" I said. "You've done enough in the kitchen. We can go for pizza or something Italian like we used to."

"Like we all used to," she said, her words drifting with the memories. Then she smiled. "Yes, that might be a good idea. Drive away the blues." She went into the kitchen to put together a take-away package for Haylee.

Irene smiled at me. "You're wonderful with her, Kaylee. It will be fine," she said. "You'll see. She's stronger now than you think."

"I hope so," I said.

I was thinking of what it was going to be like for my mother when I left, too. She would have to be strong to live alone until one of us returned. There were too many memories floating about for me. I couldn't imagine what her nights would be like for her, actually for all parents when their children left for college and a start to their own independent lives. It couldn't be all that different from what my mother faced. Loneliness was loneliness, no matter what mask it wore.

Haylee's bedroom door was still shut. I waited, listening, and then, hearing nothing, I tapped gently on it.

"Haylee?"

I tapped again and called again, and then I opened the door. For a long moment, I stood there gaping like someone too shocked to speak. Her bed looked just the way it had when I left her. Moving quickly, I checked her bathroom and then stood there trying to make sense of it. Had she gone down without any of us realizing it? Was she downstairs now? Just to be sure, I went to look in my room, my bathroom, Mother's room, and her bathroom. I returned to Haylee's room and checked for her small suitcase. It was nowhere. A surge of heat like molten lava flowed through my veins. *It can't be*, I told myself.

Then I hurried down the stairs and found Mother and Irene still seated at the kitchenette table. They looked up sharply.

"Where's Haylee?" Mother asked. "Is she still asleep?"

"She's not there," I said. The concept didn't register on either of their faces. "She's not anywhere upstairs. Did you hear her come down?"

Irene shook her head.

I went into all the rooms downstairs, calling for Haylee as I searched, and then returned to the kitchenette. Both were standing now.

"Her bag is gone, too," I said. "The small suitcase that she had with her."

"I don't understand," Mother said. "Did your father come here very, very early?"

Without answering, I went to the front door and stepped out to look up and down our street. Then I shouted for her. Irene came up behind me, so I turned to her.

"She didn't use her bed last night," I said. "She must have left after we were all asleep."

"Oh, dear," Irene said, bringing her hands to her cheeks. "We have to call your father."

I nodded and rushed to the phone.

"I was waiting to call you to see how it went," he said immediately after I said, "Daddy."

"It went well, Daddy, but she's gone."

"Gone? What's that mean?"

"She snuck out last night, and she's gone."

I could almost hear him try to swallow. "Are you sure?"

"I checked everywhere in the house. She took her bag, too. She's gone."

"You looked outside?"

"She's gone, Daddy. She's gone! Aren't you listening?"

"Okay. Keep your mother calm. I'll call Dr. Alexander immediately," he said. "She'll be calling the police, for sure. Expect them. I'll be there as soon as I can."

After I hung up, I stood there trembling. Irene and my mother stepped into the kitchen and looked at me.

"Daddy's calling her doctor, and then the police will be called."

"Why did she do this?" Mother asked. "Now they'll never let her come home for Christmas."

Neither Irene nor I could respond to that.

"She's just very confused," Irene finally said. "It's been overwhelming. Let's all just stay calm and wait to hear what the doctor and the police do. I imagine your father will be here."

"Yes," I said.

"Come along, Keri," Irene told Mother. "I'd like you to sit. I'll get you some water, and we'll all wait together."

"Where could she go?" Mother asked as we all went into the living room. "Kaylee?"

"I don't know, Mother. We're not exactly walking distance from a train station or a bus station."

Mother sat, and Irene went to get her a glass of water.

"She's just confused. I'm sure," Mother said. "When do you think she left?"

"Sometime during the night. After I fell asleep, for sure. I didn't hear anything."

"No. I didn't, either."

The phone rang. I hurried to the one on the kitchen wall. Irene waited with Mother's glass of water. It was Dr. Alexander. Her first question was Haylee loaded. I had to remind myself that Haylee was her patient, not me.

"Did something happen, Kaylee? Something to upset her?"

"No. She was a big hit, Dr. Alexander. She and I played duets on the pianos. She talked a lot. She made my mother very happy. Nothing nasty was said. We had a great dinner. We began by promising not to talk about the past. I tried my best to stay cool and not say or do anything that would ruin the evening. I was worried for my mother more than I was for Haylee. Too bad Haylee wasn't."

"Did she mention a boy named Cedar Thomas?" Dr. Alexander asked.

"Yes. She likes him a lot."

"Cedar Thomas escaped two days ago," she said. "Did she mention that?"

I wasn't simply shocked or surprised; I was angry at myself for being taken in by Haylee again.

"No. She had me convinced she was returning to be with him. She even moaned about not being able to wear the clothes she wore last night because he would like them so much. I didn't have the slightest suspicion that she would do this. You know what I do think, Dr. Alexander?"

"What?"

"I think she's better at it than she's ever been. Maybe she'll be giving both of us therapy someday," I said, unable to hide my bitterness.

"I'll be in touch," Dr. Alexander said. "It's out of my hands for the moment. The police are searching for Cedar Thomas. They'll add Haylee's name. My guess is he picked her up at your house late last night. It sounds like something they had planned."

"And under your very eyes," I said.

I hung up and looked at Irene.

"What was all that?" she asked.

"My sister had a boyfriend in the nuthouse, as

she called it, and apparently, he escaped the day before yesterday. Dr. Alexander believes he probably picked her up last night."

"Oh, my. Don't mention it to your mother yet," she warned.

I nodded, and we returned to be with Mother.

"Who called? Did they find her?"

"Not yet, Mother."

Irene handed her the water.

She drank some and looked at me. "Well, who was that? Was it your father?"

"No, it was her doctor at the institution, Dr. Alexander."

"Well, what does she think?"

I looked at Irene.

"What do you two know that I don't? Tell me!" Mother cried. She was losing it quickly.

Irene nodded at me.

"It looks like Haylee planned an escape with a boy at the institution, Mother. He escaped two days ago. He must have a car, and he must have picked her up during the night."

Mother looked like she was going to faint.

"I think it's best that your mother lie down, Kaylee. I'll remain until this is sorted out."

"Yes," I said. "Go on, Mother. I promise I'll call you the moment we know anything."

Irene helped Mother stand up and start for the stairway, practically carrying her.

I sat, thinking, reviewing everything Haylee had said to me to see if I could come up with something that might help find her.

Twenty minutes later, my father arrived. His face was swollen with rage. I told him what Dr. Alexander had told me.

"How's your mother?" he asked.

"Devastated," I said. "Irene is upstairs with her."

"I can't believe how well she worked me on the way over, how sweet she was, how grateful for this second chance. Something told me not to trust her. I swear, Kaylee. I could feel it twitching inside me, this distrust. She wasn't much different from the way she had been during the time you were trapped in that man's basement." He looked like he wanted to slam his fist into the wall.

The doorbell rang, and we both went to answer it. Two policemen were there. They started to ask questions, and my father turned to me.

"She'll tell you all she knows," he said.

"I'm afraid I don't know much more than anyone else. She talked about the boy, Cedar Thomas, but she led me to believe she was returning to the institution to be with him, was actually looking forward to it."

"You don't need a picture of her," my father told them. "Just look at Kaylee. But the similarity is only on the outside, believe me."

"We might have a lead on a stolen vehicle," the

taller of the two policemen said. "We have a good description of this Cedar Thomas."

"This might sound stupid," I said, "but he might go where there are cedar trees."

Neither policeman said anything to that. They thanked us and left.

Irene had come down the stairs and stood waiting behind us. "Keri heard the doorbell. Anything?"

"Just the police getting information," my father said. "How is she?"

"Shocked, but she'll be okay. Don't worry, Mr. Fitzgerald. I've decided I'll remain until this is settled."

"That's very kind of you, Irene." My father looked at me. "I'll go up and speak to her."

"That would be good," Irene said.

She and I returned to the living room, and then, at her suggestion, I made myself some breakfast and some for my father, too. I didn't ask him what he had said to Mother or what she had said to him. I was hoping they were beyond recriminations, that they had both realized that accusing each other of being responsible for where we were at this point was fruitless. It was a time to come together and find ways to support each other.

Irene brought tea and more toast up to Mother, hoping to persuade her to remain strong, especially now.

"The girl is a lost cause," my father said at the table. He was happy I had made some eggs and toast, the eggs just the way he liked them, over easy. "She put the last nail in her coffin, as far as I'm concerned. They can keep her in that place for years. And this was absolutely the last time I will ever ask you to do anything for her, Kaylee."

"Okay, Daddy," I said, and sipped some coffee.

He looked at me and smiled.

"What?"

"I know when I'm being humored. What a mess."

"I had suggested to Mother that she and I go for pizza tonight, Daddy. I didn't know Irene was supposed to leave today. I know you wanted me to go to dinner with you and Dana, but . . ."

"I don't think you can leave her. Of course, stay with her, Kaylee." He looked at his watch. "I have a couple of things to do today, but I won't be far away. There's nothing much we can do but wait anyway," he said.

I agreed. There was no point in his babysitting me. Irene would probably be putting Mother back on some tranquilizers for now. We said we'd call each other periodically.

"Dr. Alexander will stay in touch with me," my father said.

I walked him to the door. He shook his head, hugged and kissed me, and after gazing toward the stairway, he left.

I went upstairs and sat with Mother and Irene until Mother fell asleep for a while. It was almost impossible to concentrate on anything, but early in the afternoon, it occurred to me to call Troy. He immediately thought I was calling to hear about his talk with his sister and started to tell me. He sounded on the verge of being hysterical, so I didn't interrupt him.

"My sister absolutely refuses to admit to anything or go to a therapist, and my mother supports that. You know what she had the nerve to say? She said Jo would grow out of it. Can you imagine? Grow out of being sexually abused by her father? I went into a rage and threatened to go to the police, but that caused Jo to get hysterical, so I had to promise not to do it. Nothing will change. Maybe . . . maybe Jo will realize what she needs herself. Thanks to you, I am more hopeful about myself, Kaylee. Anyway, I'll drive over tomorrow and—"

"No," I finally said. "You can't come now."

"Why not?"

I told him what had happened. I was on the phone with him for nearly an hour, describing every little thing Haylee had done and said.

"Wow," he said. "And here I was feeling sorry for myself and my sister, while you had all this heartache. Is there anything I can do?"

"Just call me. And I'll call you if anything changes, okay?"

"Yes. Kaylee . . . you're the first person besides my sister that I care so much about."

I almost said *Ditto* but stopped myself. "That feeling's mutual, Troy. I can't wait to see you again."

I had hoped that my call to him would cheer me up, but when I hung up, I felt a terrible and deep sadness for us both. *We'll dig out of it*, I told myself. *There's nowhere else to go but up.*

The best way to pause the flow of sadness was to help Irene care for Mother. We tried to get each other to eat some lunch. It was one of the longest days I could remember. Nothing I could do would make it go faster. Constantly looking at the clock didn't move those hands quicker but only rein-forced how stuck in the tension we all were. My father called a little after three o'clock to see how we were and to tell me what I already knew: he had heard nothing.

Darkness fell like a heavy rain. I was afraid to put on music or look at television. Irene rarely left Mother's side. Mother dozed on and off, but every time she woke, she was desperate for news, and hearing there was none was like another lash of the whip for her. We got her to eat some dinner and settled her on the sofa with a blanket afterward. My father called again with the same questions and the same message.

Just before eight, Dr. Alexander called, this time

not to follow up on her patient but sincerely to see how I was doing and how my mother was doing. I sensed an underlying stream of guilt beneath her words. She, after all, had approved Haylee's temporary parole. I didn't accuse her of anything and hoped my voice didn't betray my belief that she was at fault. After all, what she had was hope; she wanted to succeed. It was simply that I, along with my father, believed Haylee was beyond redemption. Her problems were too deeply embedded in who she was.

Dr. Alexander ended our conversation by saying, "I'm sorry this has happened."

"Me, too," I said. "I didn't want it to be this way."

"I believe you, Kaylee. Don't lose faith in yourself. You're a twin, but you're not a duplicate."

I liked that, but right now, it seemed as if nothing anyone could say would bring any joy.

I told Irene who had called and that there was nothing new.

"Maybe we should all just go to sleep," she suggested. I imagined she was truly tired.

Mother didn't resist, and Irene remained with her in her room.

Before I went to mine, I looked in at Haylee's redecorated bedroom. The pink cloud, I thought. How dark it had become.

Epilogue

Our English literature teacher, Mr. Edgewater, spent a great deal of time getting us all to understand the essence of classical tragedy. He stressed that the tragic character isn't simply someone who has a terrible thing happen to him or her. He or she has to have hubris, too much pride, meaning ego. He or she therefore causes the tragedy to occur.

I will always wonder if Haylee thought she could do what the therapists couldn't when it came to Cedar Thomas. Maybe she believed he was so in love with her that she could lead him from the dark, insane world to her world of constant pleasure and happiness. She might have even thought up the whole thing, not realizing that she had gone too far. Maybe she believed that if it didn't work, no one would blame her. She would simply return to some form of treatment. There was no such thing as good or evil; there was simply a wrong turn.

The police detective informed us that they were confident the driver, Cedar Thomas, deliberately went through the guardrail and plunged the car a few thousand feet to the rocky place below. Miraculously, there was no fire, but neither the driver nor his passenger was wearing a seat belt. The medical examiner claimed that death was instantaneous.

Days later, Dr. Alexander invited us to meet at her home. Only my father and I could go. Mother was practically catatonic, under care and medication. My father almost refused the invitation, but after a second thought, he decided we should hear what Dr. Alexander had to say.

"I didn't ask you here to listen to excuses," she began after we sat in her modest living room. "I wanted to tell you what I believe happened."

"It clearly looks like he committed suicide and took Haylee along for the ride," my father said. The events had hardened him almost to the point of being unrecognizable. Once again, he was launched into a conflict between anger and sadness.

"As strange as it's going to sound to you, that's not what I think happened."

"Why not?" my father asked.

"Cedar Thomas believed he could read auras around people. He was taught to believe this, and it became a device to service his own inner rage, his deep paranoia."

"But he drove the car over a cliff deliberately," my father said.

"Because at the time, he was convinced your daughter had a demon living in her."

"Then why did he pick her up? Why did he want to be with her?"

"He thought he was doing good, destroying evil."

"But he would die, too," my father said, his face showing terrible pain.

"We would know that. We're rational and logical. But he thought he would be rewarded in the hereafter. That's my assessment."

My father shook his head. "How did you let her get involved with this nutcase?"

"Neither of them was living in solitary, Mr. Fitzgerald. I think Haylee was intrigued and fascinated by him. She appeared more energetic, more interested in doing productive things."

"And thought she could cure him?" I said.

"Maybe. More likely, she didn't think of him being cured, just free. They'd both be free."

"So she used him," I said. "Whatever the reason, she was responsible for what happened to herself."

"I don't think we should blame her now."

"So we're back to that," my father said. "Whom should we blame?"

"Either you believe what Cedar Thomas was taught, that there are demons in some people, or you accept that we all share blame. We don't mean to do harm. Things we do get misinterpreted, misdirected. They're mistakes, and maybe we miss seeing the effects of those mistakes, but we want good things for people we love. Your ex-wife wanted that. She certainly didn't want this, and neither did you or Kaylee. I simply want you to find some peace with it all."

I looked at my father.

"I don't know if you're right. I don't even know if it matters, Dr. Alexander," he said. "I don't envy you for the world you're in. It's easier to believe that there are good guys and bad guys and leave it at that. But I appreciate your telling us about the boy and sharing your thoughts with us. Kaylee?"

We stood to leave.

"What about me?" I asked. "I'm one of the Mirror Sisters. Will I make a similar mistake, overestimate what I'm capable of doing, and cause more trouble?" In the back of my mind, I was thinking about Troy and how I had advised him.

"It's not all in what's reflected, Kaylee. I think you know when to ask for help."

My father was quiet for most of the ride back. We both were.

"She's right," he finally said. "She's like the rest of us, more educated but only out to do some good. It's pointless to blame her."

"I like that, Daddy. Maybe someday I'll do what she does."

"Maybe you will. That way, I'll get some free therapy."

It was practically the only time either of us had smiled during the last few days and practically the only time we would in the days to follow.

Mother was not well enough to attend Haylee's funeral. Troy cut school to be with me. I knew his biggest worry was that I wouldn't return to Littlefield. There would be too many questions and all the astonishment at my hiding the past and my sister's existence.

"If you transfer to some other school, I'll transfer there, too," he promised.

That night, I called him after talking about it with my father.

"I'm coming back," I said. "I'm not running away from anything anymore."

"I'll be waiting," he said. "We'll go for the best sundae in America."

"In the world," I said, and we started to talk about all that we would do in the weeks and months to come.

At the end of the week, I went to Haylee's grave alone. There was no monument or footstone yet, just a small plaque with her name and dates. It was a bright day, one of those days when the sky is almost turquoise and the small clouds look like what my mother once had described as puffs of God's breath. We were only about five when she told Haylee and me that.

Haylee had blown up her cheeks and looked at the sky and said, "I want to make a cloud, too."

"And what do you want to do, Kaylee?" Mother immediately asked me.

"Whatever Haylee wants to do," I replied. It was the answer she wanted, the answer she would never hear again.

I studied the mound of earth. I had seen the coffin lowered, but it still seemed unreal to me. Nevertheless, I stepped closer to talk to her.

"I think deep down you really wanted us to be sisters again, Haylee. You ran away, but you thought you would be back, maybe even for Christmas. You'd expect Mother would have two of everything she had bought for us. We'd each kiss her cheeks, and she would kiss each of ours.

"Then we'd play Christmas songs in duet, and there would be lots of laughter and hugs and, most important, promises. We'd go to bed together, talking about boyfriends and how we were going to be married in the same ceremony and take the same honeymoon and have children at the same time.

"We were supposed to grow old and die together at the exact same moment.

"So you see, it doesn't matter what happened. I'm going to live for both of us just the way we had planned. Nothing's changed. Mother will still see two of us, and even though he doesn't want to, so will Daddy.

"To lose you, really lose you, I'd have to live in a world without mirrors. You will live on in my reflection just the way I would in yours.

"What do you think of that?"

I stood there for a moment, listening to her laughter and imagining us holding hands as we ran across the lawn to greet the guests who had come to our fifth birthday party, while we recited, "Haylee and Kaylee, Kaylee and Haylee."

I knelt, put my palm on the freshly turned earth, whispered her name, and then left, feeling renewed confidence in the happiness that would come.